Mistress

A complete list of books by James Patterson is at the back of this book. For previews and information about the author, visit JamesPatterson.com or find him on Facebook or at your app store.

Mistress

James Patterson
AND
David Ellis

**Doubleday Large Print
Home Library Edition**

LITTLE, BROWN AND COMPANY

NEW YORK BOSTON LONDON

Little, Brown and Company
Hachette Book Group
237 Park Avenue, New York, NY 10017

Little, Brown and Company is a division of Hachette Book Group, Inc. The Little, Brown name and logo are trademarks of Hachette Book Group, Inc.

The publisher is not responsible for websites (or their content) that are not owned by the publisher.

ISBN: 978-1-62490-504-9

Printed in the United States of America

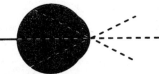

**This Large Print Book carries the
Seal of Approval of N.A.V.H.**

To the supremely talented Sally McDaniel-Smith, for your help on this book and for preserving my sanity for the past six years.
—**D.E.**

Mistress

CHAPTER 1

Let's see what she has in her medicine cabinet. I mean, as long as I'm here.

Careful, though. Before you turn on the light, close the bathroom door. The rest of her apartment is dark. Best to keep it that way.

What do we have here . . . lotions, creams, moisturizers, lip balm, ibuprofen. What about the meds? Amoxicillin for a sinus infection . . . lorazepam for anxiety . . .

Diana has anxiety? What the heck does **she** have to be anxious about? She's the most put-together woman I know.

And what's this? Cerazette for . . . birth

control. She's on the pill? Diana is on the pill? She never told me that. She isn't having sex with me. Not yet, anyway. So who **is** she having sex with?

Diana, every time I think I have you figured out, you remind me that you're a mystery. **A mystery wrapped in a riddle inside an enigma**—Joe Pesci's line from **JFK,** though Winston Churchill first used it in a 1939 radio address to describe Russia. President Roosevelt, who grew very close to Churchill during the war, once wrote to him, **It is fun to be in the same decade with you.**

Diana, it is fun to be in the same decade with you. Now excuse me while I check out your bedroom closet.

Same drill: get inside, close the door, then turn on the light. Keep the light from filtering into the remainder of the condo.

Whoa. At least a hundred pairs of shoes, meticulously lined up. Stuart Weitzman stilettos. Black knee-high Manolo Blahnik alligator-skin boots. Roger Vivier heels with a satin-rose toe. Red Jimmy Choos. Pink Escada evening sandals. Black Chanel pumps, appropriate for the boardroom or a five-star restaurant.

Woodrow Wilson favored white dress shoes with his linen suits. Lincoln had the biggest presidential shoe, a size 14, while Rutherford B. Hayes had the smallest, a size 7.

You'll have to excuse me. Sometimes my mind wanders. Kind of like Moses through the desert. Except that he had a better excuse. And a speech impediment—unlike me, unless you count putting your foot in your mouth.

Anyway, that's a long story, so back to our regularly scheduled programming: Lady Diana's Closet. And what do we have here, hanging behind a row of dresses, hidden from all but the keenest of voyeurs? Hmm . . .

Leather vests and headgear. Chains and whips. Vibrators of various kinds and colors. One of them is purple and curved on the end (I'm not sure why). Most of them are shaped like the male organ, but some have appendages for some reason. There are some black beads on a string . . . what are those for? Nipple rings—I get that, I guess. Creams and lotions. A long yellow feather—

Then I hear it and see it and feel it all at

once—movement across the carpet, brushing against my leg, circling me—

"Hey, Cinnamon," I say after the momentary terror dissipates and the prickling of my spine ceases. Diana's Abyssinian cat, three years old. The word **Abyssinian** is Ethiopian, but the origin of the breed is believed to be Egyptian. Isn't that weird? Abyssinians have bigger ears and longer tails than most cats. Their hair is lighter at the root than at the tip; only a handful of breeds have hair like that. I told Diana she should have named her cat Caramel, because it more accurately describes the color of her coat. Plus I just like caramel more than cinnamon, especially those candy chews.

Okay, time to get to work. I turn off the closet light before I open the door—still dark in the place. I feel like Paul Newman in **Thief.**

Start with the bedroom. There's a desk on one side, near the balcony. Next to it, a pair of electrical outlets. I plug the AC adapter into the lower outlet and drag the cord behind the window curtain toward the desk. It looks just like any other AC adapter for a computer or appliance. But it's a high-resolution, motion-activated video recorder with thirty-two hours of memory that will film the entire room in color. It can be switched to continuous recording if necessary, but motion activation is the smarter play here. I like this one because it doesn't need a battery, as it's plugged into the wall. And it doesn't transmit signals—it only records them to an SD card that can be played on a computer—so it wouldn't be detected in a bug sweep.

Keeping low, I move out of the bedroom into Diana's main living space, which has an open floor plan that encompasses a small kitchen area and a large living and dining area. Her place is on the top floor of a condo building in Georgetown, which means she's paying for location, not square footage.

I don't want to use another AC adapter; if one is discovered, the other will be found. Diversify, I say. But this one will be more complicated than plugging something into a wall, so I need my night-vision goggles—like the serial killer in **The Silence of the Lambs,** except I've never murdered anyone, much less skinned them.

Murder can be made to look like suicide,

and suicide can be made to look like murder.

Tired of worrying about house fires and home intruders? Want to spy on your party guests while you protect them from unwanted smoke inhalation? Introducing Benjamin's functional all-in-one smoke detector and covert color camera. This easy-to-use gadget mounts to any ceiling and comes in three attractive colors to match any decor. Best of all, its 3.6-millimeter pinhole camera and audio microphone let you see and hear everything in the room. But that's not all: if you act now, we'll throw in a twelve-volt power adapter absolutely free!

Trust me, I'm not as normal as I seem.

Okay, all done. The kitchen looks the same as it did when I entered. I drop Diana's old smoke detector and my night-vision goggles into my gym bag and stop for a minute to make sure I haven't left anything behind.

I check my watch: it's 9:57 p.m. My instructions were to be done by ten. So I made it with three minutes to spare.

I reach for the doorknob and then it hits me—I've made a terrible mistake.

Paul Newman didn't star in **Thief.** It was James Caan.

How could I mix up Paul Newman and James Caan? Must be the nerves.

I lock up and move quickly down the hallway to the fire escape, accessible with a key. I pop the door open and slip into the night air just as I hear the **ding** of the elevator down the hallway.

CHAPTER 2

I take the stairs down the fire escape, all six stories, at a slow pace, gripping the railing fiercely. I don't like heights. Presidents Washington and Jefferson wanted DC to be a "low city." I'm with them all the way.

In the 1890s, the Cairo Hotel was built on Q Street to a height of 164 feet, towering over its neighbors. In reaction to the uproar that followed, Congress passed a law called the Height of Buildings Act a few years later. But they amended the law in 1910, making it even more restrictive. Now the heights of buildings in the capital are limited to the width of the streets they face plus twenty feet. Most streets in DC are no wider than 110 feet, so most buildings are no higher than 130 feet, which usually means thirteen stories or fewer.

Still too high for me. I can't stand near ledges. I'm not so afraid of losing my balance or slipping. I'm afraid I'll jump.

When I reach the bottom, I walk through the parking lot and take the stairs up to the brick path that follows the C&O Canal. Diana lives on a tiny, two-block stretch of 33rd Street between the Potomac River to the south and the Chesapeake and Ohio Canal to the north. Hers is the last building before the dead end at the canal, so it's a secluded walk for me as I come around to the front of her building again.

It's sticky-hot outside in August. The capital was built on swampland, and our humidity is unbearable this time of year. I don't blame Congress for staying away.

Two younger guys are standing outside the loft building across the street, smoking cigarettes and checking out my bike.

"Sweet ride," one of them says. He's small and mangy, like Joaquin Phoenix in **To Die For**—Nicole Kidman's break-out role, in my opinion, in which she showed for the first time she could carry a movie.

"You like it?" I ask. I do, too. It's a 2009 Triumph America. Dual overhead cams, 865-cc, twin four-stroke engine, twin reverse cone pipes, phantom black with chrome detail. Yes, like the one Colin Farrell drove in **Daredevil.** I'm not saying I bought it for that reason. Not saying I didn't. But yeah, it's a pretty sweet ride.

"You get this thing out on the open road much?" the guy asks me.

Colin Farrell was terrific in **Phone Booth.** I liked that cop movie he did with Edward Norton and that futuristic movie he did with Tom Cruise, **Minority Report.** He's underrated as an actor. He should do a movie with Nicole Kidman.

"Yeah, I try to stretch her legs when I can," I tell the guy. I'm not supposed to be advertising my presence here, and yet here I am chatting up a couple of guys about my bike.

I look up into the darkness at Diana's apartment, at the triangular brick balcony that juts out over 33rd Street. The balcony serves more as a garden than anything else. The ledges on the sides are all lined with potted plants and flowers, and some small trees sit on the balcony floor, all of which she treats with loving care.

A light has gone on inside her apartment, illuminating the kitchen window.

"What do you got on the front there?" the guy asks me, kicking my front wheel.

"A 110/90 ME880," I say. "I like to ride with 880s front and back."

Diana's home already? That's . . . interesting.

"Cool," says the guy. "My tire guy doesn't do Metzelers. I've been running Avons all these years."

I look back at the guy. "They handle pretty well so far."

He asks me for the name of my tire guy. I tell him while he scribbles it down on a scrap of paper. Then I jump on the bike and take one last look up at Diana's balcony. Good night, Lady Di—

—what—

"No!" I cry.

A body is in free fall from Diana's balcony,

plunging head-first six stories to the ground. I close my eyes and turn away, but I can't close my ears to the sickening **whump** of a body hitting the bricks, of bones snapping and crunching.

CHAPTER 3

I jump off my bike and sprint toward her. No. It can't be. It can't be her—

"Did you see that?"

"What happened?"

I reach her second, after two women, from a car in the circular driveway, have jumped out and knelt down beside her.

Oh, Diana. Her body lies just short of the street, spread-eagled and facedown. Her luminous hair spills over her crushed face and onto the curb. Blood runs over the curb onto the street. I stand by the two women, looking over their shoulders at the only woman I've ever—

Why, Diana? Why would you do this to yourself?

"Did anyone see what happened?" someone shouts.

"That was Diana's balcony!" someone running toward the building shouts.

A crowd has quickly gathered. Nobody can do anything but stare at her, as though she were a museum object. She is—I can't say the word, but she isn't breathing, her body has been crushed, she . . . isn't alive.

Leave her alone, I say in my head, maybe out loud, too. **Give her space. Let her have some dignity.**

At least it's dark, which, mercifully, shrouds her in a semblance of privacy. You can't see her damaged face, can't see the pain. It is, in a strange way, consistent with Diana's fierce pride that she would hide her broken face from the public even in death.

Somebody asks about an ambulance. Then ten people at once are on their cell phones. I sit back on my haunches, helpless. There is nothing I can do for her. Then I see, to my right, between the feet of some onlookers, pieces of a broken clay pot and dirt. I even detect a whiff of cinnamon. I look up at her balcony again, not that I can see anything from this angle in the dark. Must be her apple geraniums, which she kept in pots outside during the summer, near the tip of the triangular balcony overlooking the street.

I pull back and part the growing crowd of people, moving back onto 33rd Street, suddenly unable to be part of their morbid curiosity.

I turn and vomit on the street. Before I know it, I'm on all fours on the pavement.

Diana's hand on my cheek. Diana giggling when she spilled creamer all over herself at that new coffee shop on M Street. Diana showing me her hair a month ago, when she dyed it brown, wondering what I thought, caring about my opinion. That look she had when something was on her mind but she didn't want to say anything. Turning and looking at me, realizing it's me, and smiling. Smiling that carefree smile but maybe not so carefree. **She was taking lorazepam, you idiot; how did you miss that? How did you miss the signs?**

She needed my help and I wasn't there

for her. I didn't take the steps necessary to be proactive. It never occurred to me that **suicide** could be an option.

Murder can be made to look like suicide, and suicide can be made to look like murder.

"Hey, bro—"

The apple geraniums.

"—dude's freaking out over here!"

Run, Benjamin, run.

Sirens now, flashing lights cutting through the darkness, sucking away the air—

"Hold steady," I coach myself. "Hold steady, Benjamin." I take a deep breath and get to my feet.

"Okay." I jump on my motorcycle and speed away.

CHAPTER 4

I avoid the highway and take Independence home because I don't trust myself to drive my bike at a high speed right now. I keep my motorcycle steady and don't try to pass anybody. I'm looking through cloudy, tear-soaked eyes, and my hands are trembling so feverishly I can hardly keep my grip.

Independence is a slightly more direct route—4.44 miles door-to-door, to be precise, compared to 4.8 miles on the highway—but it's slightly longer, 15.8 minutes compared to 13.2. This time of night, with traffic more sparse, the gap should narrow. Over the last nine months, the Independence route has varied from twenty-two minutes and eighteen seconds to eleven minutes and five seconds, but I've never been able to compare the routes during rush hour because Constitution and Independence have turn restrictions those times of day, so I have to adjust the route, and that obviously throws the comparisons out the window. Like apples to oranges. Oranges to apples.

Apple geraniums.

Fiona Apple should be a bigger star. She should be as popular as Amy Winehouse was. They remind me of each other, those throaty, soulful voices, but Fiona never seemed to take off after "Criminal." Not that Amy fared much better, ultimately.

Yeah, the way my mind wanders? It gets worse when I get stressed. Dr. Vance had a fancy phrase for it—**adrenaline-induced emotional sanctuary**—but I always thought he was just trying to justify all the money my father was paying him to "fix" me. It took me a long time before I figured out that I suffered from "Pater Crudelis" disorder.

I take Pennsylvania within a block of the White House and, like everything, like a song or a tree or oxygen, it makes me think of Diana. **He's so talented,** she'd said of the president. **He understands what we're trying to do like nobody before him.**

Oh, Diana. Intelligent, caring, idealistic Diana. Did you do this to yourself? Did somebody kill you? Neither possibility makes sense.

But I'm going to figure it out. It's what I do for a living, right?

An oncoming SUV honks at me as it passes me in the other direction on Constitution. Only two presidents signed the Constitution, Washington and Madison. Madison was also the shortest president. And the first to have previously served in the United States Cong—

I swerve to avoid the Mazda RX-7 in front of me, gripping the brakes with all the strength my hands can muster. I end up sideways, perpendicular to the cars at my front and rear. Red light means stop, Ben. Focus! You can do this.

Benjamin, the sooner you learn your limitations, the better.

You're not like everyone else, Benjamin. You never were. Even before— well, even before everything happened with your mother.

You'll have plenty of time to make friends when you grow up.

Diana was my friend. And she could have been much more. She **would** have been.

I can do this. I just need to take some medicine. I just need to get home.

Light turns green. I right the bike and move forward.

Diana Marie Hotchkiss. Marie was her aunt's name; Diana was her grandmother's name. Born January 11, 1978, in Madison, Wisconsin, played volleyball and softball, won the award for outstanding Spanish student from Edgewood High School of the Sacred Heart, from which she graduated in 1995—

Honking; someone's honking at me for something I did; what did I do?

"Shut up and leave me alone!" I yell, not that I expect a response from the car behind me—or that they'll even hear me.

"Pull your motorcycle over and kill the engine!" booms a voice through a loudspeaker.

I look in my rearview mirror and notice for the first time the flashing lights. It's not an angry motorist.

It's a cop.

This should be interesting.

CHAPTER 5

I pull my motorcycle to the side of Constitution and kill the engine.

The first reported murder of a cop was in 1792 in New York in what is now the South Bronx. The perpetrator was a guy named Ryer, from a prominent farming family, who was involved in a drunken brawl at the time. Want to hear the funny part?

"How we doing tonight?" says the cop, walking over to me. I'm illuminated by the searchlight from his car, which he's trained on me.

The funny part is that one of the police

precincts in the Bronx is located on Ryer Avenue, named after that same family.

I give him my license and registration. He probably already traced my plates. He already knows who I am.

"You wanna take off your helmet, sir?"

Actually, no, I don't. But I do it anyway. He takes a long look in my eyes. It can't be a pretty sight.

"Do you know why I pulled you over, Mr. Casper?"

Because you can? Because you have the power to stop, frisk, search, seize, and arrest pretty much whoever you want whenever the mood strikes you? Because you're a constipated, impotent, Napoleonic transvestite?

"I lost control back there a bit," I concede.

"You just about caused an accident," he says. He has a handlebar mustache. Is this cop on loan from the Village People?

I don't favor facial hair, but even if I did, I wouldn't shape it like a handlebar. I'd probably go with the two-day stubble Don Johnson wore in **Miami Vice.** That would be cool.

"You crossed the centerline three times in one block," he says.

I decide to exercise my right against self-incrimination. And pray that he doesn't ask me what's in my bag—like night-vision goggles or a used smoke alarm or some rudimentary tools. Or the body frosting I took from Diana's closet.

I need to get home. I need time to think, to figure this out.

"Have you been drinking tonight, sir?"

He's standing pretty close to me. One of the hazards of pulling over a motorcyclist. I could reach over in jest and grab his baton or the handcuffs on his belt, maybe his holstered weapon, before he could say **doughnut.** He probably wouldn't think it's funny.

But if he gets too inquisitive, I might not be joking. I may have mentioned that sometimes I don't trust myself.

"Sober as a priest," I answer. Actually, my priest when I was growing up, Father Calvin, was a raging alcoholic.

"Something upsetting you tonight?" he asks.

Well, the night started off okay, when I successfully planted surveillance equipment in the home of the woman I love. It took a turn for the worse when she later plummeted to her death. **HOW DOES THAT SOUND, COP?**

"Fight with my girlfriend," I explain. "Sorry about my riding. I was just a little worked up. I'm totally sober and I'll drive home carefully. I'm on the Hill, just five minutes away."

I can play normal when I have to. He looks me over for a while, watches my eyes, and then tells me to sit tight. He takes my license and registration back to his vehicle. He isn't going to find anything interesting. I don't have a criminal record—not one that he'd find, anyway.

Ulysses S. Grant was once stopped for speeding on his horse. The fine was twenty dollars and he insisted on paying it. Franklin Pierce was once arrested for hitting an old lady with his horse, but the charges were dropped.

"You're a reporter," the cop informs me when he returns. "The **Capital Beat.** I've read your stuff before. Thought I recognized the name."

Actually, I'm the White House correspondent, and I also own the company. The benefits of having a wealthy grandfather. Does that mean he won't write me a ticket?

Nope. He cites me for reckless driving and crossing the centerline. It seems duplicative to me, but now is not the time to engage in a debate about logic. I just want him to let me go, which he's going to do, albeit with tickets for moving violations. That's the good news. The other good news is that, in a bizarre way, this cop has calmed me down, forced me somewhere toward normal.

The bad news is that now I've been placed near Diana's building within an hour of her death.

CHAPTER 6

I don't sleep but I dream: of a gun on a bathroom floor; of a woman prone on a sidewalk; of blood spatter on a shower curtain; of vacant, lifeless eyes; of a scream nobody can hear; of a blood droplet in free fall, taking the shape of a sphere before striking a surface without a sound.

"Diana," I say aloud. My head pops up. I get up from the second-floor landing and rush downstairs. Did I hear her voice?

"Diana?"

I check the kitchen, the family room, the bathroom.

Outside, the darkness is gently dissolving. Dawn. Seven hours have passed in what felt like seven decades, torturous, agonizing. My body is covered in sweat and my pulse is just starting to slow. My limbs ache and I'm breathing as if someone is standing on my chest.

I race to the front door and look through the keyhole: a white panel truck is parked directly outside my town house. Coincidence? A couple of joggers are running through Garfield Park, across the street. My neighbor's giant schnauzer, Oscar, is urinating on my brick walkway. Giant schnauzers freak me out. People should only have the small kind. They don't make sense being that tall. They remind me of Wilford Brimley for some reason. That guy's been sixty years old my entire life.

President Johnson had at least three dogs, mostly beagles, including two he named Him and Her. George Washington kept foxhounds, but he loved all dogs. During the Battle of Germantown, his troops came upon a terrier that belonged to British general Howe, his sworn enemy. His troops wanted to keep it as a trophy, but Washington bathed it, fed it, and then called a cease-fire so that one of his men could return the pooch to his owner across enemy lines under a flag of truce. FDR had a dog he took every—

Just then, a kid appears out of nowhere and hurls a newspaper at my front door.

I duck down, which makes no sense, then silently curse Paper Boy—he'll get his, one day soon—and then decide that I should probably have taken my medicine last night. But no time for that now. I need to get out of here.

First I need to shower, because I stink with sweat and that vanilla body frosting from Diana's closet. I think you're supposed to have somebody else in the room when you use it. Calvin Coolidge liked to have Vaseline rubbed on his head while he ate breakfast in bed. "Vasoline" is second only to "Interstate Love Song" as the Stone Temple Pilots' best song. I probably should have taken a pill last night, but I don't like the side effects, which include mild nausea, ringing in the ears, and, oh yeah, impotence. **It keeps you from getting down, and it keeps you from getting it up.**

Not that impotence is my number one

problem right now. You need another person in the room for that endeavor, too, last I checked. I've had sex with eight women a total of ninety-nine times. The shortest encounter, from foreplay to climax, was three minutes and roughly fourteen seconds. I say **roughly** because sometimes it's a little awkward to go straight to the stopwatch afterward, so you estimate: it takes five seconds to withdraw and between five and ten seconds to pay her a compliment before checking your wrist discreetly.

The longest encounter, if you're wondering, was forty-seven minutes and roughly thirty seconds. Taking all my encounters together, and using round numbers, the mean duration is twenty-one minutes, the median is eighteen minutes, and the mode is seventeen. My math tutor, Miss Greenlee, would be proud. Because every time with her was over thirty minutes.

I've never had a long-term girlfriend, though. For some reason, most of them thought I wasn't romantic.

Until Diana. We connected. We're all

puzzle pieces on a huge board, and she and I, well, our jagged edges just fit together. Even if she hadn't figured it out yet.

I turn on the shower water but whip my head back around. What was that?

I throw a towel around my waist and rush to the bedroom window, overlooking F Street. The white panel truck is still parked directly across from my town house. My quaint little tree-lined street is blossoming as the city awakens. More dogs are running around now in Garfield Park, but not that giant schnauzer.

I walk to my staircase and remain still, listening for anything on the two floors below.

Nothing.

Satisfied, I return to the bedroom. A blast of music erupts, thrashing guitars, thumping bass, almost knocking me to the carpet. "Fine Again," by Seether. I take a moment to recover from what could have been a coronary. It must be 6:30 a.m. I have my clock radio alarm set to DC101.

I turn the shower water past hot and let the scalding water punish my neck. My eyelids are heavy and my legs are rubbery. Staying up all night has handicapped me now, when I need to focus more than ever.

Because now I'm going back to Diana's apartment.

CHAPTER 7

I take my motorcycle back the same way I came last night. The streets are relatively quiet, as it's not quite seven in the morning, plus Congress isn't in session, which means its coattails—staffers, interest groups, lobbyists, even reporters—have thinned out considerably. We're still packed into the city like sardines, but everything's relative. I can feel the heat index rise as I move down Constitution again. It's going to be hotter than yesterday.

There's so much I don't know at this point. I don't know what Diana was doing yesterday, either in the daytime or in the evening. I just know that my instruction was to be out of her apartment by ten o'clock.

Ten o'clock was Calvin Coolidge's typical bedtime. He usually slept until somewhere between seven and nine the next morning, plus he took an afternoon nap. He used to joke, **When I'm asleep, I can't make any bad decisions.** President Arthur rarely went to bed before two in the morning. President Polk routinely worked late into the night and rose early, but then he died from exhaustion three months after completing his one term. He did purchase California, though, which some people consider a plus.

What happened after I slipped out of her apartment a couple minutes before ten? The elevator door I heard opening—was that Diana? Was she alone? And why was it so important that I be gone by ten?

I feel my pulse ratchet up as I cruise along K Street, driving along the Georgetown Waterfront Park, watching some kayakers on the Potomac, approaching 33rd. Truman was our thirty-third president but the thirty-second to hold the office, as Grover Cleveland was elected to two nonconsecutive terms, losing his reelection bid to

Benjamin Harrison in 1888 even though he won the popular vote. But then he thwarted Harrison's reelection bid and won a second term four years after his first, when Harrison was unable to campaign because of his wife's illness.

Maybe I should have taken my medication.

I take a right onto 33rd and ride north toward the canal and Diana's apartment building. I park my ride a block short and walk up the street, sweating from the humidity—already—and probably some nerves, too.

I feel like Bruce Willis in **Pulp Fiction,** returning to his apartment after he killed his boxing opponent and betrayed a mobster. If John Travolta were waiting for me inside, I'd ask him why he did **Battlefield Earth.** If I had a Bruce Willis film festival, I would watch **The Sixth Sense, Die Hard, Unbreakable,** and **Pulp.** And probably **Ocean's Twelve,** even though he just played himself. Hey, it's my film festival, my rules.

This could be risky. I have to be careful about being seen. I have a key to her place, but some people might recognize me. I wish I had one of those realistic masks like they wore in the **Mission: Impossible** movies, the ones they dramatically rip off to reveal their true identities. But it's just lonely old Benjamin. I don't particularly stand out. I've become good at blending into the woodwork. People used to tell me I look like my father, which they meant as a compliment, even though I welcomed it like a tetanus shot. Diana said I looked like Johnny Depp. Maybe I should be disguised as a pirate. Or John Dillinger. Or Willy Wonka.

As I get closer, I feel my chest constricting, my throat and mouth drying up, my limbs becoming unsteady. This is where Diana's life ended last night. It hasn't really sunk in yet. I've been punched, but the bruise hasn't yet formed. My brain knows it, and my body is physically responding, but somehow it doesn't seem real yet.

And then it does. Then it crystallizes. The image of her falling comes into focus and I want to rewind time, like Superman did to save Lois Lane, and find out what was happening with Diana that I didn't know, what caused someone to kill her or prompted her to take her own life. **Tell me,**

**Diana, give me something, tell me how
I can figure—**

A man in civilian clothes is standing
very close to the spot where Diana landed,
looking up at the balcony. Unless he's an
architect or a real estate agent or a big fan
of balconies, he's probably one of DC's
finest. He looks over at me and I see the
mustache, which seals it. This guy's a cop,
investigating Diana's death.

And having lost myself in my thoughts,
I've made a terrible blunder. I'm only ten
feet from him, and now I've seen him and
come to a complete, dead stop in response,
in the middle of the sidewalk. Which, of
course, makes me stick out to him. He turns
and looks at me. I stare back. Neither of
us says a word. This is getting worse with
every second that passes. This is what
Uma Thurman in **Pulp Fiction** called an
uncomfortable silence. I wonder if he can
hear the throbbing of my pulse.

It's way too late to start up again and walk
past him casually. Headlong flight is an
option, and, looking the guy over, I see that
I could probably take him in a footrace, but
all in all that seems like a last-resort idea,
and maybe he saw me park my bike, so

even if I got away clean, it would take him one call on his radio to know all about me—including the fact that I was in the neighborhood last night, driving erratically and acting upset.

Oh, this is really going well, Ben. Nice idea, coming here.

He takes a step toward me. He folds a stick of gum into his mouth and nods to me.

"Morning," he says with a practiced calm. But I can tell. He can see it in my eyes. He's better than handlebar-mustache patrol guy from last night. His antennae are up. He knows. **He knows.**

What now, smart guy?

"You live around here?" he asks, like it's just idle curiosity, like he's about to ask me for directions to the Washington Monument.

I don't answer. Instead, my left hand reaches around behind my back. I move casually, with a smile on my face to keep his threat radar low.

In one seasoned, fluid motion, he disengages the cover on his hip holster and eases his hand over the revolver.

CHAPTER 8

Turns out this cop's a lefty. I guess the holster on his left hip should have been a clue. President Garfield was a lefty. So was Truman. In the modern era—

I brandish my MPD press pass, which was folded up in my back pocket. "**Capital Beat.**"

The cop takes a breath and decelerates, releasing his grip on his sidearm. "Jesus Christ," he says.

"No. Just a reporter."

Actually, Garfield was ambidextrous. He could write ancient Greek with one hand while writing Latin with the other. Lefty was

Al Pacino's character in **Donnie Brasco.** In my opinion, it was his finest acting job, restrained and despairing.

The cop does a quick read of my credentials. They're issued annually by the Metropolitan Police Department. "Benjamin Casper," he reads. "Well, you sure as shit gave me a nervous moment there, Benjamin Casper."

Great. He said my name twice, quadrupling the likelihood that he'll remember it later.

President Buchanan often cocked his head to the left because one eye was nearsighted and one was farsighted.

"You're supposed to keep your credentials in plain sight, pal."

"Guilty as charged." I nod in the direction of Diana's building. "Jumper last night?"

He looks me over again. "PIO will release something later. Still working on identification."

That's a dodge if I ever heard one, and White House correspondents hear them every day. Most detectives or uniforms will feed you the basics even before the public information officer releases an official statement, especially if you promise to spell their names correctly in the story. That tells me something: this case is being treated differently.

The area where Diana landed is roped off with yellow tape. Pieces of the clay pot and some soil from the apple geraniums still remain. There is the bloodstain, which is amassed primarily on the sidewalk, with traces beyond it onto the curb.

Once blood has left the body, it behaves as a fluid, and all physical laws, including gravity, apply.

"Help me out, Detective," I say. "No leads at all?"

He's already begun to tune me out. Now that he makes me for a reporter, I'm about as welcome as a flatulent cockroach.

But my question gets his attention. He turns to me. "Leads on what? On a lady jumping from her balcony?"

"Have it your way," I say, sounding like a reporter getting the stiff-arm.

"Sorry, Benjamin Casper. This is dark for now."

What's with repeating my damn name?

I decide to cut my losses and beat it. This was a net loss, all told. I didn't get into Diana's apartment, and one of the investigating detectives said my name three times, virtually guaranteeing it would be burned into his memory. But at least I used my reporter angle to avoid a catastrophic misstep.

And the trip wasn't a total waste. I came away with three things I didn't previously know. First, the Metropolitan Police Department is treating Diana's death as a homicide investigation. Second, they're acting like they're not, for some reason.

And third, there are two guys wearing sunglasses, parked down the street in a Lexus sedan, who seem awfully interested in me and this cop.

CHAPTER 9

I kick the Triumph to life, throw on my shades, and turn in the direction of the Lexus with the two guys just to get a quick look. Each of them is Caucasian, steel-jawed, muscular, and constipated. Okay, constipated is just a guess. I don't know their deal, but now is not the time to find out—not when I lack the element of surprise, they're two and I'm one, and they're in a car and I'm on a bike. Besides, I've aroused enough suspicion for one morning.

I drive back to my house slowly, giving them a chance to follow me. They don't. So maybe they have no interest in Diana.

Maybe they just wanted a glimpse of the Potomac from their vantage point. Maybe they're bird-watchers.

Diana would ride with me on the Triumph sometimes. It was the best time I ever had on the bike, with her arms nestled around my waist, her chin on my shoulder, sharing an adventure. I haven't yet come to grips with the fact that she'll never ride with me again.

We were going to be a couple. I know that. The best couples are the ones who start out as friends first, like Billy Crystal and Meg Ryan in **When Harry Met Sally.** Except let's face it—she was way too cute for him. Anyway, most people come together through sexual attraction and then try to figure out if they're compatible. The sex distracts them, then they realize too late that their pieces don't fit together. Diana and I, we were different. We were pals. Buds. True, I wanted more, but her resistance forced us to develop a different kind of relationship. Once we got to the romantic part, we would've already checked off all the other boxes.

Or maybe I was just dreaming. I'll never know for sure.

Because somebody killed her. I'm sure of it now. She loved those apple geraniums. Even if she wanted to die, she would've taken care to step around them before taking the plunge. She wouldn't have willy-nilly barreled over the side and taken them with her.

I can imagine a cop laughing at my analysis. The Case of the Fallen Geraniums. **Someone in this room is a florist!**

You'd have to know her like I do.

Anyway, the video surveillance in her apartment will tell the story. I'll just have to wait until the police clear out—

Wait. Wait. Did Diana **know** somebody wanted to kill her?

Is **that** why she asked me to put the surveillance equipment in her apartment? She never volunteered why, so I never asked. But it makes all the sense in the world.

Why would Diana go to the trouble of having me install eavesdropping devices in her apartment if she were going to commit suicide the same night?

She wouldn't. That confirms it. Diana Marie Hotchkiss was murdered.

Oh, Diana. Were you afraid for your life?

Why? What did you do? What situation were you stuck in? Did you know something you shouldn't have? Did you **do** something you shouldn't have?

And why didn't you trust me enough to tell me?

I should go to the police with this. It's a critical piece of information. They'll know Diana was afraid of somebody, plus the surveillance cameras should solve the crime.

But I'm left with the same problem I've had since the moment I left her that night, dead on the sidewalk: I was in her apartment only minutes before she fell. And I fled the scene.

The minute I go to the police, I become the prime suspect in her murder.

CHAPTER 10

They come at me all of a sudden, face-less, but big and strong, with quick hands that take hold of me, seize me by the neck and the wrist, forcing me into submission as my feet slip on the wet bathroom tile, placing the gun in my hand but gripping it fiercely, maintaining control, pressing it against my temple. I resist, moving my hand, angling my head away from the barrel, but their fingers grip my hair, force my head forward, press the barrel against my temple, and reach for the trigger. I stretch my fingers outward, off the

trigger, but they're too strong, they're too strong and I'm too weak, and I see the blood spatter on the shower curtain before I hear the bullet, before I feel it penetrate my brain, before I know that I am dead.

I lurch forward and almost break my laptop computer in half. I expel a loud breath and take a moment to reorient myself. I'm sitting in the corner of my bedroom. I was online doing research for a story and I guess I dozed off. I've been doing that a lot since Diana died—not sleeping in any regular fashion but rather nodding off until the violence of my dreams shakes me awake. I can count on one hand the number of hours I've slept in the last forty-eight.

I place the laptop, hot in my sweaty lap, onto the carpet and rise to a crouch. I stay that way, keeping low, as I move toward the window, careful to stay below the sight line.

Then I rise up just enough to look down at the street level. The sun, recently risen, sends stripes through the trees into the park and onto F Street below.

The white panel truck is still parked along the curb across from my house, two days running now. I have passed it several times in the days since Diana's death. Never have I seen a single person inside. Then again, I can only see inside the driver's compartment. I have no idea what's going on in the back.

One of my neighbors, a grad student named Alicia who won't let you forget she studied the classics at Radcliffe, is walking her Doberman along the brick sidewalk across the street. A Frisbee sails to a rest at her feet and she pauses, concerned, as another dog, a yellow Lab, races to retrieve it. She hustles her Doberman away to avoid a confrontation. The Lab manages to scoop up the Frisbee in his mouth and gallops back to his owner, who is standing in the middle of Garfield Park.

No sign of Oscar, the giant schnauzer.

Someone's playing Frisbee with his dog this time of morning? The guy is big and athletic—is he one of the guys from the Lexus a couple days ago, watching me and the cop outside Diana's building? Could be. I don't know.

I turn away from the window and catch a whiff of myself. I didn't shower yesterday. I don't remember much of what I did yesterday, which is not to say that I have amnesia but rather that it feels like a blur. Somewhere in there, while hunkered down in the house—the benefits of owning an online newspaper—I banged out an article on a power struggle between the president's chief of staff and the secretary of homeland security, something I dug up from a source inside DHS, an assistant to the deputy secretary, one of the few women I ever dated who actually liked me when it was over.

Music pops on over a DJ's voice—my clock radio. Six thirty in the morning in the nation's capital, and it's going to be a great day, he tells me.

No, it's not. Today's going to be a bad day.

I move slowly, trudging along, bitter and wounded. Over the last two days, I have veered wildly between depression and bitterness and fear, depending on whether I consider that (a) Diana is gone forever; (b) someone violently took her from this world; (c) someone might have similar thoughts toward me; or (d) somehow, in some way I can't fathom, I am being set up for Diana's murder.

The instinct comes naturally to me, bred into me since childhood, to turn inward, to hide, to keep everything and everybody out.

Benjamin, the sooner you learn your limitations, the better.

You'll have plenty of time to make friends when you grow up.

Diana was my friend. And that's why I can't stay in the house today.

Today is Diana's visitation in her hometown of Madison, Wisconsin, and I owe it to her to attend.

Even if it gets me killed.

CHAPTER 11

I shower, shave, put on a suit, and take the Triumph over to the airfield for my flight to Madison. The fresh air does me some good, snaps me out of my funk for the moment. I need my head screwed on tight.

I park my bike and walk right through the lobby out onto the tarmac. Potomac Airfield is just a few minutes from downtown DC, yet there are still no fences, no cameras, no real security checkpoints. Go figure. The guy who runs this place has some kind of guts. But when he's got an empty spot, he'll let me tie down or hangar for practically nothing, as long as I talk him up with the other correspondents. Politics in the District isn't limited to elected officials.

I walk over to my plane, a Cessna 172N Skyhawk, 1979 model. I bought it two years ago, tapping the trust fund my grandfather left me. Never knew the guy, but Grandpa did well in the convention business and even better in the stock market, and I have a plane, an online newspaper, and a pot of money invested in bonds to show for it.

The Cessna's a beauty. Four seats with just enough cargo space. Blue stripes, the color of a peaceful sky. The color of Diana's eyes.

I'm going to say good-bye to you today, Diana.

President Kennedy was the first to use the plane that became known as Air Force One, a modified Boeing 707. He didn't want an overtly military look, so he went as far as to remove the words **Air Force** from the side of the fuselage. Kennedy flew in it the first time to attend Eleanor Roosevelt's funeral in Hyde Park, New York. His last time on the plane was his flight to Dallas in November of 1963. President Johnson took the oath of office on board that aircraft.

I remove the chocks, the triangular blocks that prevent the wheels from moving. I walk around to remove the wing and tail tie-downs. I get a funny look from a pilot tying his plane down next to me. Most pilots just use chocks for short stops of an hour or so and only use tie-downs if the plane remains outside overnight or longer. I use both. You can never be too safe.

President Kennedy fantasized about his own death. He talked about assassination frequently and even reportedly made a playful home movie about it.

The routine of the preflight inspection comforts me, freeing my mind from weightier subjects. No frost on the wings—fat chance in this sweltering August heat. Sufficient oil; external lights illuminated. I've already called in the flight plan, so I won't have an unexpected air force escort. The SFRA—the Special Flight Rules Area all around the District—isn't really a big deal unless some idiot pilot forgets to notify anyone that he'll be flying through. Then he just might have the nation's finest airmen using him for target practice.

Cargo door secure. Rudder control and elevator control cables okay. VOR antennas in good condition. The VOR antennas, radio beacons that create the "highways" in the sky, are crucial to instrument-guided flight. With two or more bearings to or from a station, I can triangulate my position on a map—but only if my antennas are working properly.

One of Kennedy's favorite poems was "I Have a Rendezvous with Death." He would often ask his wife to recite it to him.

I climb up in the cockpit and start the next checklist. Seat belt: fastened. Brakes: set. Mixture: full rich. Carb heat: cold. Prime the fuel. Throttle in one-eighth inch. Master and beacon: on. Open the window, yell out "Clear!" Crack the throttle and hit the starter. The plane rolls forward.

I have a rendezvous with Death
At some disputed barricade,
When Spring comes back with
**   rustling shade**
And apple-blossoms fill the air—

Or apple geraniums, tumbling to the sidewalk six stories down.

A blood droplet in free fall will take the shape of a sphere.

A crackle of muted static, frantic squawks from the radio. To my right, the pilot who shot me the funny look is screaming and pointing. I hear a strange loud thrumming, like the metro rumbling by the Eastern Market while I walked with you, Diana, in the cherry blossom–scented spring sunlight—

No!

I slam on the brakes. The prop on the front of my Skyhawk nearly takes the wingtip off a Piper Mirage as it taxis past me. Jesus, Ben, wake up!

The three most important things to remember when you're in the cockpit, Benjamin. Fly the plane. Fly the plane. Fly the plane.

Breathe, Ben.

My heart creeps back down my throat to its cage in my chest, and I taxi out for takeoff with trembling hands.

I have a rendezvous with death.

CHAPTER 12

I take a rental car from the Dane County Regional Airport to this place, the Partridge Funeral Home, which is bordered on the north by its cemetery, on the south by residential housing, and across the street by some kind of forest preserve or park. The building looks like an elementary school, a one-story structure of faded brown brick with simple shrubbery and a small lawn that's withering in the blasting summer heat.

I slow my pace as I approach the front door. Through the glass door I see a blown-up photograph, placed on an easel, of

Diana from long ago, a high schooler in her purple homecoming dress, her hair poofy and sprayed, wearing a gaudy white corsage and, as always, that carefree, crooked smile.

A tremble runs through my body. I stifle the instinct to turn and run, to return to the capital. But I have to do this.

There are some things in life you just have to do. That from my dear father as he knotted my tie on the morning of Mother's funeral. I always thought that was a stupid thing to say, but now I guess I understand what he meant.

I enter the building, take one more look at the photo of the smiling Diana, and follow the directions on a sign. At the end of the hallway, a large parlor area hums with the quiet, respectful tones of those paying their last respects. There are flowers everywhere. More photographs are displayed throughout the room: Diana as a newborn; as a toddler in a Halloween princess costume; as a teenager setting a volleyball; as a graduate in a posed yearbook photo, her eyes full of promise as they look off into the distance. In the middle of the room, several women who look to be Diana's age gather around a laptop computer that plays a slide show of images.

Where's the casket? With my question comes relief. I'm not sure I'm ready to see her lifeless. It was one thing to see her facedown in the dark; it would be another to see her posed in cruel artificial lighting, broken and damaged and on display.

Then it hits me. Diana's body isn't in Madison. It's in DC, in the custody of the Metropolitan Police Department. They haven't released the corpse. For now, they're only having a visitation, to be followed by a funeral at a future time after they determine the cause of death.

Just as they did with Mother.

To the far right of the room, an elderly couple and a guy in his midthirties shake hands with well-wishers. Her parents and brother, a receiving line.

I do another survey of the room. About thirty people here and I don't recognize a soul. It's probably asking a lot for people from DC to trek out here to Wisconsin. Most people don't have a trust fund, as I do.

A woman in a crisp black suit, somewhere around forty, stands in a corner, looking at a collage of photos of Diana.

Except she's not really looking. Her eyes move casually about the room, keeping an eye on the entrance. She's chosen the corner that maximizes her view of the entire parlor. She avoids eye contact with me when I try to establish it. She's pleasant-looking and unremarkable, which is smart—she's a good choice, somebody who won't stick out. Whoever sent her, they aren't stupid.

I mean, in **The Firm,** one of the henchmen, the one who killed Gary Busey and the lawyers in the Caymans, and who tried to kill Tom Cruise—that guy was an albino. If you were going to pick someone to anonymously carry out your wet work, would you choose an albino? Anybody, but anybody, could identify him: **Well, let's see . . . don't remember much, 'cept, oh, yeah, he had white hair and red eyes and was completely pale.**

This woman here—dirty-blond hair, normal-looking, medium height, simple black outfit, etc. She could be anybody.

I take a breath. Okay. I can do this.

I stand in a small line of people waiting to speak with Diana's family, my heartbeat accelerating. Why would an albino go into acting in the first place? Are there a lot of roles out there for people lacking pigment? Maybe you figure you have a niche, and you do minor roles just to put food on the table, awaiting that one part, that film that will define your career, **The Color of Nothing,** the story of the albino kid from Detroit who everyone said wouldn't amount to anything, who lifted himself up by his bootstraps working at carnivals and tanning salons until he rose to prominence as Alfie the Clown, the star of a Nickelodeon—

"Hello."

I turn to see a woman standing behind me, alone, dressed in a loose-fitting blouse and blue jeans, more casual than I might have expected for a visitation. She looks to be about Diana's age, so I'm guessing local, a high school classmate or neighbor.

"Hi," I manage. It comes out weak, through a full throat.

"I'm Emma."

"Ben."

"You're from DC?" Emma asks. She's a tad overweight, a round stomach, possibly pregnant, but I don't dare ask. I'm not **that** stupid.

I nod. "You?"

"High school," says Emma. "I still live in town. My husband's a math professor at the university. Do you work at the same PR firm as Diana?"

PR firm? Diana didn't work at a PR firm.

"Yes," I answer. "I do."

She shakes her head—bemusement, not admiration. "That must be something, living out there. All the fighting and spinning and talking heads."

"Diana—Diana talked about it a lot?"

"Oh, I don't know about 'a lot.' We'd lost touch. I'd see her when she came back in town, maybe once a year around holidays, that sort of thing." She smiles absently, recalling a memory. "I remember when she graduated from UVA—"

She didn't graduate from UVA. She didn't even **go** to UVA.

"—and she took that job on the Hill."

She didn't take a job on the Hill after college.

Here: Diana was a sophomore at Wake Forest, a poli-sci major, when she got pregnant. The history professor who knocked her up talked her into an abortion. She complied, it tortured her, and she dropped out of school and moved to DC. She was a housekeeper at then-congressman Craig Carney's apartment. Then, history repeating itself, she started an affair with Congressman Carney. He recognized her brains as well as her beauty, and when Carney became deputy director of the CIA he elevated her to her current position as a CIA White House liaison. He also put her up in a nice place in Georgetown. The affair ended, Diana picked up the rental payments on her own, and she kept the job with the CIA.

"That's what she called it, the Hill. She was so excited. She said she might run for Congress someday." Emma shakes her head, lifts her shoulders in frustration. "What—I mean, does anyone know why she would take her own life?"

I look up at the ceiling. This is an interesting development.

"Sometimes," I say, "you just don't know a person."

CHAPTER 13

George Hotchkiss is retired, a former middle manager with Madison Gas and Electric. He was born in pre–World War II London and came to America in the 1950s to study engineering at Purdue University. There he met Bonnie Sturgis, whom he married on November 23, 1963, the day after JFK's assassination.

He's also a domineering, violent prick, according to Diana.

"George Hotchkiss," he says to me with a dour expression, slowly extending his hand. He looks like he once had significant upper body strength, probably pumped iron, but now has about twenty pounds layered over that flabby muscle.

"Ben Casper, Mr. Hotchkiss. I'm very—"

"Say the name again?"

That stops me a moment. "Benjamin . . . Casper."

It doesn't register with him. "How did you know Di?"

Cognizant of Emma, whom I'd just told that I worked with Diana, I keep it vague. "I was a friend of hers in DC," I say. "She was wonderful," I add, to change the subject. "The best."

He takes the measure of me. I don't get the sense he's coming back with a positive read. The feeling is mutual.

"She never mentioned you," he informs me, which is sweet of him.

"Well, she loved you very much, sir." That's a lie. Diana couldn't wait to get out of Madison. It had nothing to do with the town and everything to do with her parents.

Moving right along. Diana's mother, Bonnie, is no picnic, either. She appears to be a couple of vodka martinis past the intersection of sober and appropriate. Her eyes are bloodshot and her words are a bit slurred. I'm offended for Diana's sake. A mother should be strong for her daughter at a time like this, right?

We have to be strong today, Ben. It's what Mother would have wanted.

Well, maybe I'm being too judgmental. Everyone grieves differently.

"I don't remember ever hearing your name," Bonnie tells me.

"Right, your husband mentioned."

Next up, brother Randy. Diana had a weakness for the kid. He had a rough patch in his early twenties. He's supposedly interning now at a local TV news station in the sports department, though as I look at him—short, rough complexion, small, liquid eyes, hair in all directions—I see that he has a face for radio.

"She talked about you all the time," I say, which is a stretch. "All good."

"I doubt that."

I almost laugh. "It's a very nice visitation."

"Wake," he says.

"I'm sorry?"

"It's a wake. We're Catholic. We call it a wake."

Well, then. "I'm very sorry for your loss."

His eyes narrow. "You knew her how?"

"We were friends."

"Good friends?"

I think of many ways to answer that but just say, "Yeah."

"Hmph." He nods slowly. "Well, if you were good friends with her, Mike—"

Ben. My name's Ben.

"—then maybe you can tell me why she would kill herself."

Another one I could answer many ways. What does he expect me to say? How about, **Murder can be made to look like suicide, and suicide can be made to look like murder.** I opt for respectful silence instead.

"So maybe **not** such a good friend." He dismisses me with a pat on the arm. "Thanks for coming, Mike."

I don't say anything in response, though I'd like to. This guy just lost his sister, so he gets a long rope.

So! That was the family. Can't imagine why Diana didn't like coming back home.

The fortyish woman in the stylish black suit is still loitering at the other end of the room. She looks up every time someone new enters the parlor and studies him or her a moment. She finally catches on that

I'm watching her, but she still won't lock eyes with me.

Detective LaTaglia did the same thing at Mother's visitation. Except she didn't watch the other people entering and exiting the funeral home in Rockville, Maryland. She didn't even watch my father.

She watched only me.

You're a strong little boy, Benjamin. Eight years old and all grown up! Your mother would be proud.

She loved you a lot, didn't she?

You loved her, too, right?

"They're grieving."

I spin around. It's Emma again, the possibly pregnant high school friend. She likes to sneak up on me.

"The family," she says. "Especially Randy. He can be nice, believe it or not. But it's gotta be tough for him right now."

It must be tough, Ben. Not being able to give your mother a proper Christian burial. They say your soul doesn't go to heaven until your body is buried.

"Yeah," I tell Emma. "It must be tough."

But here's the thing, Ben. We can't let your mother be buried until we figure out what happened to her.

Do you know what happened to her, Ben? I kinda think you do.

Emma smiles at me, subdued for the occasion. "A bunch of people are getting together later," she says. "Someone rented a room at Jack's. If you want to stop by?"

I glance back at black-suit lady. For the moment, at least, she is gone.

"I just might do that," I tell Emma.

CHAPTER 14

Jack's Pub is an off-campus bar populated by grown-ups and students from UW who have decided they're too mature to be hanging out at a campus bar. They would be the outcasts, the rebels, the ones who didn't go Greek, didn't play a sport, didn't join the student council or any of the clubs, who lived off campus and made the decision to rebel before they knew what it was they were rebelling against.

They would be me.

Someone rented the back room so we could celebrate the life of Diana in the proper way, meaning with alcohol. In my experience—as an adult—wakes and funerals provide an opportunity for reunions, and despite the depressing premise for the occasion, people are generally happy to reconnect with old friends.

The back room is all brick, with televisions in the corners, well lit, full of maybe fifty or sixty people, with music from the '90s—a rap song, then a dance song—playing overhead. Almost everyone in here is the same age. They are, presumably, members of the class of '95 from Edgewood High School of the Sacred Heart, or their significant others.

I love that PC term "significant other." It means you're someone special—you're significant!—but either you can't get married because you're gay, which nowadays is only true in some states, or you're unmarried and for some reason object to the word **boyfriend** or **girlfriend.** The next time the person you're with says, "I love you," respond by saying, "You're very, very significant to me."

I slip between some people and head toward the bar when I hear someone say, "That's the guy who worked with Diana at the PR firm." I turn to a group of people looking my way, including Emma and Randy, sitting on a bar stool in the center of the pack.

"Is that right?" Randy says too loudly. He's had more than his share already tonight. "Hey, Mike—"

Ben. My name's Ben.

"—what was the name of that PR firm again?"

In **Spy Game,** Robert Redford taught Brad Pitt the fine points of espionage, including how to recruit foreigners to be undercover spies for the United States. Don't lie to them, he advised Brad, because from that point on, that lie will have to be true.

I wave a hand. "I don't want to talk business."

"I don't wanna talk business, either, Mike. I just wanna know the name of that PR firm you worked at with my sister."

I prefer some of Pitt's earlier roles—the felon in **Thelma & Louise** and the stoner in **True Romance.** He was great in **Seven,** too.

I move to the bar. Randy calls after me, "Hey, Mike," and I hear Emma say, "I thought his name was Ben," and then Randy calls, "Hey, Ben!"

I order a vodka and pay too much for it. Then I head back, trying to decide if I should talk to Randy or not. That is, in fact, my primary reason for sticking around Madison tonight. I'm a reporter, after all, and if I'm looking for the skinny on someone, the chance to talk to that someone's brother is irresistible.

"There he is—Mike-or-Ben." Randy salutes me by raising his pint. He's goading me. But I'm not in the mood.

"I prefer Ben-or-Mike," I answer. A couple of ladies in the group like that. Randy doesn't, but that's too bad for Randy. It's my parting shot, so I part.

I see the lady in the black suit nursing a Bud Light at a corner table, fending off a couple of boozers who think she's the cat's meow.

I stop dead. Cinnamon. Who's taking care of Diana's cat?

The lady in black senses a hitch in my giddyap. She doesn't know why, but it interests her. She's pretty good, but not as good as Detective LaTaglia thirty years ago.

Tell me what happened, Ben, and your mother's soul can go to heaven.

Now, Robert Redford, as much as I loved **The Sting** and **Butch Cassidy** and **The Natural**—actually I thought **The Natural** was boring, but everyone else raved about it so I went along—to me his most amazing work was behind the camera on **Quiz Show** and especially **Ordinary People.**

I find a table not far from black-suit lady and watch her and everybody else for a long hour. Luckily the music is decent, and, even more important, there's a waitress walking around (my "significant other"), so I'm four drinks in when I see Diana's brother part the crowd and sit next to me.

"Please have a seat," I say after he already did.

He whacks my arm with the back of his hand. "Hey, man, didn't mean to come on so strong. I was just—Diana didn't say a lot about what she did, y'know? So I was wondering, if she worked at a PR firm, maybe I could, at least, know the name of it."

Overhead the song changes from "Groove Is in the Heart" to "Smells Like Teen Spirit." Someone has dimmed the lights without me noticing.

Randy probably wouldn't be good at this kind of sleight of hand on a good day, but with half a gallon of booze in him, he can hardly keep a straight face.

I lean in and speak directly into his ear. "I don't feel like being tested, Randy. I don't know who or what you think I am, but I'm really, truly, a friend of Diana's. We both know she never worked at a PR firm, and she didn't attend UVA, either. But that's what she told everyone around here, and I, for one, am not going to contradict her."

Randy, his eyes forward while I speak into his ear, remains motionless.

"She loved the hell out of you," I say. "I can't imagine why, but she did. And my guess is she would be unhappy to see you drinking yourself down a hole tonight, especially after she spent all that money sending you to New Roads that summer while your parents thought you were living with her and interning on the Hill."

With that, Randy's face contorts and he lets out a low moan. He covers his face with a hand and has himself a good cry. I pat his back a couple of times but generally leave him to himself. I hardly know the guy, after all, and I'm not a big hugger.

After ten minutes or so, Randy takes some deep breaths and rights himself in his chair. "I couldn't be sure of you," he said.

The hair on the back of my neck stands at attention.

"What's going on?" I ask.

"Hey, don't ask me. Nobody tells the dopey brother anything." He spits out the words like he's expelling a pill. He pushes himself off the chair and starts to leave.

"Well, who **should** I ask?" I try.

Randy turns and looks at me. "Ask the guy she was fucking," he answers. "Ask Jonathan Liu."

CHAPTER 15

I wake up with a nasty hangover in a mediocre hotel room. I need more sleep, but the gong banging in my head won't allow it, and anyway, I need to get back to DC. I need to learn more about Jonathan Liu.

The two attendants at the desk at Wisconsin Aviation give me a friendly glance and a wave on my way through to the tarmac. They don't ask for any kind of identification, even though I've never flown from here before this trip. The rules for general aviation just aren't the same as those for commercial flight. No metal detectors here. As long as I have the pilot "look," nobody asks any questions. And I'm not even wearing my aviators.

I know what you're thinking—a Leo Di-Caprio mind-scroll, right? Sorry, too tired.

I rush through the preflight check, eager to be rid of Madison, of Diana's family, of the lady in black, of Diana's diminutive drunk of a little brother, with his furtive reference to the most powerful Chinese lobbyist on the Hill.

Chocks up, preflight checklist complete, tower cleared for takeoff. I never go to the big airports. Nearly all airports are public, and they can't refuse to let small aircraft land or take off, but they can leave a tiny plane like mine on the tarmac until I'm roasted or rusted through. Dane County Regional gets me off the ground in an hour.

Flaps up and trim set for takeoff, I release the brakes and open the throttle to full. About fifteen hundred feet down the runway, I hit sixty-five miles per hour and the wheels are bouncing before we're airborne, climbing at full power.

The ground falls away beneath me. Funny how the fire escape at Diana's makes me shake with fear, but throttling up to eighty knots and hurtling through space, supported by faith in the invisible power of lift, is no problem.

I reach altitude and check the GPS, banking east and settling into the flight plan, which will take me to Mansfield, Ohio, for a quick refueling stop before the last leg home.

The engine suddenly brings my mind back to the moment. It sputters. Coughs. I change the fuel mixture to rich, adding more fuel to the mix of fuel and air, and turn on the carburetor heat. The temperature at the airport was ninety degrees when I took off. There can't be ice in the carburetor. Can there?

The engine roars for a moment. Then there is a horrible clatter, like the time we were sitting in the café on G Street, Diana, and a city bus making a right turn tore the side mirrors off two parked cars, and you laughed at the crowd that gathered.

And then, more horrifying than any noise, there is silence. I hear the wind rushing past and nothing more.

"The Sound of Silence" is a nice song, and a nice thought, too, in moments of contemplation or serenity. But it's not a nice sound when you're nine thousand feet off the ground in a single-engine Cessna.

Easy, Ben. You know what to do.

Airspeed at eighty miles per hour. Switch fuel tanks. Mixture to full rich. Carb heat on—check. Primer in and locked. Ignition to left, then right, then . . . start.

I said, **Start.**

Nothing. Not even a click.

That engine is not going to start.

I try again, just to be sure.

My heartbeat kicks into my throat. There are no atheists in Skyhawks that lack engine power. She's a sturdy aircraft, but she's no glider. Watertown is too far. There's no way I can coast all the way there.

This plane is going down.

CHAPTER 16

Breathe in, Ben. Fly the plane.

Look around.

Wind out of the north. I need to find a field. This plane doesn't need a runway, remember? That crazy kid from flight school landed his on the eighteenth green. Oh, how I'd love to be playing golf right now.

> **I have a rendezvous with Death**
> **On some scarred slope of**
> **battered hill,**
> **When Spring comes round again**
> **this year**

And the first meadow-flowers appear.

Just find someplace flat, Ben.

I bank left, into the wind. At least my instruments are still working. For now.

Seat belt and harness tight. I can do this. Just like power-off landings during training. Except without the pesky runway.

I see a long stretch of two-lane highway, and I'm sorely tempted. No, Ben. Power lines. They'd tangle you up like a fly in a spiderweb.

The most beautiful sight I've ever seen appears in front of me—a level pasture, dead ahead. Never have I been so happy to see a bunch of cows.

I can make it. I prepare for landing: Airspeed down to sixty-five knots. Fuel shutoff valve on. As if that mattered. But an engine fire on landing would complicate things.

Focus, Ben. This can still have a happy ending.

Fly the plane. Flaps down. Airspeed to sixty knots.

I tune the radio to 121.5 MHz. That's one I never thought I would see on the dial—

the international aeronautical emergency frequency.

I open the frequency, and with a voice so calm that it doesn't sound like my own, I say the words that haunt a pilot's dreams:

"MAYDAY, MAYDAY, MAYDAY. Watertown tower, this is Skyhawk three-one-six-zero Foxtrot. Repeat: Skyhawk three-one-six-zero Foxtrot with total engine failure attempting a forced landing in a pasture. Last known position 43°6′46″ north, 88°42′13″ west, at fifteen hundred feet, heading twenty degrees. One person on board. I require immediate assistance."

The radio silence compounds the silence of the engine as the seconds tick away. Don't panic, Ben. Fly the plane.

The radio crackles to life. "Cessna three-one-six-zero Foxtrot, this is Watertown tower. I read you five by five. Assistance is en route."

Okay, great. Now, if you could please get here in the next five seconds and toss me a parachute.

The ground hurtles up at me—too fast, too fast. Flaps full down. Nose up, tail down. The wings groan in protest. That's strange—I didn't really notice that sound when the engine was running. Slow it down. Float, Ben. Don't hurtle. Slow it down . . . but don't slow down too much or you'll drop right out of the air altogether and real damage will be done.

Here it comes, here it comes, here it comes—

I unlatch the cabin doors and lock them open so that when the frame is twisted on impact I can still get out. The door bangs deafeningly against the frame, flapping open and shut in the gusts of wind. The noise is a relief after the silence. The quiet engine, like the silence of death, with the wind whistling past.

Did you hear the wind, Diana, as you fell to the pavement?

Dammit, Ben. Fly. The. Plane.

I wait until the very last moment and pull up hard, just before my wheels hit the soft earth. The back wheels collide with the ground, then the front wheel. Perfect. It would have been a shaky landing on a runway, but I feel a premature rush of pride anyway.

Immediately, pride disappearing into panic, I bounce back up, still moving too fast to stay on the ground. Keep her level, Ben. The plane falls back to the ground again with a great thud, and I can see the black and white of the resident cows running frantically from the horrible sound of my Skyhawk skidding through their pasture. I slam on the brakes with every last ounce of strength I have. Full up elevator.

Oh, God, **please stop please stop please stop.** The noise is excruciating. The plane shakes and shudders so hard that sound and sight and smell and taste and touch all blur together. I stand on the brakes completely, straining against the seat belt and harness.

I hear the sickening shriek of twisting metal, and I suddenly slam forward, smashing my head into the instrument panel. The plane tilts suddenly to the left and the ground is shockingly close to my window. As if in slow motion, the wingtip scratches through the earth and shreds, cracking with the force of the impact. I must have lost a wheel back there. I skid forever, my eyes covered with my blood, and then everything goes black.

**It may be he shall take my hand
And lead me into his dark land
And close my eyes and quench
     my breath—
It may be I shall pass him still.**

"Hey, airman, you okay in there?"

I open my eyes, blink away the blood. I kick the door open and crawl out. My head throbs with every heartbeat.

My nose pricks up. I smell . . . kerosene. What the hell?

Kerosene?

I can see fuel dripping from the damaged wing.

I reach out and catch a few drops with my hand. Drops, like blood, forming a perfect sphere in free fall.

Murder can be made to look like suicide, and suicide can be made to look like murder.

Avgas, or aviation gasoline, should evaporate almost instantly. And 100LL—the kind of gas I use for this plane—is dyed blue. But the drops coming from the wing are not the right color. And they leave an oily residue on my hand.

This isn't avgas. This is jet fuel.

One of the guys who rushed to help me says, helpfully, "Someone musta put jet fuel in your plane, son. Who'd do something dumb like that?"

I look at him and shrug.

It's the right question. And it's a question I intend to ask Jonathan Liu.

CHAPTER 17

The aftermath is like a dream, like I'm floating. After a couple of minutes on my feet, my legs buckle, ink blots flash and disappear before my eyes, and I collapse to the ground. The first responders ask me if I'm all right, and I'm thinking—I don't know if I say this out loud, but I'm thinking—if I could survive a fall of nine thousand feet, I can probably survive a fall of six feet and one inch. An ambulance is there a few minutes later and they rush me off before the media arrives. They transport me to Watertown Regional Medical Center, or at least that's what they tell me. I'm weaving in and out of consciousness, picking up a few words here and there, **blood volume** and **saline** and **cyanosis.** A nice paramedic who looks like Demi Moore, but blond, and with a different eye color— okay, maybe she doesn't look totally like Demi—

"God must have been with you today, Benjamin," she says.

"Was He the one . . . who put the jet fuel in . . . my plane?"

I'm leaving on a jet plane. Don't know when I'll be back again. But I'm still here. **I'm still standing, yeah, yeah, yeah.** I hate that song. **She loves you, yeah, yeah, yeah.** A little better. But she didn't love me. She would have, someday. Diana would have—

"My . . . mother loved me," I say.

"Your mother loves you?" It seems like she's trying to keep me talking. She looks kind of like Demi Moore.

"She . . . died."

"Oh, I'm sorry. Was that just recently?"

"Plane crash," I say. If you can't have a little fun, what's the point? Oscar Wilde reportedly said on his deathbed, **My wallpaper and I are fighting a duel to the**

death. One or the other of us has to go.
I don't know if that's true, but I like it.

"Oh, this one's a real joker," says the woman who doesn't look like Demi Moore totally, but kind of. "Stay down, Benjamin. Lie flat."

"I'm . . . fine."

"You're not fine. You're concussed and hypersomething blah, blah, blah."

And then there's a light in my face, and they're poking and prodding me in a bed and . . . and . . .

". . . pain medication, Mr. Casper."

". . . someone you'd like us to call, Mr. Casper?"

". . . reporters want to speak with you, Mr. Casper."

". . . with the National Transportation Safety Board, Mr. Casper."

". . . ask you a couple questions, Mr. Casper?"

"Casper the friendly ghost, Mr. Casper."

"The friendliest ghost you know, Mr. Casper."

Demi Moore in **Ghost** made every red-blooded male want to take up pottery. No, Mr. NTSB investigator, I have no idea how jet fuel got in my tank, and yes, I'm going through some tough times right now, but no, I'm not suicidal. If I were suicidal I wouldn't have **landed** the fucking plane, and I don't care what anyone says, I'll take Demi Moore on her worst day, even in **G.I. Jane.**

"Morning, Benjamin." A woman's authoritative voice.

I open my eyes slowly, like a garage door lifting. "What time is it?"

"Oh-five hundred," she says. A nurse, heavyset, with a warm face.

Five in the morning? I slept for almost eighteen hours. I touch my face. There's a thick bandage on my forehead.

"What happened?" I ask.

"You don't remember what happened?"

"I mean, am I hurt?"

"You suffered a concussion and you went into shock. But no broken bones, by some miracle. How do you feel?"

I shake myself fully awake and let reality reintroduce itself. But it doesn't shake my hand. It goes straight for my balls.

Someone killed Diana and then tried to kill me.

"I have to go," I say.

"Well, you **might** be ready for release.

But I know the guys from the NTSB want to come back. You weren't able to answer their questions last night."

I wasn't? I thought I told them all they needed to know about Demi Moore's film career. They want to come back to talk about her time on **General Hospital**?

I shake my head. I can't stay here. I'm a sitting duck if they're looking for me. And after surviving a free fall from nine thousand feet, it would be a crying shame if someone just walked in and shot me.

"I'm leaving," I say.

CHAPTER 18

I take a cab to Watertown's airport and charter a flight back to Potomac. I know, I know, but I figure my odds of crashing in a plane twice in forty-eight hours are fairly remote, and I'm way too stubborn to let my fear ground me. The guy who flies me is a young Asian guy who keeps asking what it's like to crash-land a plane until I offer to show him. The whole time I'm thinking, if we crash and end up in some remote mountains and get to the point where we're starving to death, like in **Alive,** I hope this guy doesn't eat me.

When I land at Potomac, my fear reawakens. I can't go home. I make a snap decision and drive my Triumph ninety miles south to my lake cabin in Virginia. Anyone wishing to do me harm wouldn't be expecting this move. Only problem is, I wasn't, either, so I don't have my keys. I have to break into my own cabin.

The place has log siding and a stone chimney and sits on four acres of waterfront property on Lake Anna. The land's been in my father's family for three generations, but the lake, in its current form, wasn't created until the early '70s as a cooling mechanism for Virginia Electric and Power's nuclear reactors. My grandfather built the original log cabin on this land, but within a month of his death, in 1983, Father knocked it down and built a two-story, four-bedroom, two-bath structure. Father wasn't exactly the sentimental type. He didn't keep a single picture from his childhood and never talked about his parents. My grandfather worked in trade shows. I think that meant he brought shows in and took a commission from the convention center or something like that. He made millions and invested exceptionally well, ergo my trust fund. That's all I know about Grandpa. Never met the guy and never heard a single intimate detail about him except from Aunt Grace at Father's funeral, who said that Father hated his dad. So we Caspers are keeping a pretty consistent generational theme going.

I stop and gaze a moment at the serene lake, breathe in the clean air. Down by the water there is a long, L-shaped dock and boathouse. No boat, though. It's stored in town and I've been too busy this summer to get it out. No matter. Just being here instills a sense of calm. This place is good for the soul.

Father was a closet drinker, which is a very difficult thing to be, because you're not fooling anybody when you're slurring your words and stumbling around like a toddler learning to walk. But he limited his boozing to the evening, so only Mom and I were granted front-row seats to the Marty Casper Show. In the thirty-four years he worked in the history department at American University, I'll bet there wasn't a soul there who had any clue that Professor Casper emptied a bottle of Scotch per night.

I circle the cabin, looking for the best

point of entry for my break-in. I settle on the wraparound deck on the lake side of the cabin, which is almost entirely a wall of glass. The view of the lake is breathtaking. Others who live here, in the so-called mid-lake, who like to check out everyone else's cabins as they motor up and down the water, call our cabin the house of glass.

I decide on a kitchen window because it's a standard model that will be easy to replace. I pick up a rock, but it falls from my hand. I poise my hand in the air and watch it quiver. It's the first time I recognize the tremble in my body. My legs begin to buckle again and I realize that I've underestimated the effects of what happened to me. I'm surprised I made it down here on the Triumph without killing myself. Mother would have said, **You didn't have your thinking cap on.**

Mother wasn't the warmest of people, either. She took a lot of pills and thought I didn't know. Some days, she'd put me in front of the TV and lock herself in the bathroom for hours. One time, I walked over to the door to ask her what was going on and heard her sobbing and sniffling inside. I never made that mistake again. I just sat in front of the television, ready to turn up the volume when necessary to drown out her cries or her singing. She'd come out eventually, having mustered the courage to face the world, and would wrap her arms around me and hum softly to me while I watched whatever was on TV.

So maybe she wasn't everyone's idea of the ideal mommy, but she was still mine. And she didn't deserve what happened to her.

Instead of a rock, I use my elbow to break through the glass of the kitchen window. It's not an easy fit, but I slide through the window face-first into the kitchen sink, one of those old-fashioned farmer's sinks of stainless steel.

I manage to fall to the floor without doing serious damage to myself. I won't be giving any Olympic gymnast a run for his money, but I don't break any bones. Maybe I'm like Bruce Willis in **Unbreakable.** Nothing can stop me—not a plane crash, not breaking into my own cabin, not even a giant schnauzer.

I let out a forty-eight-hour sigh. After all that, I'm home, in some sense of that word, safe and sound. But safe for how long?

CHAPTER 19

Night falls, and, as if on cue, as if the weather is being controlled by Edgar Allan Poe, the winds kick up and a healthy rainfall follows. The windows rattle and the cabin groans. Outside is nothingness, black as ink, interrupted only by dramatic strikes of lightning.

Dark thoughts invade my brain as I settle into bed on the second floor with my laptop and a bottle of Absolut, in pitch darkness save for the illumination of the computer screen. Someone tried to kill me but wanted it to look like an accident. And they followed me to Wisconsin, a place they couldn't be sure I'd go—it was no foregone conclusion that I'd attend Diana's wake—so they had to be watching me and be capable of moving fast. Which means they're smart, and they're sizable in both resources and numbers.

Which means money. And Jonathan Liu stands behind plenty of it. A reporter in DC knows how to access the lobbyist database, and that told me part of the story— the amount of money Jonathan Liu spread around, either through his own firm, Liu Strategies Group, or through his clients. Jonathan Liu represented BGP, Inc., the Chinese national petroleum company; Tongxin, Inc., an international telecommunications giant; Huò wù Global, a Chinese shipping company; and Jinshu Enterprises, one of the world's largest producers of steel. The annual earnings of those four companies alone are larger than the GDP of most civilized nations.

When you talk about Chinese influence in Washington, you talk about Jonathan Liu. Each of the companies Jonathan Liu represented, plus Jonathan Liu's lobbying firm and then Jonathan Liu himself, maxed out their donations to the political action committees of every major player in Congress, then tripled it in "soft" money to the noncandidate PACs. And that's to say nothing of the gifts—

What was that?

I rifle forward in bed and hold my breath. There's not much activity on Lake Anna this time of night, at least not in the remote area where I am now. On an ordinary evening, you could hear a car approach from a hundred yards away. But the swirling wind and the slapping rain would conceal that tonight.

It sounded like . . . a scraping sound. Metal on wood. The sound of a piece of patio furniture moving across the wooden deck a foot or two.

The rain and wind could have moved the chair a bit.

So could a person who accidentally bumped into it.

My bare feet land softly on the rug. I tiptoe across the bedroom and peer into the hallway. I'm at the far end. Between me and the staircase to the ground floor are three doors on the left—two bedrooms and a bathroom. To my right is a partial wall that ends about ten feet before the staircase, and then it's just a railing and a view down to the ground floor. A partial loft, Father called it.

I move with caution, stopping and listening for anything unusual. The rain smacks the cabin with such ferocity, the wind whips so feverishly, that it's hard to hear anything else. But there's usually a muted quality to it, given the shelter enclosing me, and this is different. It sounds . . . closer. Not muted.

Then I remember the kitchen window and relief floods through me. After I broke into the cabin, I put a makeshift cardboard cover over the window, and that was probably it—it blew off in the storm, so now the outside sounds are streaming into the cabin. Sure. That must be it.

Still, I move on, inching along the wall until it ends. Now it's just the railing, which will do just fine preventing you from falling to the ground floor, but it won't conceal you.

I listen. Nothing but the storm, a loud crack of thunder, the wind crying out to me in a plaintive wail, and the urgent drumbeat of the raindrops overhead.

My heart in my throat, I steal a quick

peek down below, then retreat to the safety of the wall. Not long enough for anyone to see me.

But long enough for me to see, very clearly, that the sliding glass door to the deck is wide open.

CHAPTER 20

My heart thumps so fiercely it robs me of my breath. Someone is in the cabin.

He's downstairs, probably checking the single bedroom and bathroom down there. But it won't take him a minute to realize they're empty and that, other than the living room and kitchen, everything else is up here.

Think. **Think think think.** What does he know? He knows I'm in the house. But he doesn't know where. Every light in the house is off. I could be anywhere.

I move on the balls of my feet down to the bathroom adjacent to my bedroom. I tiptoe in, flip on the light, and turn on the shower water. I get back out, sure that he's heard me, absolutely certain he's already in the hallway waiting for me, that I'm going to walk into a bullet, but I don't have a choice, so I move back into the hallway and duck into the next bedroom and I don't think he saw me. I press myself flat against the near wall and silently name the presidents in order and try to control my breathing. I need to stay near the door.

When I get to Van Buren, I hear the stair groan, that third stair up that I've always meant to fix.

Then I hear it groan a second time.

Two people.

They're up here now, in the hallway. By now they've noticed the light emanating from the bathroom and have probably heard the soft, consistent hum of the shower water. Their footfalls suggest they're not being as cautious now, that they're moving with more purpose. They're headed my way, which means they didn't stop at the first upstairs bedroom.

I'm in the second one.

I can feel their body heat now and pray

they can't sense mine. If I spun around to my right, I could reach out and touch them. Sweat drips into my eyes and I squeeze them shut and hold my breath.

They pass me.

They move to the next door down, to the bathroom, where they're sure I'm taking a shower.

Then there's a burst of rapid-fire gunshots, automatic weapons unloading.

That's when I race out of the bedroom to the staircase.

The **rat-a-tat-tat** of the gunfire provides me with audio cover. I'm bounding down the stairs before I hear the first sounds from them.

"Shit!"

"Staircase!"

I take the stairs in twos, all my weight forward, barely able to keep my balance as I bound toward the ground floor. I feel the bullets whiz past me in the dark, hear the sounds of them penetrate wood and cloth in staccato thumps. The wall of windows shatters in a violent crescendo, raining glass on me as I duck my head down and blast through the open sliding glass door onto the deck. Time is not on my side, so I don't turn for the stairs on either side. I meet the outer railing without breaking stride, jump onto the top plank, and vault over it and down, fifteen feet, to the grass.

CHAPTER 21

I land hard on the ground and feel sure that I've damaged myself in various ways, but now is not the time for assessment. I pop up and sprint for the boathouse and the dock. The men are shouting behind me, but it's white noise to me, drowned out by the furious adrenaline rush.

They can't see you.

But surely they know the direction I'm headed. The bullets blasting into the beech and pine trees all around me confirm it. I don't have a choice. I don't know what I'm up against on land. Lake Anna at least evens the playing field. But the water's still half a football field away.

My legs burn. The undergrowth tears my ankles and calves. My bare feet take a beating over the terrain. And I'm making too much noise. I've always been a noisy runner. In high school, I would come home from a thirteen-mile tempo run, and our housekeeper, Dominga, would say, **Lord above, Mr. Ben, you breathe like a cow.**

Glass shatters in front of me, by the water. The boathouse windows. They must be running and shooting at the same time.

Well, Dominga, you should hear me now. I'm gasping for air, filling my lungs down to the bottom, and clearing them out with a giant **wheesh** before breathing in again, intentionally hyperventilating to maximize the oxygen in my bloodstream. I've never tried it while running, but I'll need all the air I can get for what's coming.

I tear off my T-shirt just before I hit the dock and pound out the last one, two, three, four, five steps, just as I did when I was a kid, count out the five steps and leap, arcing up first to look across the water at the lights of Anna Cabana, and then down to the water, tucking my head between my arms in a tight streamline to get as much distance from the dock as possible.

I slice into the water and keep it deep and flutter-kick like mad. I've got to make it to the neighbor's dock without coming up for air.

I wait until I just start to slow down, then I start the pull-kick-glide of the underwater breaststroke, just as Matt Damon did at the end of **The Bourne Ultimatum,** when it looked like he was dead in the water, like he'd been hit by a bullet before he jumped off the building, but then he started swimming and the music kicked in and we were all relieved that he'd survived.

When Nicholas Cage jumped off that building into the ocean while escaping from prison in **Face/Off,** they just presumed he was dead and didn't search for him. That seemed like a stretch to me, but I guess when you're watching a movie premised on the idea that someone could have surgery done overnight to transplant another person's face onto his without any scarring or recovery time, then you're already on board with the suspension-of-disbelief thing.

Pull. Kick. Glide. I need oxygen. Johnnie

Shaw from the tri training club could make it fifty meters in one breath. That's just crazy, though. Thank God the dock isn't that far. I hope.

My lungs are already begging for air. I let small puffs of air out through my nose with each stroke to help stop the spasms of panic from my lungs.

Was your mother breathing when you found her, Ben?

My son won't be answering any questions, Detective.

My son won't be answering any questions.

I open my eyes underwater, but it makes no difference. I can't see a thing. Utter blackness. There's no horizon to reference, no way to know if I'm swimming in a straight line. All I know is that I was pointed toward the dock when I jumped. Every part of my body is on fire. My legs, arms, back—everything screams for air. All that time training for triathlons, training to get away from my father, I never did a workout with sprints first and swimming after. Hundreds and hundreds of brick workouts over the years, jumping off the bike after a fast ride and then running, to get used to the transition. But why would I need to transition from sprinting to swimming? So I never did. Until now.

Pull. Kick. Glide.

Pull. Kick. Glide. I don't think I can make it much farther. My fingers and toes are buzzing and my chest is throbbing, struggling for a great racking sob of inhalation. I must be getting close. I hope I'm getting close.

The police are going to try to blame you, Ben.

Don't ever talk to them, son. They can't make you.

Pull. Kick. Glide. I can feel my feet brush the surface of the water. Oh, I've never wanted anything so much as the sweet night air just inches above. But bullets travel remarkably well through water, no matter what the movies say.

I fight every instinct to breach the surface. I pull back down, away from precious oxygen, and I want to die.

Did your mother ever talk about wanting to die, Ben?

My son won't be answering any questions.

Pull. Kick. Glide.

My arm brushes something solid. I reach out and feel it. All the mermaids in the sea never sang a song as beautiful as my heart sings to the solid wooden pylon of the dock. I scramble up the post and my head breaks the surface of the water. The air sears into my lungs and I gasp delicious, choking breaths of oxygen while trying to avoid too much rainfall in my mouth. I'm alive. I'm still alive.

But whoever was chasing me can't be far behind.

CHAPTER 22

After a minute or two of panting like a desperate animal while I regain full consciousness, I pull myself onto the dock and lie flat. The rain's lightened up a little, but it's still coming down strong. I listen and hear nothing, but then again, the rain might be drowning it out.

I slither along the dock toward the boathouse and silently thank Steve for not having the light on. Maybe he's not even at the lake right now.

Steve Sykes used to let me escape to his house whenever I could get away. I would assure Father I was training again, on a nice century ride somewhere—a hundred miles can take hours—and I'd sneak over and watch old movies for the afternoon. Steve would always leave the side door unlocked. But it's been years. With any luck, old habits die hard.

I try the handle. It's locked. It's a glass-panel door, so I grab the canoe oar engraved with SYKES from over the top of the door and break out the windowpane by the door handle.

Sorry, Steve. Getcha back for that one.

I carefully reach in through the broken pane, unlock the door, and sneak into the quiet house. The side door opens onto the laundry room. I rummage quickly through the basket by the dryer and find dry clothes and slip on the flip-flops by the door. I peer around in the kitchen. The fridge is still right there by the door, and it looks like his old offroading Jeep keys are still hanging there. At least that habit stuck around. I take the keys and creep back out the side door.

I don't hear anything from outside except the rush of the wind and the beat of the rain, so I dash quickly over to the old Jeep, a 1986 CJ-7 with THIS END UP in big yellow block letters across the top of the windshield. Steve liked extreme sports before they were called extreme sports.

It's been a long time since I drove a stick shift, but she roars to life, along with Brian Johnson of AC/DC singing "Back in Black," and I have no trouble remembering how to crank up a manual transmission and let her rip. I floor it out of the driveway, kicking up gravel behind me. Thank God for the hardtop in this rain.

What are those guys with automatic weapons thinking right now? They don't know, that's what they're thinking. Maybe they hit me and I died in the water. Maybe I'm still in the water, swimming somewhere, could be anywhere, they have no idea. Lake Anna's an enormous lake. Probably they've given up on me.

I take Halls Drive up to a fork. The soft left will take me west. I slow down only slightly and follow the fork west, just as I see headlights to my right, the east—the direction of my cabin.

It's them.

(This is when Mel Gibson, in some action flick, would say, **We've got company.** I always wanted to say something cool like that.)

I floor the gas and kick the old Jeep as hard as it can go, but now the headlights behind me have negotiated the fork and are bearing down on me. The beams are high. It's probably an SUV. I can't outrun it. I hear a staccato burst from behind me and see the flash of light from the automatic weapon, but the first round misses completely. I weave along the road, trying to be as unstable a target as possible while drilling the gas pedal to the floor.

The SUV closes ground on me and then my back window shatters and bullets rip into the passenger seat, **thump-thump-thump,** and the radio blows out just as Angus Young was starting into his guitar solo and the windshield takes two or three pops as well. I'm ducked as low as I can go and the wind is whistling in through the holes in the windshield and another staccato burst, **rat-a-tat-tat,** drums into the body of the vehicle and I know it's any second now, any second, and the SUV is getting so close that they probably think they're going to ram me and force me off the road and I veer left, to the far left of the road, and they're staying along the right side, probably because the shooter needs a steady ride so he can aim and they probably like the angle, with them all the way on the right side of the road and me on the left, it makes it easier to shoot at me but guess what? it's about to create a serious problem for them because—

This road is about to veer sharply to the right.

Bullets rip across my windshield and tear through the dashboard and I cut the steering wheel hard right and navigate the turn and pray that this Jeep doesn't topple over, especially on a slick road, praying that the angle I've given myself will make up for the centrifugal force and the SUV behind me is completely out of position and I make the turn but the SUV slams on the brakes and it's too little too late and I look in my rearview mirror but I don't **have** one anymore so I crane my neck around while I keep driving forward and the SUV has . . .

Yes, it's gone off the road, missing the curve and sending it into underbrush and, if there's any justice, an unforgiving tree.

I let out a breath. You narrowly escaped again, Benjamin.

But the bell tolls for thee.

CHAPTER 23

I double back to my cabin, taking a different route to avoid the bad guys. I hate to say that I hope they died in a collision with a tree, because I hate to wish death on anybody, but let's just say it wouldn't ruin my day.

I stay for a grand total of two minutes, long enough to pack a bag full of possessions. I try not to linger too long on the hundreds of bullets lodged in the walls, furniture, and floor, or on the fact that most of the glass wall on the lake-facing side of my cabin is in tiny shards now. I'll never feel safe in this place again. And I owe

Steve Sykes a new Jeep (or at least an old one).

I decide to stay close by and find a hotel for the night, or what remains of the night. There's no real reason why those guys shooting at me, even if they are in one piece, would stick around Lake Anna, and if they were still on the hunt for me tonight, they'd likely be watching the highways. Plus I don't trust myself driving long distances in the rain and dark on my Triumph.

I get a single room with a queen bed and a tiny bathroom at a chain hotel. There's no couch in here, but there's one of those cheap little love seats. I push it up against the door. Then I take my car keys and balance them on the manual latch on the door so that if any weight pushes on the door from the outside, the keys will drop to the floor and land on a strategically placed tiny hand mirror that I found in Steve's Jeep. The sound of keys falling onto glass will, I hope, alert me if anyone's trying to join me tonight. Clever, right? I saw that in **Conspiracy Theory.** Mel Gibson, Julia Roberts. I might have been the only one who saw it.

I probably won't need that warning,

because I doubt I'll be able to sleep. I know this much: I need to. I still have a hangover from that little thing with my plane crashing to the earth, and tonight hasn't exactly been a picnic, either. My heart is racing and my head is pounding and my limbs are jangling, but I know that underneath the nerves, I desperately need rest.

I pace the cheap carpet while my mind scatters in twenty directions like cockroaches fleeing light. Was President James Buchanan gay? Did John Wilkes Booth's fiancée have an affair with President Lincoln's son Robert? Isn't it odd that Robert Todd Lincoln was present at two presidential assassinations but not his own father's? I mean, what kind of odds are those—

Stop. Focus, Ben. Concentrate on another set of odds: your odds of survival. Whoever's trying to kill me only has to succeed once, after all. I have to succeed every time in avoiding them.

I turn the shower dial as hot as it goes and let the water punish me. I put my forehead against the wall and try to think about that lobbyist Jonathan Liu and what Diana might have known that got her killed and might get me killed, and then I'm thinking of

Janet Leigh in the shower in **Psycho** and then that remake with Vince Vaughn, and that probably wasn't his best career move, but then again he got to have sex with Anne Heche—or wait, that wasn't **Psycho,** that was **Return to Paradise**—anyway, I'm vulnerable, because how well can you defend yourself when you're wet and naked?

Not very. I mean, I'm not much of a threat to anyone when I'm clothed. Naked, about the only thing I could do is scare somebody for a few seconds.

I dry off and put on some clothes that I brought from the cabin, stuff I haven't worn for ten years, and try to relax, to think of something that won't freak me out, to take a small break from all this so I can get some rest.

By 2:00 a.m., I'm convinced that Buchanan was gay.

By 3:00 a.m., it's clear that, while Julia Roberts can obviously hold her own in a lead role, I prefer her in ensemble casts like the ones in **Mona Lisa Smile** and **Mystic Pizza** and **Steel Magnolias,** which makes me briefly consider whether I'm gay, too.

By 4:00 a.m., I've put the presidents in alphabetical order.

And then I'm back to wondering about the odds of my surviving whatever is happening to me, and there's literally an equation on a blackboard, and then Matt Damon puts down his janitor's mop and picks up a piece of chalk and navigates through this complicated algorithm with confident strokes and then Ben Affleck shows up, first to apologize for **Gigli** and then to tell Damon that he should be doing more with his life than scrubbing floors, then Robin Williams walks in and tells me to seize the day, and I try to tell him he's got the wrong movie but then Damon has completed the foot-long equation on the blackboard and just as he turns to me there's a loud, tinny sound that startles all of us, and Damon says to me, **Hate to say it, Ben, but you're toast—**

My eyes pop open and I lurch forward on the bed. I scramble to get a view of the door.

The keys aren't teetering on the latch anymore.

They've fallen onto the mirror on the floor.

Someone just tried to open my door.

CHAPTER 24

I quietly slide off the bed and slither along the carpet. I can't see below the door frame. I have no way of knowing if someone is standing outside my door.

But those keys didn't just fall off by themselves. Someone must have pushed against the door.

I hold my breath, count down the first twenty presidents, and wait for any further movement. I stare at that door until my eyes are playing tricks on me, until that door is breathing in and out, expanding and contracting.

I lie there perfectly still for at least ten

minutes, my face pressed against carpet fibers of cheap quality and questionable hygiene. Maybe the sound of the keys landing on the glass mirror, meant to alert me, had the additional effect of spooking them. But it's kind of hard to believe that men armed with automatic weapons would be scared off by a set of car keys and a hand mirror.

I push off the carpet to a crouch, then tiptoe toward the door, careful to stay out of the line of the door frame. If these guys are inclined to unload their weapons through the door, I don't want to be on the receiving end.

I approach the door and hold my breath again and listen. Nothing that I can hear but the quiet hum of the cheap air conditioner in my room.

Okay, it could have been gravity, not an intruder. But I have to be sure.

From my position outside the door frame, I leap into the line of fire, so to speak, and peek through the peephole. Nothing. Nobody out there.

Okay. Maybe it **was** just gravity. Maybe I need to get a grip.

"It's time to end this," I announce to no one but myself. I'm not even sure what that means, because I'm not exactly in control of events, but it sounded cool and I'll take any relief right now. Something Eastwood or Stallone would say before engaging the villain in a climactic scene. Load the chamber, cock the weapon, and say, **This ends here.** No—**This ends now.**

"This ends now," I say to the mirror.

I have one card left to play. I'm going back to Diana's apartment to grab the surveillance tapes. They'll tell me who pushed her off the terrace.

Then I jump as I hear a short, loud buzz, then the same sound a second time. Terror fills me and disintegrates in the time it takes my brain to register that my smartphone, resting on the nightstand, has just received a text message.

I reach for my phone as though it were a hot burner on a stove. The sender has been blocked. The message is a photograph. It takes me a moment to get it in full view.

"Oh, no," I mumble.

It's a photograph of Diana's brother, Randy Hotchkiss, lying facedown in a pool of blood.

And underneath it, these words:

Randy couldn't stop asking questions. Can you?

CHAPTER 25

Riding the Triumph in the misty morning air, I take a different route to Diana's place this time. I'm not going to turn up 33rd Street and just walk right into a police detective—not to mention catch the attention of any mysterious guys in a Lexus. No, this time I'm entering Diana's building from the rear, up the fire escape.

Cue the theme to **Mission: Impossible.**

I park the Triumph a couple blocks away and walk along the C&O Canal's path, keeping company with joggers getting in their exercise before the workday begins. Then I head to the back of Diana's building and take the rickety steps of the fire escape up to her floor.

Wouldn't it be cool if you could play theme music when you were walking around doing things? Especially during dramatic moments. I think it would inspire people.

I still have the key that opens the fire-escape entrance and her door. What I don't have is any idea who might be watching this building right now, or whether I'm committing a crime just by entering. But I'm out of choices at this point.

I feel a wave of nausea as I take the wobbly steps, but compared to my other challenges the last couple of days, this is a walk in the park. I reach the top and enter the building, my heartbeat fluttering ever so slightly.

Her apartment is at the end of the hallway. There is yellow police tape across the door, so that removes any question about whether I'm supposed to go in there.

But I do it anyway. I walk in, and my breath is whisked away, memories cascading through me in waves. Diana. What were you doing, Diana, that brought all this down on you?

Focus, Ben. It won't take two minutes to get those tapes and leave.

I look up at the smoke detector in her kitchen, the pinhole camera inside it. I grab the stepladder Diana always tucked next to her refrigerator and find the Phillips screwdriver she kept in a tray in her pantry and get to work. I'm unscrewing the second of two screws when I hear a noise from the other end of the apartment, a bottle falling over and rolling on glass.

Panic spreads across my chest. I climb down from the ladder as Cinnamon, Diana's Abyssinian, comes jogging toward me.

"Hey, girl!" I cry out, surprised at how happy I am to see the cat. Maybe because I'm happy to see anyone these days who isn't pointing a firearm at me. Or maybe it's because Cinnamon is now the last vestige of Diana.

The poor thing is a nervous wreck. Has anyone been feeding her? I really don't know. So I find some cat food in the pantry and give her a bowl. She forgets all about me and goes to town on the food.

I get the last screw out of the smoke detector and pop the bottom lid and—and there isn't any camera or microphone. The surveillance equipment has been removed.

I jump down off the ladder and head into Diana's bedroom and see that the motion-activated video recorder, disguised as an AC adapter plug, is also missing. I look behind Diana's desk and check every outlet, but no, it's gone.

Both of the surveillance devices I installed are gone.

And with them the identity of Diana's killer.

I have no leads and nowhere to go.

CHAPTER 26

After parking my Triumph, I walk the streets of the capital, stopping often to double back and watch for anyone paying close attention to me. I find a coffee shop in Georgetown and sit with my back to the wall, watching everyone who walks into the place. A muscle-bound Asian guy. Two cute college girls. An elderly woman and two grandchildren. A slick suit talking into his earpiece.

I don't know whom to suspect. Anyone could be watching me anywhere.

At 10:00 a.m., I get a text message from the White House. The president is back from a week on Martha's Vineyard and is holding a press conference at 2:30 this afternoon. It's my week to cover the briefing room, and I consider asking my partner, Ashley Brook Clark, to cover it for me. But today it's a welcome diversion.

Inside the Brady Room, the major network reporters are dolled up in their makeup, coiffed hair, and neatly pressed clothes, doing stand-ups, predicting to the audiences at home that the president will comment on the next secretary of agriculture, the unrest in Libya, and the resumed fighting in Chechnya. Me, I have an online newspaper, so I don't need to care much about my appearance—but even for me, I'm looking worse for wear today. I've only slept a handful of hours over the last forty-eight, and, not being able to return home, I was forced to buy clothes at Brooks Brothers. My shirt is still creased from the package, and the sport coat is too big in the shoulders. I look like a disheveled kid.

The press secretary, Rob Courtney, is prepping us with some details of the president's schedule over the next week and some background on the appointment he's announcing today. I don't need it. I've

known who was going to be the next secretary of agriculture for two weeks now. It
pays to know people on the inside. And
when I say it pays, I mean that literally.
Usually it's Redskins or Nationals tickets.
Several years ago, I flew a source in the
State Department and his girlfriend to
Manhattan and back for the evening in my
Cessna. She had a wonderful birthday
dinner at Moomba and I had a nice headline story about how the ambassador to
Australia was planning to resign to run for
governor of Ohio.

"Blue shirt, red tie," predicts the reporter
next to me, Wilma Grace. A running joke
with us, and a running bet. Being the gentleman that I am, I always let her pick first.

"White shirt, blue tie," I counter.

I look around the briefing room and
slowly calm. I'm safe, if nothing else, within
the confines of the West Wing, and seeing
familiar faces is comforting.

"The president of the United States,"
says Rob Courtney.

President Blake Francis strides in with
the fluid ease that accompanies power,
with a fresh tan from vacation, and with a
blue shirt and red tie.

"You saw him today already," I whisper to Wilma.

"Never said I didn't."

"That's cold, Gracie. That's cold."

"You might want to take the price tag off your sport coat," Wilma suggests. Yeah, I'm feeling better. I'm glad I came.

"Afternoon, everyone," says the president. "It's nice to be back. I can't tell you how much I missed all of you."

Polite laughter from those of us in the peanut gallery. The aides flanking him laugh like he's just told the funniest joke ever uttered.

"Before I discuss the appointment I'm here to announce, I'd like to make one comment. Many of you were as saddened as I was to learn of the recent death of Diana Hotchkiss, who worked for several years on Congressman Carney's staff and then as a liaison for the CIA."

I blink. Did he—did I hear him correctly?

"And I understand that her family has suffered a second tragedy recently with the death of her brother," he continues. "I'd just like to say that Libby and I send the Hotchkiss family our very best." President Francis gives a presumptive nod. "Okay.

Now, as you know, I promised that before I appointed the next secretary of agriculture, I would search high and low . . ."

I look at Wilma, who returns my glance but doesn't seem to be registering any undue surprise. She shrugs her shoulders. "Some staffer on the Hill, I guess?" she whispers.

I nod back. Wilma obviously didn't know Diana. She meant a great deal to me, but to most people Diana was one of thousands of faceless, ambitious staffers toiling behind the scenes of power.

So how did she warrant a mention in a nationally televised news conference with the president of the United States?

CHAPTER 27

After the presidential briefing, the pain returns to my stomach. Out of the sanctuary of the White House, I'm once again exposed and vulnerable to whoever is out to get me. I'm confused and scared and out of ideas.

Good ideas, at least.

The building on Connecticut Avenue is five minutes north of the White House. It is ten stories of gray stone with a green awning over the entrance. I park my Triumph and go in. The lobby security asks me if I have an appointment and I lie and say yes. I sign my name in a register and pass through a metal detector. I get off at the tenth floor and turn right and go through a thick glass door. The reception area is ornate, intended to impress. The visitors' sitting area has sleek black-and-purple furniture and a nice floor-to-ceiling window overlooking Connecticut Avenue. The reception desk is a half-moon; the woman sitting behind it could grace a magazine cover. The name of the company is stenciled in a fancy font—the same one Porsche uses, I think—on the wall behind her.

"May I help you, sir?" she asks. She's wearing a headset with a receiver that curls around to her mouth.

"Ben Casper of **Capital Beat** for Jonathan Liu," I say, showing my press credentials.

Admittedly, this is a less-than-subtle tactic. Ideally, I would investigate this guy under the radar, gather what information I could, and confront him when it was strategically optimal. But I can't think of another move I can make right now.

"Is he expecting you?" the bombshell asks me.

"He should be." That's pretty close to the truth.

She pauses. "Can I tell him what this is in regard to?"

Behind the woman is a glass wall and a door. An earnest, well-dressed man pushes through it and passes me on his way out of the office. The door clicks shut behind him.

I say, "I'm doing a story about how lobbyists are underpaid and why we need more money in politics, not less."

The receptionist thinks about that for a second.

"It's a story about how lobbyists are making the world safe for bloodsucking Fortune Five Hundred companies that rip off the little guy and then get bailed out by the government. It's high time corporate America had a voice in politics."

She's still thinking.

"Just kidding," I say. "I'm holding a garage sale this weekend to help raise money for Mr. Liu. A million dollars a month hardly pays the groceries these days. I'm worried about him."

The woman mumbles something into her mouthpiece.

"Okay; I'll be straight with you." I lean forward so I'm sure she can hear me. "The story I'm writing is about how Jonathan Liu murdered a senior Capitol Hill staffer. A staffer he was having an affair with. The story's going to press in an hour. I'm wondering if he'd like to hear me out first."

I walk over to the window by the sitting area and wait. It's near the end of the business day and people are hustling about. People always seem to move more quickly when they're exiting work than when they're arriving.

After a few moments, a well-dressed man opens the glass door and holds it open.

"Mr. Casper?" he says. "Right this way, sir."

CHAPTER 28

I'm escorted by two serious Chinese men, each approximately the size of a small house, down a spacious corridor filled with expensive artwork and canned lighting and purple carpeting. The Liu Group is doing okay these days, at least from appearances. I'm not a big fan of purple, but I will admit that Prince's **Purple Rain** is one of the best albums of my generation. You could argue that **1999** was superior, but **Purple** showed more emotion.

The two guys escorting me, on the other hand, show none. If they weren't moving, I'd swear they were statues. They walk me past a series of offices, each one bigger and fancier than the previous one. We turn a corner and then we're going down another hallway. We stop at an elevator.

"Where are we going?" I ask Frick and Frack. "I'm supposed to be meeting with Jonathan Liu."

"You're mistaken," says the bigger of the two.

The elevator opens and they push me inside.

"I should warn you," I say. "I know karate, jujitsu, and a lot of other Asian words."

Nothing. Not even a smile. When the elevator opens again, we're in an underground garage. A black limousine pulls up and a side door opens.

"Get in," says one of the men.

Well, I asked for this. This could be the biggest mistake of my life.

I step inside the limo and the door closes behind me. It automatically locks. I'm alone inside the passenger area, staring at a black screen that obscures the driver.

We pull out onto Connecticut Avenue and then cross over Dupont Circle to Massachusetts Avenue. It occurs to me that they could be driving me to some deserted location so they can put me out of my misery.

But then we take a roundabout and turn right onto Q Street. That's when I figure out where we're going. They're not taking me to an undisclosed location.

They're taking me to the Chinese embassy.

CHAPTER 29

A couple of years ago I attended a ceremony in the Grand Hall of the Chinese
embassy, an immaculate limestone building in the northwest section of the capital.
The room I'm escorted to now, though, is
anything but grand. The walls are gray and
red. The room is cramped and poorly lit
and cold. The two men who take me from
the limo underground are about the same
size as the other goons, but not sparkling
conversationalists like Frick and Frack.
They don't put their hands on me until
we're in the room, at which time they each
take one of my shoulders and force me

into the lone chair in the center of the room.

A door that I didn't even know was a door opens, and two Chinese men enter. They are in suits and ties. One has a tight haircut and the other is bald. The bald guy looks like he's spent some time in a gym. The one with the tight haircut looks softer, like a diplomat.

"Mr. Casper," says Bald Guy.

"That's me."

"What is this you are saying about Jonathan Liu? You told the receptionist that he is responsible for the death of a government worker?"

I look from one of them to the other. "It was a conversation I intended to have with Jonathan Liu."

"Mr. Liu is not here." There is a trace of his native accent but his English is perfect.

"And you are . . . ?" I ask.

"I am . . . the one asking you questions."

"I meant, what's your name?"

"I know what you meant. Tell me of these accusations you make against Jonathan Liu."

I don't know if this guy is on my side or

against me. I could take a wild guess. "I've written an article that explains how Jonathan Liu murdered the White House liaison for CIA deputy director Craig Carney."

Bald Guy is impassive. "And your proof is?"

"Read the article." There is no article. Not yet. I'm nowhere in the vicinity of proving what I believe. The truth is, I'm fishing.

"There is no article," says Bald Guy.

What is this guy, a mind reader? "Have it your way," I say. It reminds me of those Burger King commercials from the '70s. Great, now that stupid **Hold-the-pickles-hold-the-lettuce** song is in my head. But it beats the hell out of their later commercials, the ones with that freaky king character. That guy could haunt my dreams.

"Relations between our country and the United States are rather . . . tenuous, wouldn't you agree, Mr. Casper?"

"If you're a fan of human rights, then yes, I'd agree."

"Human rights." He allows himself a small chuckle. "Mr. Liu does not represent the People's Republic. Yet we are aware that he is a man of considerable influence.

What is accused of Mr. Liu will be accused of the People's Republic. Bombastic, ridiculous accusations will not do."

I lean forward and one of the goons behind me takes my shoulder. "I'm an American journalist in the United States. I will print what I want. In America, we have something called a free press. You should look it up."

Hold the pickles, hold the lettuce, freedom of the press upsets us . . .

Bald Guy moves closer toward me. "You may be an American journalist," he says, "but you're not in America. Not at the moment."

"Because you kidnapped me."

"We did nothing of the kind. We have you signed in at the front entrance. You asked to speak with me and I'm granting you that audience."

I let out a nervous sigh. I'm trying to play cool but I'm feeling anything but. "Listen, Reverend Moon—"

"Ah, a slur. That's to be expected of an American. All us slant-eyed Asians are the same, yes? That's fine, Mr. Casper. Keep thinking of yourself as morally superior while our country runs circles around yours economically. The People's Republic is flourishing while the United States of America is sinking deeper and deeper into a hole."

Bald Guy walks within a foot of me and leans forward, staring at me eye-to-eye. "Now, sir, before I become impatient. Tell me what you know of Jonathan Liu."

"Diana Hotchkiss," I say.

He nods slowly. "A tragedy."

"He had her killed."

"And why did he do that?"

"Read the article."

A smile crosses his face. "There is no article. What is it going to say? That you, Mr. Casper, had a relationship with Ms. Hotchkiss? That you, Benjamin Casper, were at her condominium the night of her death?"

I do a slow burn.

"A person of interest in the death of Ms. Hotchkiss—a spurned lover who had, as you Americans say, motive and opportunity—is writing a story about her death? Would this not be considered something of a conflict of interest?"

These guys are all over this. What stone have I turned over?

Bald Guy puts his nose within a hair-breadth of mine. "There is no article," he says.

He stands straight again and paces the room. "And if there is, it will get, shall we say, ugly for you, Benjamin Casper. Perhaps everyone will learn the interesting background of your own life. Including your childhood."

Ben, you remember me, right? Detective Amy LaTaglia.

My dad says I'm not supposed to talk to you.

I know, Ben. So don't. I'll talk to you. I just wanted to let you know that we got back the fingerprint analysis. Did you know that we found fingerprints on the gun that was in your mother's hand?

"Those records are sealed," I hiss.

Bald Guy waves a hand. "Then perhaps it gives you a window into the resources at our disposal that we were able to access that sealed information."

Do you want to guess whose fingerprints we found on that weapon, Ben?

My dad says I'm not supposed—

They were yours, Ben. Your fingerprints were on that gun.

"On the other hand, Benjamin, I suppose we can forget about that information if you forget about your wild and unsupported accusations against Mr. Liu."

I lower my head and try to contain my emotions while memories cascade toward me in waves.

You're in a lot of trouble, Ben.

You need to tell us what happened in that bathroom with your mother.

"If my accusations are so unsupported," I say slowly, "then why am I here?"

Bald Guy lets out a hideous laugh. "Oh, Benjamin," he says, "you were never here. And you better hope you never are."

CHAPTER 30

They dump me back on Connecticut Avenue, near the building where Jonathan Liu's company takes up space. I relish the thick air and freedom after my unplanned visit to the Chinese embassy. So now I know that the Chinese—and probably Jonathan Liu in particular—were involved in this somehow. But how? How did my Diana gain the attention of the Chinese government and the president of the United States?

I ride over to Idaho Avenue, where the MPD's Second District station is located. I ask for Ellis Burk, a detective I profiled a few years back when he solved a murder involving a congressman's daughter. We've kept in touch since then, because he's a pretty good guy and because it's my job to have friends everywhere.

I'm good at that—having friends, the superficial banter over dinner or drinks, the wisecracks, the false flattery to get them to open up, always leaving them with a favorable impression so they'll be receptive next time you need them. I even have a database of my acquaintances, noting how I met them, any significant events that tie us together (in Ellis's case, it was the Dana Manchester murder), a carrot to use if I need a favor (for Ellis, it's Cuban cigars), and any return favors I may need to remind them of (a flattering profile of the detective who solved the Manchester murder).

That's my specialty, superficial friends. But I don't get too close, and I don't let them too close. Keep your fingers away from the cage, and everyone will be okay.

When I arrive, they tell me Detective Burk will be a few minutes, then they put me in a room. It's a windowless, gray room with a mirror running horizontally along one wall and a single table surrounded by four chairs. I assume this is an "interview" room, where they watch you through the mirrored wall as you're interrogated.

Hold the pickles, hold the lettuce,
First Amendment rights upset us;
All we ask is that you let us
**   censor your words.**

Sure, now I think of it.

"Ben-jamin Casper," Ellis sings as he comes through the door. "The man who survived a plane crash."

Oh, right. The AP must have picked up the story. "Hey, Ellis."

He shakes my hand. His expression changes after he gives me a once-over. "Took a toll on you, looks like. Well, listen, most people don't survive a plane crash, so just consider everything that happens in your life from here on out a bonus."

Actually, that's pretty much what I've been doing.

"You okay, man?" Ellis asks me. "You look a little . . . stressed-out."

I try to manage a smile but can't. No sense putting lipstick on this pig.

"It's been a rough week," I say. "A friend

of mine died. I think she was murdered. And since then, somebody's been trying to kill me, too, starting with—"

Ellis raises a hand to calm me. He's tall and wide, an African American guy who grew up in Boston when it wasn't so easy for a black man to become a police officer. He looks thinner than the last time I saw him in person, more than a year ago. Maybe a diet, maybe illness.

"One step at a time," he says. "Start from the beginning. Tell me about this friend of yours."

I blow out a sigh. "Okay. My friend works as a staffer for the CIA. She lives in George-town and someone pushed her, I think, off her balcony—"

Ellis cocks his head. Recognition dawns all over his face.

"—and I was there, in her apartment, just be—"

"Stop." Ellis scoots his chair back. "You're talking about Hotchchild, or Hotch-something—"

"Hotchkiss. Diana Hotchkiss."

He nods his head. "Diana Hotchkiss."

"You know the case, I gather."

He studies me for a moment. "That's

not a case you want to be connected with. There could be some trouble for you, Ben."

You don't say.

"This is a case you're working on?" I ask.

He gets up from the table and paces. "I wasn't the lead, but we had it here in the Second."

I pick up on the use of the past tense. "Not anymore?"

He laughs without humor. "Couple days ago, the CIA comes waltzing in here. They announce that the Diana Hotchkiss case is a matter of national security and they're taking over. They demanded all our files, right there on the spot. I mean, they literally carted everything off. Over twenty years on the job, I've never seen it handled that way."

This is getting stranger by the minute. The feds are all over this case now. The president of the United States mentions Diana in his weekly press conference. The Chinese haul me in for a friendly off-the-record inquisition.

What the hell is going on?

"If I were you," says Ellis, "I'd take some of that money you inherited and fly to some remote island for a month or two."

Probably good advice. "I'm not going anywhere, Ellis. I need some kind of a lead. Something. Anything. The CIA took everything from you?"

Ellis stares at me for a long, sober moment before his expression breaks.

"Maybe not quite everything," he says.

CHAPTER 31

Ellis returns to the interrogation room with a thin file containing glossy photographs. "Crime scene shots," he says. "And a few witness statements. I might have forgotten to give every copy to the feds."

I recoil as he drops the file down on the table and a few photographs spill out. I'm not really in the mood to see photos of Diana's crushed face and body. "Anything from the witness statements?" I ask.

"Not much." Ellis shakes his head. "Except that the first people to attend to the victim were also the first ones to leave."

I think back before I realize he's talking, in part, about me.

"Two women got to her first," Ellis recites from memory. "They were parked in some kind of a blue compact car by the building. They apparently reached her, and it seemed like they were checking her vitals, that kind of thing. But they got in their car and left before the ambulance arrived."

I remember the first part of that, the two women getting out of the car. What happened to them afterward I have no idea.

Ellis looks squarely at me. "Then there was a man who was talking with some people across the street about his motorcycle. He was second to reach the victim. After a few minutes, he staggered back into the street and puked his guts out. Then he jumped on his motorcycle and left before the authorities arrived." Ellis shrugs his shoulders. "Any idea who rides a 2009 Triumph America with . . . let me see . . ." He looks down at some notes and then back up at me. "Metzeler ME80 tires?"

"No—880s," I say, correcting him.

"Right. ME880s." He smirks at me.

"Apparently those witnesses knew their motorcycles," I say.

"So did the guy who owned the bike. They said he was a real nice guy. Real friendly."

"Handsome, too," I add.

"Yeah, they said he looked like . . . Skeet . . . Ulrich, whoever that is."

I let that wash over me. This is, to say the least, an unwelcome development. Skeet Ulrich? Diana said I looked like Johnny Depp. I mean, I loved Skeet in the original **Scream** and thought they should have kept him on that new **Law & Order** series, but Depp was Donnie freakin' Brasco, for God's sake. In one week I go from Johnny Depp to Skeet Ulrich? What's next—Ralph Macchio?

"I had nothing to do with her death," I say. "But yeah, I was there. I already told you that before you showed me the witness statement."

"So you did, so you did." Ellis shrugs. "Well, maybe if the CIA hadn't ordered me and my colleagues to back off this investigation, I might sit you down for questioning. But seeing as how I've been taken off the case and all . . ."

Ellis is a good egg. Like a moth to a flame, my eyes move back down toward the photos of Diana lying crushed and broken. I can't look. I can't **not** look. A photo from above; her auburn hair, which she'd colored only a month earlier, cascading across her face. Her left leg askew, the long, smooth limb, her fashionable suede leather low-heeled shoe perfectly set on her foot, ironically enough, though I imagine she would be glad to know she died in a decent pair—

I step backward, my pulse suddenly surging with adrenaline.

"I know it's hard," says Ellis. "You must have cared about her."

I manage to nod and mumble something incoherent as I excuse myself and head back out to the parking lot. Yeah, I cared about Diana.

Or maybe I shouldn't use the past tense. Maybe I should use the present tense.

Because Diana has a butterfly tattoo above her left ankle, and the dead woman in that photo doesn't.

CHAPTER 32

I leave the police station with a growing set of facts spread out all over the desk of my brain, but in no discernible order, no logic. Think, Ben. Ultimately, everything is a link in a chain. I just have to put them together.

I hop on my Triumph and spot a car across the street from the Second District parking lot, two guys inside a dark Chevy sedan looking my way. Can't tell if they're Chinese or not, but I suppose the Chinese are capable of having Caucasians in their employ, right? I mean, why would I assume that Chinese only hire Chinese?

Maybe they'll get that albino guy from **The Firm**—

They start their car up just as I kick the Triumph to life. Coincidence? I don't believe in them.

Is it just a coincidence, Ben? Did your fingerprints just leap onto that gun?

I should call Father.

We'll call your father, Ben. For now, you're coming with us. We're taking you into custody. You'll be provided a lawyer and a guardian ad litem and you probably won't be able to live with your dad for a very long time.

Unless, Ben, you want to explain to me what happened.

The Chevy backs up to get out of its parking space and bumps a Toyota compact in the process as I maneuver my bike out of its spot, not sure of where I'm headed—

The compact. The two women in the blue compact car who reached Diana—or whoever it was who fell from her balcony—before I did. They took off before the police and ambulance arrived, Ellis said.

I tear out of the parking lot, suddenly sure of where I'm headed.

I turn onto Wisconsin Avenue, passing a bar that used to be the Alliance Tavern, where Ellis and I once got drunk on cheap whiskey. I don't see the Chevy behind me, but that doesn't mean it isn't following me. Traffic is pretty thick, for some reason. I take a quick right onto M Street and then I get on Route 29 going south, crossing into Virginia. The rush of air, the best thing about this bike, provides me some measure of relief, but there is a permanent tremble coursing through me now, and the only antidote I can think of is speed, speed, speed, but I'm back on main roadways until I hit Jefferson Davis Highway and I floor it, topping ninety, and then I'm thinking of Jefferson Starship and all the other names they used, **We built this city on rock and roll,** and I almost throw up in my mouth—

Within thirty minutes, I'm at the Delta ticket counter at Reagan Airport. I use my corporate credit card, not a personal one, and just book the flight there, not a return, knowing that a last-minute, one-way flight is sure to subject me to the most stringent of security checks, but I don't care anymore. Maybe that's my problem—I'm too afraid, afraid of dying. Maybe if I'm more reckless, if I'm fearless, like James Bond or something, a cool smile in the face of mortal danger, I'll be okay. That new James Bond guy is freakin' awesome. I try for a cool smile, but it doesn't work.

Turns out I missed the last flight of the evening. So I'll sleep in the terminal tonight.

And tomorrow morning, I'll be on the first plane to Madison, Wisconsin.

CHAPTER 33

The Hotchkiss family is home at just after ten in the morning. Home and intoxicated, at least the missus. But I'm sure as hell not going to blame them. As far as they know, they've lost both their children in the space of a week.

Before I knock on their door, I read and reread on my smartphone everything the media had on the death of Diana's brother, Randy. The theme is familiar: Randy Hotchkiss, distraught over the death of his sister, committed suicide by jumping off the roof of Van Hise Hall on the University of Wisconsin campus. No sign of foul play.

No pending criminal investigation. Case closed. Yeah, right.

The parents don't really remember me from Diana's visitation, and they aren't thrilled about my being a reporter, but I assure them that I'm not here on the record. When they allow me in, it feels more like a function of their exhaustion than their willingness to speak with me.

Their home is an old Victorian with a dated living room lined with color photographs of their children and black-and-white shots of their ancestors. The whole room has a musty smell overlaid by the smell of burned coffee—not that either of the Hotchkisses appear to have been drinking it this morning.

Bonnie's eyes are bloodshot and aimless, looking through the fog of grief and alcohol. George is more alert, but he's clearly suffering as well. Each of them snaps to attention, though, when I tell them a story that every parent who has lost a child longs to hear: somehow, miraculously, their child didn't really die.

"Is this . . . some kind of a cruel joke?" George asks.

"I didn't come all this way to joke, Mr.

Hotchkiss. I saw the photos. Diana had that tattoo above her ankle."

"Then why aren't the police here, asking us about that? You're the only one who noticed the missing tattoo?"

"I don't think the DC police had time to notice something like that," I answer. "The feds swooped in right away and took over the investigation. Before the local cops could do much of anything, the whole case was snatched from them."

Bonnie shakes her head. "What does all of this even mean?"

I open my hands. "I—I guess I'm not sure. Diana was involved in something. What it was I don't know. Was she part of something, or did she discover something—I don't know. All I know is that the person who fell from that balcony wasn't her."

George slowly turns to Bonnie. Each of them is incredulous—I can hardly blame them—but hope is a powerful fuel for suspension of disbelief.

"And you say—the people who found her—"

"The two women in the compact car, right. I think they were plants. They were supposed to be there. They made **sure** they were the first ones there. I think they covered her hair over her face. I mean, you could hardly see her face to begin with. It was nighttime, there was poor lighting, and anyway she'd fallen face-first, so— forgive me, I know that's graphic, but it's not like I could really identify her, anyway."

"But they made sure," says George.

"They made sure. Her hair was covering her face by the time I got there. It was Diana's clothes, it was her shoes—the woman was made to look like her, no doubt. But whoever did this missed that detail about her tattoo."

Bonnie shakes her head. Tears have formed but they haven't fallen. This is, in the end, potential good news to them, however mind-blowing it may be.

"Did you know that Diana dyed her hair dark a month before this happened?"

"No," Bonnie says.

I nod. "Thinking about it now, I bet she probably dyed her hair to match the hair of whoever it was who fell from that balcony."

"You're saying Diana helped **murder** some girl?" George asks. "Is that what—"

"No, sir. I doubt she knew about it. But

the truth is, I don't know. Listen, Mr. and Mrs. Hotchkiss. I know this is crazy. I do. But there's an easy way to figure this out."

They both look at me. It's a fairly obvious conclusion, but their brains aren't fully functioning at the moment.

"Demand that the federal government release her body," I say.

CHAPTER 34

I'm back at Dane County Regional Airport within two hours. I'm not sure how I left things with the Hotchkiss family. There's no manual on how to react when someone tells you, hey, guess what, your daughter might not be dead after all. And if I'm wrong, then I've performed just about the cruelest act that could be inflicted on a grieving parent—giving false hope.

I won't board the return flight for another hour, so I stroll along the brown-and-gold tiled floors, checking out the Wisconsin Marketplace and briefly considering an Aaron Rodgers jersey, because c'mon, how cool is that guy, even with the mustache, and then I head to the men's room closest to my gate.

One overweight guy passes me on the way out and one of the bathroom stalls is occupied. I use the urinal, then wash up, making the mistake of looking in the mirror. What stares back at me is a pair of dark, deep-set eyes and a pale, ghoulish face. Not my best day, clearly. Maybe I **do** look like Skeet Ulrich. If I played a cop on TV, I'd want to be one of those hardened, wisecracking veterans who bitches about his ex-wives and delivers the punch line after they find the body. **Looks like he lost an argument with a switchblade. Well, I guess I won't be having spaghetti for dinner tonight.** Something like that—

Two things happen at once: the door of the bathroom stall kicks open behind me just as someone enters the bathroom to my right. Two men, one black and one white, both of them big and serious, both of them wearing dark suits and white shirts, converge on me simultaneously. I throw an elbow behind me and connect with some part of the white guy's face. It feels like I hit some meat and bone, so it probably hurt.

If I had any talent for this kind of thing, I would follow up with a forward kick at the black guy coming directly at me.

But I don't. I'm off balance from the elbow toss, and the front guy has both hands on my sport coat before I can say **ambush.** He pushes me up against the wall, right next to the hand dryer, while the white guy recovers from my elbow.

"Take it easy, take it easy," I say.

He thrusts a knee into my groin and I double over. **Pain** is a word you can look up in the dictionary, but you don't know what it means until someone drills you in the balls. And this guy knew how to throw that knee. He got the frank **and** the beans.

Franks and beans! Franks and beans!

The white guy grabs me by the hair and stands me up straight again. My hands go south, primitive instinct to protect what's left of the family jewels, while I try to catch my breath.

"This is your last warning, Benjamin," says the black guy, fixing his tie in the mirror. "Stop asking questions about Diana Hotchkiss."

The mention of her name shakes me awake, reminds me why I'm doing this.

"I'm not afraid of Jonathan Liu," I manage to say.

"Jonathan Liu?" The black guy chuckles, then looks in the mirror at his partner, who has a bloody face. "There's a lot you don't know about Jonathan Liu, Benjamin."

From behind, the white guy delivers the next blow, a sharp punch to my kidney, and I crumple to the ground. Searing pain shoots from my groin and back and head, synapses firing in all directions. My vision goes spotty and I struggle to remain conscious. I'm not sure I'll ever be able to urinate again.

The black guy squats down next to me. "You're going to go back to DC and you're going to call the Hotchkiss family. You're going to tell them you've made a big mistake, and you're very sorry, but you're sure that Diana is dead and you won't be bothering them again."

These guys know everything we said to each other. Whoever they are, their resources are unlimited.

"And . . . why . . . would I do . . . that?" I manage.

"Because if you don't, Benjamin, they're both going to die." The man stands again, his polished wingtips inches from my nose. "Don't you see the pattern, Ben? Everyone you try to talk to ends up dead. It's like you're pulling the trigger yourself."

Speaking of pulling the trigger. They've kneed me in the balls and sucker punched me. But compared to the things that have happened over the last week, that's like a peck on the cheek.

Point being, they aren't here to kill me. These aren't the same guys with automatic weapons who tore up my cabin.

So who are they?

I try to move, but the pain kicks up with the faintest of motions. I'm curled up in a fetal position on a skanky bathroom floor. At least I don't have any question about whether I'll be able to urinate again. A warm stain has spread across my pants.

"I'm not . . ." I start, but it's hard to even speak, and anyway they've left. It's just me, myself, and I in the bathroom.

"I'm not going . . . to stop," I say.

CHAPTER 35

"George, you're going to have to trust me," I say into my cell phone as I walk through the covered parking garage near Reagan Airport.

"Trust you?" George Hotchkiss screams through the phone. "You tell me my daughter is still alive, and now you tell me to just forget the whole thing?"

That about covers it, yeah.

"Just for now, George. Give me some time to figure this out."

"Why the hell should I do that? Why should I wait one damn second?"

"Because your wife already lost a son, at least, and maybe a daughter, too. Don't make her a widow on top of all that."

That seems to quiet him. "Just give me a couple of days, George. Promise me that much. Then you can make whatever noise you want."

I punch out my cell phone after I finally get a concession from Diana's father that he'll keep quiet for forty-eight hours. I don't know if those guys in the bathroom were bluffing, but somebody is taking this very seriously, and I don't want the deaths of Diana's parents on my conscience, however she may have felt about them.

I pull out my keys and start to climb on my bike when I hear a squeal of tires, a car racing down the ramp from the upper level of the parking garage. It's a black stretch limousine. And it stops right in front of me.

I brace myself. I'm a sitting duck. I'm standing in a parking space with cars on either side of me and this limo cutting off my only route of escape.

I have no good options. I don't even have time to panic.

The tinted passenger-side window rolls down. A handsome, well-appointed Asian man stares at me.

"Well, well," I say.

"You've been looking for me," says Jonathan Liu.

CHAPTER 36

Opposite me in the back of the limo sit the notorious Jonathan Liu and a stocky white guy holding a firearm in his lap who looks formidable. Not barroom-brawl formidable but special-forces formidable.

Up close, Jonathan Liu is everything you'd expect—the nattily attired lobbyist, the slick look. But beneath the facade there is more—hands that tremble, eyes that dart about. Jonathan Liu is scared.

"Are you going to kill me?" I ask, which if you think about it is kind of a dumb question.

Liu studies me a moment. "If I wanted

you dead," he says, "you'd already be dead."

That's a pretty cool line. Something you'd hear in a movie. And convincing, too. But if I were going to kill somebody and didn't want that person to resist while I drove him to some undisclosed location, that's exactly what I'd say to him. **If I wanted you dead, you'd already be dead.** Then the guy would relax, I'd drive him to a garbage dump and say, **Just kidding!** and pump him full of lead.

(I mean, if I were the kind of person who'd shoot a guy.)

"Then how 'bout your friend puts away his gun?" I suggest.

Liu shakes his head. "That's to make sure that when we're done talking, you get out."

"I hate to shatter your ego, but this isn't the first time I've had a gun pointed at me." Samuel L. Jackson's line in **Pulp Fiction.** Always loved that line. Never thought I'd use it. Never thought it would be true.

Jonathan Liu observes me awhile. "I'd heard you could be stubborn. Relentless, actually, is the word I heard."

I look back and forth between Brutus and Liu. "You heard that from . . . Diana?"

He nods but doesn't speak.

"How is she, by the way?" I ask, as though I'm asking him about his folks or something.

The comment doesn't register with him immediately. "What kind of a sick thing to say is that?"

"C'mon, Jonathan. I was born at night, but not **last** night."

"I—don't understand that reference."

"Oh, now you're the foreigner who doesn't speak English so good? Give me a break, Jonathan. You speak English better than me."

He leans forward, elbows on his knees. "You're not suggesting Diana is **alive.**"

This guy's a lobbyist by trade, so his entire job description comes down to two words: **bullshit artist.** He'll look you in the eye and promise you that deregulation won't lead to corporate misbehavior, that Fortune 500 companies need government subsidies so they can put people to work, even if the money goes to golden parachutes for their CEOs. He'll piss on your leg, as they say, and tell you it's raining.

"That would be news to the US government," he says. "I even heard the president gave her a ten-second eulogy at his press conference."

"And why would he do that?" I ask. "I've covered over a hundred presidential briefings, and other than at the death of a world leader or some other elected official I've never heard a president do that. For your run-of-the-mill staffer? Why is it so important to the federal government that we believe Diana is dead?"

He doesn't have an answer for that. He has an agenda today; he planned out the whole rendezvous, so he obviously has something to tell me. I might as well hear what he has to say.

The limo reaches the ticket booth of the parking garage and we exit. The driver, whoever that may be behind the shaded glass, pulls the car over instead of heading toward the highway.

Jonathan Liu rubs his hands together and wets his lips—tells, giveaways, indicators that something or somebody has put the fear of God into him. A good reporter recognizes all the signs.

"You're asking the wrong question," he says.

"And what question should I be asking, Jonathan? I have a hundred for you."

"Have you ever heard of Operation Delano?"

I haven't. My expression probably answers for me.

"That's where your shovel should be digging, Mr. Casper."

"Help me," I say. "Tell me where to dig."

He gives me a smile that on a normal day I'd interpret as condescension. But the sweat trickling from his brow gives me an indication of the struggle he's experiencing.

"Delano," I repeat. "FDR's middle name. This involves the president? I should be digging at the White House?"

Jonathan Liu looks me squarely in the eye. His expression never cracks, but he's not saying no.

"Now we're done," he says. "Get out."

"No," I say.

"Yes. Listen to me, Mr. Casper. You've created a lot of trouble for me, coming around my office and accusing me of all sorts of things. I may not even survive this."

"Hang on a second, Jonathan. Let me

reach for my hankie. I've been shot at, I've had to crash-land my plane, Diana's brother was murdered, and I don't know what's happened to Diana at this point. And I'm pretty sure that you have some-thing to do with all of that—"

"I don't. I didn't even know that any of that had happened to you. I knew about Diana and her brother. Not you. But now that I do know, Mr. Casper, I want you out of my car more than ever."

"Yeah? And why's that?"

Brutus the bodyguard clicks off the safety on his handgun. He isn't aiming it at me yet, but it won't be long.

Jonathan Liu says, "Because apparently you're closer than you even realize."

CHAPTER 37

I ride the Triumph back to the capital, taking an unusual route toward K Street in case someone is following me. The capital is sweltering today, and it's so bright you have to squint. It makes it more challenging to look around for people watching you, following you, hunting you.

I feel a measure of relief and comfort as I push through the revolving door of the ground-level offices of **Capital Beat.** The chaos of the street noise is immediately replaced with the hushed urgency of a newsroom. The **Beat** is small, taking up only the ground floor of the four-story building I inherited, but I've packed it with a maze of cubicles—enough to accommodate the staff who keep the business running.

An unfamiliar face greets me at the front desk. She must be the new receptionist I haven't been in to meet yet. "May I help you, sir?" she asks politely.

A head pops up from within the maze, and the advertising layout coordinator, Shari—in the newspaper business known as the "dummy"—breaks into a grin.

"Hey!" she says, more loudly than necessary. "Look who decided to grace us with an appearance!"

Immediately, five other heads pop up from different cubicles and shout greetings.

"You guys look like prairie dogs when you do that," I retort.

"It's an act we're perfecting," says Shari. "We're hoping someday we'll be good enough to hide on the lawn of the West Wing and blend in with the native fauna." She looks furtively around, makes a few rodentlike noises, and disappears back into her cubicle.

I sigh. It's good to be here.

We don't print any publications on paper, but the newsroom still smells like ink. We get all the major papers, and someone reads them thoroughly every day. And the ink smell is mild compared to the smell of hot computer parts. So the aroma is a combination of hot plastic, dust, and damp newspapers. I think it smells like hard, honest work.

The office is pretty quiet. Most stories are filed remotely these days. The few employees I pass on the way back to my office look pretty much like you'd expect DC journalists to look. Lean and hungry, but sleep-deprived and stressed-out. Blue jeans, moccasins, no color coordination, zero fashion sense. Just like me.

The newsroom is divided into sections. The department editors—politics, grapevine, opinions and features, and photography—have large cubes surrounded by tall walls. Around each editor, the staff writers for each department have tiny cubicles, small enough for you to be able to touch both sides when you're sitting down. The writers are usually out newsgathering, anyway. No sense in making them too comfortable at the office.

The copy editors all sit in a row down

the far left-hand side of the room, their enormous monitors displaying the soon-to-be-published stories in huge type. The sales department—the only department that actually receives visitors at this location—is the most visible and most comfortable. There's a reception and greeting area immediately to the right of the entrance in front of well-appointed cubicles furnished with large screens for displaying online advertising at each station.

I reach the large cubicle of Ashley Brook Clark, who runs the politics department and shares White House duties with me, and poke my head in. I'd called ahead and asked her the big question.

She spins on her chair and looks up at me. "Never heard of it," she says. "Operation Delano, you said?"

"Right."

"Don't know it. Want me to cast a net?"

"I'm not sure. I think I like you in one piece, Ashley Brook."

She draws back. "It's that serious?"

I tap the side of her cubicle. "I'll get back to you."

My office is in the back, the only one with actual walls, though they're all clear

glass, so there's not much privacy, anyway. The door reads BENJAMIN CASPER,
EDITOR. I don't need a title with "chief" or
"executive" in it. At least an "editor" sounds
like he works for a living. Of course, since
Diana . . . well, one of the perks of owning
the business is that I can count on Ashley
Brook to run it for me while I'm away. I'll
need that perk for now.

Everyone wants to talk to me about the
plane crash—my phone exploded with
e-mails and texts after the news leaked
out—but I brush them off because I'm
tired, and it's only a fraction of the story of
my life over the last week.

I called ahead and had my secretary
buy me some shirts, pants, underwear, and
toiletries—on the company card, of course,
which means on my dime—so I could stay
mobile. I pick up a set and head for the
bathroom.

When I turned this place into a newsroom, I blew out the walls in both bath-
rooms and added showers, a feature that
suits the lifestyles of employees with ir-
regular hours. Good for me now, because
I need a hot shower. I'm going to wash up,
change, and get the hell out of this office

before whoever's chasing me finds me here and shoots up the place. I'm radioactive right now.

When I'm done, I feel better, refreshed, and I wish like hell I could put my feet up in my office and snooze.

The buzzer on my intercom cries out. It's the new person up front. Our last receptionist would just turn and yell back to me across the entire space.

I'm not sure I even remember how to use this thing, but I push a button and say, "Yes?"

"Mr. Casper?"

Who else would it be? "Yes."

"Someone named Anne Brennan to see you," she says. "She says it's urgent."

Anne Brennan is Diana's best friend.

"Send her back," I say.

CHAPTER 38

I greet Anne Brennan at the door of my office and offer her a chair. She looks like she could use it. She looks tired and out of sorts—frazzled, as Diana used to say.

I don't know Anne very well. I met her just a handful of times, but other than Randy she was the only person Diana ever talked about in terms of personal intimacy. So I feel like I know her through Diana.

Anne is cute, a petite woman with curly brown hair to her shoulders, attractive in a warm, nonthreatening way. Mary Ann to

Diana's Ginger. That would make me Gilligan.

"I'm not sure why I'm here," she says. "I'm not sure where to go. Diana trusted you so much."

"Tell me," I say. I'm debating what I might tell **her.** She should go first.

"I mean, first it's Diana, and now people are coming around, asking me all kinds of questions about her."

"What people?" I ask.

"The CIA," she says. "They want to know what I know about Diana. Why she would kill herself. Was she romantically involved with someone? Things like that."

"What did you tell them?"

I admit, I'm hoping her answer will be, **You, Ben. She was romantically involved with you.**

"I—I didn't—" She gets out of the chair and starts to pace. She's been shaken up by the feds. They have a way of doing that. "I didn't know what to say. I didn't want to tell them, y'know? I wanted to keep her privacy. But it was like they knew I was holding back. And then they start threatening me. They say they've pulled all my tax returns for the last ten years and they're sure they can find something wrong with them. 'You can always find something,' they said. They said I could lose my home and my catering business and—"

"Anne. Anne. It's okay. It'll be okay. I promise."

She bursts into tears, her face in her hands. I put an arm around her shoulder and help her back into the chair. I fetch some water from the tiny fridge behind my desk and hand her the sweaty bottle.

She finally composes herself, taking a couple of sips and some deep breaths. "This is really embarrassing, coming unglued like that."

"Nothing to be embarrassed about. They rattled you. It's their specialty." I squat down next to her. "Listen, Anne, they're not going to do anything to you. They just wanted to make sure you didn't hold back. Did you hold anything back?"

She doesn't respond. A nonanswer that is, in fact, an answer.

"I didn't tell them about . . . a friend of hers."

"Jonathan Liu," I say.

She looks at me. "Jonathan Liu they knew about."

I recoil. "There was **another** friend?"

Her eyes part from mine. She inhales and exhales slowly.

"The Russian," she says. "I didn't tell them about the Russian."

CHAPTER 39

"His name is Alex," says Anne. "I only met him once. I ran into Diana with him and they looked—very cozy. But then a few weeks later, I saw an article about him in the **Post.** I recognized his photograph. His name is Alexander Kutuzov. He owns a soccer team in England and a bunch of specialty bookstores around the world, including one here on Fifth Street. I've actually been in it. It's called AK Collectibles. Anyway, he's made billions in oil in Russia and he flies all over the world, that kind of thing."

Despite the importance of what she's

telling me on so many levels, I can't help but feel jealousy and resentment creeping in. Diana had two paramours—Jonathan Liu and now this Alexander Kutuzov—and I didn't know anything about it? She must have thought I was a puppy dog following her around, eager for any attention she might throw my way. I must have been a joke to her.

Reality is a bitch.

"Okay, Alex Kutuzov," I say. "You didn't mention him to the feds."

Anne shakes her head. "I'm not sure why, but something about how Diana reacted when I brought up the topic. I was, like, 'Hey, y'know, I saw the **Post** article, what's up with this hotshot billionaire?' But Diana looked mortified. She made me promise I wouldn't mention him to anybody. Ever. So I kept my promise." She touches my hand. "Except I'm telling you, aren't I?"

"You are."

"Diana said she could trust you. She said you were the only man she could trust."

Okay, a trustworthy puppy dog. Still a puppy dog.

"I don't know where else to turn, Ben. I don't know what to do."

Enough is enough. I don't know what to think of Diana anymore, but I make a decision right then and there that I'm not going to let anything happen to Anne. There have been enough innocent casualties already.

I put my hand on top of hers. "I'm going to take care of this," I say. "I'm going to figure out what's going on. Let me tell you how."

My words seem to reassure her. I wish I could say the same for me.

I'll find out tonight.

CHAPTER 40

Midnight. A man without a home, with no-where to go, hiding out in coffee shops and department stores, showering at work, living out of a bag of clothes, afraid to use his cell phone, afraid to use his credit cards, standing half a football field from a gigantic Tudor home in a sleepy residential neighborhood in the northwest quadrant, where people don't usually have problems like being afraid for their lives.

I approach the house from the front but move slowly, cautiously, my hands stuffed in my pockets. I don't really have any kind of an excuse for being here. It's not like a guy like me has any reason to be strolling the streets of Forest Hills, just killing time in a sleepy neighborhood tonight.

Still, once I commit to this, I have to walk like someone who isn't afraid of being seen. This isn't my first time doing something like this. I've bullshitted my way into buildings and exclusive cocktail parties and all sorts of places looking for stories or hoping to confront people with hard questions when they don't have their high-priced assistants there to feed them a line.

Okay, I've never busted into a home. This is something new. But desperate times, as they say, call for desperate measures.

Desperate Measures had a pretty cool premise. A cop needs a bone marrow donor for his son and the only person who qualifies is a convicted multiple murderer who uses the trip to the hospital to escape. The cop has to catch him but needs him alive. Gotta love a movie with Andy Garcia and Michael Keaton.

Stop, Ben. Shake out the nerves.

I walk up onto the driveway and my heartbeat cranks up a level. The closer I get to this house, the less easily I can turn back. I walk slowly along the driveway and go around to the back of the home.

My favorite Garcia movie is **Things to Do in Denver When You're Dead.** Great cast. I loved Keaton in **Batman,** a small guy to be playing that kind of a role, but he had those eyes. **Pacific Heights** was a pretty freaky flick, but it had that scene with the bugs, and I hate bugs.

I get to the back of the house, and it's got to be an acre if it's an inch. I found the listing online earlier today, and it mentioned the "spectacular grounds." You know you're rich when they call your backyard "grounds." If you have "grounds," you probably also have an aging butler with a dry English accent who goes by a name like Hughes or Jeeves.

Actually, that's a point I hadn't considered. There might be more than one person in this house right now.

It's dark back here; not necessarily what I would have expected. That probably means there's a burglar alarm.

An alarm, possibly multiple people in the house. What else lies ahead for me?

I look over the place. Two stories, fancy enclosed deck. The listing that's still online

described the ornate furnishings inside—
no surprise.

Jonathan Liu paid $4.9 million for this place eleven months ago. He's made a fortune representing Chinese industries. He's made a career out of playing both sides. He's had a good life.

He's not going to have a good night. This time we're having a Q and A on my terms.

CHAPTER 41

I try the back door. It's locked.

I wrap my fist into my shirt and punch a hole through the pane of glass. Then I step back. Smashing glass alone could trigger some people's alarms.

Nothing. Nothing but the thumping of my pulse.

I reach through the broken pane and unlock the door. Now, opening a door would trigger **most** people's alarms.

And there's such a thing as a silent alarm, though I never saw the logic. So it's a calculated risk.

The door pops open and I hold my breath.

But no sound comes, no whiny shriek or bullhorn. As far as I can tell, Jonathan Liu didn't set his alarm.

The interior is huge, as the online description of the house advertised. I tiptoe through the to-die-for kitchen, which is perfect for entertaining, with its soapstone countertops and designer cabinets, past the charming half bath, with its imported marble pedestal sink—everything imported—and make my way into the living room, with its built-in bookcases, picture windows, pitched ceiling, and fireplace, which boasts a mantel of marble that was probably also imported, though they never mentioned it in the listing.

Then I hit the staircase. I take each step carefully, transferring my weight with caution. I can spare the two or three minutes of time. I can't spare Jonathan Liu hearing a creak on the staircase and popping awake and reaching for the pistol on his bedside table—

Stop, Ben.

I can't believe I'm doing this. What am I doing? What am I going to do, put him in a choke hold?

I take another step. Another. Get him

out of his comfort zone, that's what I'm doing. Catch him off guard and interrogate
him. Right. This could work.

I reach the top of the staircase. I could
turn in either direction, but it looks like the
master bedroom is down to the left.

Then I smell something. I can't place it,
but it triggers memories from long ago.

**I am an eight-year-old boy. I am home
from school but I don't call out. I don't
know why but instead of heading into
the kitchen, I go immediately upstairs. I
walk into the master bedroom, Mother
and Father's room, and I see Mother's
hair cascading across the bathroom
floor in the small corner of the bathroom that is visible to me.**

**And then I see Father stepping out
of the bathroom in a white undershirt,
holding a garbage bag full of something.**

**Benjamin, he says. You're . . . home
early.**

**My feet keep moving forward, even
as Father tries to block my view of the
bathroom, and I see her lying prone, a
pool of blood coming from her head, a
handgun two, maybe three, feet away
from her on the bathroom tile—**

No! No! No! I say it so many times I lose count. And then Father catches me, and he holds me by the shoulders so he can see me eye-to-eye. There's been a terrible accident, he says. He picks me up and carries me out of the room and locks me in my room. I scream and plead and slam my fists against the door and lose my breath.

As I approach Jonathan Liu's bedroom, my pace begins to slow. My heart is hammering, sounding a gong between my ears.

The door reopens. Father lets me out and holds me tight, walking me back into the master bedroom. As I said, there's been a terrible accident, Ben. I'm sorry you had to see this. But I guess you have to.

Not letting go of me, he allows me to peek in again. Mother's eyes are lifeless, her lips have formed a soft O, her body is sprawled out along the tile next to the pool of blood. It's the same scene I saw when I first walked in.

Only this time, the gun is in Mother's hand.

Jonathan Liu has a nice love seat in the

corner of his gigantic master suite. He is resting in it now, with his chin on his chest, the left side of his head blown off. In his limp right hand is a handgun.

Murder can be made to look like suicide, and suicide can be made to look like murder.

No doubt there is a note somewhere, not in his handwriting. I don't know all the evidence that has been left behind. I don't know what information Jonathan Liu could have given me.

All I know is that I have to get the hell out.

But instead, I walk into the room.

CHAPTER 42

I step slowly onto the hardwood floor of Jonathan Liu's bedroom, my heart in my throat, my pulse echoing throughout the room, my limbs quivering. His bedroom is in tidy condition. The Oriental furniture—the two chairs by the bay window, the chest of drawers—is perfectly in place. The area rug is positioned evenly at the foot of the king-size bed. The bed itself is made up, complete with the turndown revealing maroon silk sheets. All that's missing is the mint on the pillow.

The United States Mint was authorized by the Coinage Act, passed by Congress in

1792 and advocated by Alexander Hamilton. The Mint building was the first federal building constructed under the Constitution. Did you know it has its own police force—

Enough. Take a breath, Ben.

I walk carefully into the master bathroom, itself a model of cleanliness and order. The white hand towels are hung in perfect symmetry, like they'd been hung by the psychotic husband in **Sleeping with the Enemy.** The double vanity is empty save for an electric toothbrush resting in its cradle and a bottle of vitamins with a Chinese label.

I walk back over to Jonathan Liu, not focusing on him so much as on the scene surrounding him. The gun is resting in his lap. I don't dare touch it.

Do you want a moment with Mother, Benjamin? Before the police and ambulance arrive? If so, you should go do it now.

Can I . . . touch her or kiss her or . . .

She's your mother, Benjamin. You can do whatever you like. If you want to hug her one last time and say good-bye and tell her how much you love her, go ahead, son.

But son? Make sure you take the gun out of her hand first. Just slip it out and place it next to her. You can put it back in her hand when you're done.

Stop, Ben. This isn't . . . helping. Father isn't here, and it's long in the past.

To Jonathan Liu's left, blood and brain matter have splattered against the wall above a dark pool that's formed on the floor below. The bullet has lodged into the wall at a point just slightly below the point where Jonathan Liu's head would be if his head were upright.

Statistically, less than 10 percent of suicides with an entry wound in the temple show a bullet path directed downward.

I look at Jonathan's face. His eyes are hooded and vacant. His mouth is slightly parted. His skin has already begun to take on a waxy pallor.

When John Wilkes Booth shot Lincoln in the back of the head, he yelled, **"Sic semper tyrannis."** What did they say to you, Jonathan Liu, before they shot you in the temple?

C'mon, Ben. Operation Delano.

I look under the bed. I enter the walk-in

closet and open drawers, using my shirt to avoid fingerprints. I look behind his clothes, his shoes, the sweaters on top—

Nothing. Nothing in the closet, nothing in the—

Wait.

On a small desk tucked in the corner on the east side of the bedroom, there is a laptop computer that displays a screen saver—a cube bouncing around as if weightless, in orbit. I approach it slowly. This could be it. If Jonathan Liu has any information about Operation Delano, it would probably be on his computer.

I tap the mouse with my middle finger and the screen saver disappears, revealing the following text:

I cannot live with myself after what happened to Diana. She deserved better, and this is my just penance.

I read the note a couple of times. It reveals very little. It doesn't say whether he killed Diana or whether she killed herself, but he somehow feels responsible. Whoever wrote this wanted to keep all options open.

But there's no way Liu wrote this himself. Whoever wrote this wanted to convey regret. Jonathan Liu, the one time I spoke with him, was not regretful. He was flat-out scared.

I hear the squeal of a car's tires outside. Not close, I don't think, but no sense in waiting around to find out. I back away from the computer and do a final once-over of the room. There's no sign of a struggle, and there's a suicide note for good measure—one that doesn't have to match Jonathan Liu's handwriting, because it was typed.

Someone wants Jonathan Liu's death to look like a suicide.

Or a **staged** suicide.

Which explains how it was so easy for me to break in.

And which means I'm in more trouble than I realized.

I start out of the room, then stop. I run back, detach Jonathan Liu's laptop computer from the mouse and power cord, and take it with me.

CHAPTER 43

I run through yards and sidewalks, not breaking my pace, not wondering if anyone can see me or whether my actions seem suspicious, just racing back toward my Triumph with Jonathan Liu's laptop tucked under my arm.

Q: Were you able to determine a manner of death for Mrs. Casper, the decedent?
A: No. The deceased sustained a fatal gunshot wound to the head. The evidence points to either homicide or suicide, but does not rule out either possibility.

Q: But can't you examine the scene of the death and the body and determine how she died?

A: Usually. The crime scene, autopsy, toxicology, and ballistics reports usually are enough to tell the story of how someone died. But sometimes forensic pathology can be manipulated to mislead and misinform. Evidence can be warped to hide the truth.

Q: Murder can be made to look like suicide, and suicide can be made to look like murder.

A: Precisely.

I reach my bike, parked a half mile down on Albemarle Street. I zip the laptop into the satchel on the back of the Triumph and kick the bike to life. My chest is burning and sweat is dripping into my eyes, but at least now I have wheels. The sky is making noises about rain, which on a list of things I need in my life right now is just about dead last.

Q: Who discovered the body?

A: The juvenile, Benjamin, did. At least according to his father, Professor Casper. His father retained counsel for him and never allowed us to interview Benjamin.

Q: Can you describe the scene he found?

A: Her body was lying flat on the floor, with the gun resting in her left hand. There was significant blood spatter on the walls, shower curtain, floor—well, virtually every-where. It was a fairly small bathroom, and as I'd said before, he hugged and held his mother postmortem. In doing so, the body was moved somewhat, and some of the blood spatter was disturbed.

I ride the Triumph down Connecticut, past the UDC's Van Ness campus, my mind racing through the scenarios and wondering how I can figure this all out. C'mon, now, Ben, focus—drive slowly, ob-serve traffic rules, and FIGURE OUT WHAT THE HELL IS GOING ON—

Wait. There's a cop across the way, idling at the light, westbound on Tilden. Take it slow, but not too slow, don't look over too much, just cruise through the intersection—

Q: Did your bloodstain pattern analysis in-dicate where the decedent had been standing at the time the weapon was fired?

A: Yes. You see, a blood droplet in free fall will take the shape of a sphere. When it strikes a surface and a well-formed stain is produced, it's easy to determine the angle at which the droplet struck the surface. If there are enough bloodstains, it's possible to determine the location of the victim and the relative position of the weapon.

Q: And Doctor, in doing that analysis, the area of origin—in this case the exit wound—was nearly six inches lower than you would have expected based on Mrs. Casper's height and the location of the exit wound, true?

A: That's true.

Q: Which might lead you to conclude Mrs. Casper was crouching, leaning over, flinching—something like that?

A: It might.

Q: So it would be consistent with a murder scenario. It would be consistent with the juvenile overtaking his mother by force, placing a gun against her head, and pulling the trigger?

A: It could be.

Q: Or sneaking up on her while she was bent over?

A: Possibly.

Q: And the fact that the juvenile's finger-print was found on the weapon—would that not make this possibility more likely still?

A: Yes, it would.

Rain starts to fall. Shit. It's hard enough to navigate the Triumph with electricity running through my veins and my thoughts scattered in twenty directions. I need to keep this bike upright and moving. I need to get to a hotel in one piece.

I need to find out what's on Jonathan Liu's laptop.

Q: Professor Casper, I know this is difficult, but please tell us how you came upon the scene in question.

A: When I got upstairs, I knew immediately something was wrong. I could see my wife sprawled out on the bathroom floor. I—I knew—I'm sorry. I just—it's so hard—

Q: That's okay, Professor Casper. Take your time. If you'd like a glass of water . . .

A: Our son, Benjamin, was bent over her, crying. His arms were tucked under her, like he was trying to hug her. He was . . . saying good-bye to her, I think.

Q: And where was the gun?

A: In my wife's hand. I'm sure Benjamin didn't do this. I'm sure he didn't kill her. As much as I loved my wife, I have to believe she did this to herself. Please, Your Honor—don't take away my son, too.

The rain is kicking up now into a full-scale downpour. I have to get off the road. I can't think straight right now and I can't afford—

Wait, Calvert Street, the Omni hotel—do I have time to turn?

I make a late right turn, my top-of-the-line wheels doing their best—

But I got too greedy. The bike flies out from under me, skidding across the slick intersection and crashing into a light pole.

I'm not doing so well, either. I slide about ten feet on my right side. My leg is going to need some work. But no broken bones. At least I wore my helmet. A lesson to all you kids out there.

The intersection is empty this time of night. Good for me. More good news: the bike stayed in one piece, too, I notice as I get her upright.

The bad part?

The screen on Jonathan Liu's laptop is splintered into pieces.

CHAPTER 44

When Anne Brennan comes out of her condo building the next morning, she catches my eye from across the street and does a double take. She points to herself as a question and I nod.

"Ben," she says when she crosses the street. I can only imagine how I look to her. Another sleepless night at another hotel after I tried in vain to resurrect Jonathan Liu's laptop.

She reacts badly when I give her the news about the Chinese lobbyist. Bad as in scared, which is the appropriate reaction. Everyone associated with Diana

Hotchkiss seems to be falling on hard times these days.

"What in the world is going on?" she whispers to me, shading her eyes with a hand. She's a nice midwestern girl, fun-loving and sweet—not cut out for this kind of thing.

"I don't know, Anne. That's what I'm trying to find out." This isn't exactly an ideal locale for a conversation, standing in the middle of a busy sidewalk in the U Street Corridor, but this whole affair is so bizarre that this rendezvous seems to fit right in.

I take her by the shoulders. "Listen, Anne. I thought I knew Diana. But I guess I didn't. I didn't know about Jonathan Liu or Alexander Kutuzov. And I didn't know she was taking medication for depression."

I can see from Anne's reaction that she didn't know that last part, either.

"What I'm saying is, I don't know what I don't know. But something was going on with Diana. And whether you've been holding back purposely or you don't realize it, I think you know something you haven't told me."

She draws back, like she's been accused. She places a hand at the nape of her neck.

"I'm not holding back. I swear. Ask me anything."

I struggle to even **know** what to ask. "The White House," I say, recalling my conversation with Jonathan Liu. "Did Diana have any connection to the White House?"

"Well, c'mon, Ben. She was Craig Carney's aide. Isn't he one of President Francis's best friends?"

I sigh. She's right, of course. Craig Carney is deputy director of the CIA and one of the president's closest allies. He probably calls the White House his second home. Diana probably did, too.

"Diana was there all the time," Anne says. "She was on a first-name basis with Libby."

The First Lady, she means. Back when Blake Francis was a member of Congress, before he was elected governor of New York, he married Libretta Rose, a socialite and heiress to a jewel company's fortune. Libby Rose Francis bankrolled his successful gubernatorial race, and eight years later he was elected president.

"And you know how Diana talked about President Francis," she adds. "It was like he walked on water."

I do recall that. "What about Operation Delano?" I ask. "Does that ring a bell?"

Anne's darting eyes freeze. Recognition. Her mouth parts and she looks at me, then thinks twice about responding.

"Tell me," I plead.

"I know that word. Delano, I mean. Not Operation Delano, but—I heard Diana say it over the phone one time. She was on her cell phone. I don't know who she was talking to. But I remember it because it's not a name you hear often. It was FDR's middle name, right?"

"Right."

"I think what she was saying was, 'I don't care about Delano,' or something like that. Like she was mad, arguing with someone. I remember asking her, when she got off the phone, if she was having an affair with FDR. Y'know, making a joke."

"What did she say when you said that?"

The wind blows Anne's bangs off her forehead. She looks younger than her years. Under different circumstances, I might— well, under different circumstances. "She changed the subject, that's what she did. What do you think this means, Ben? What's Operation Delano?"

"I don't know," I say. There's no point in engaging in rank speculation, especially with Anne, who's probably freaked out enough as it is. So I don't tell her what I think.

I don't tell her what I get when I add up Diana's suspicious death, the involvement of the CIA, the Chinese government, and what appears to be a massive cover-up.

I don't tell her that I think Diana Hotchkiss might be a spy for the US government.

CHAPTER 45

Detective Ellis Burk drums his fingers on the steering wheel of his sedan. He says to me, "This story gets odder and odder the more you tell me."

And he doesn't know the half of it. I decided to leave out my trip to Jonathan Liu's house last night. The cops can find out about his death on their own.

"Alexander Kutuzov." Ellis nods. "I think I've heard of him."

"Diana was sensitive about her relationship with him. That must mean something."

"According to your friend Anne Brennan."

"Right. According to Anne."

"So I'm working on a secondhand account of how someone thinks someone else felt about something. That's not exactly a rock-solid lead, Ben."

"That's why you're an investigator, Ellis. Last time I checked, you follow up on leads. Does any of that sound familiar?"

"For cases I'm working on? Sure it does." He looks over at me. "But this ain't my case, partner. You'll recall the CIA took it away from us local crime fighters. Does **that** sound familiar?"

Ellis is a good man. He could have told me to jump in a lake when I asked him to accompany me today. He'd have every right and every reason to. But something has raised his antennae, and Ellis is one of those cops who's more concerned about right and wrong than he is about technicalities like jurisdictional boundaries.

Or maybe he just took one look at me and took pity on me. I'm sure I must look terrible. I peeked at myself in the mirror this morning and I looked like a character in a Tim Burton movie. And I'm not thinking clearly anymore. I'm seeing shadows where there are none, hearing footsteps that don't exist. I need help.

"I owe you one, man," I say.

"You're damn right you do." When I don't answer, Ellis glances at me. "We'll check this guy out, Ben. Don't worry."

We drive to 5th Street in Dupont Circle, where AK Collectibles is located. It sits in the middle of the block, just as Anne Brennan said it did. Inside, the place is like a rich person's study, with soft lighting and dark oak bookshelves, some chocolate brown leather chairs, every book covered in a protective sheath. There is classical music playing overhead and a dour gentleman looking over his glasses at us from the cash register.

Ellis flashes his badge and tells the guy he wants to talk to Alexander Kutuzov. You'd think he'd asked for a meeting with Santa Claus or the tooth fairy from the salesman's reaction. He picks up a phone and whispers into it.

We loiter for a few minutes. I nod to a locked glass case containing a three-volume set of **Pride and Prejudice** by Jane Austen. I had a tutor, also named Jane, who liked the author so much she went to Jane Austen conventions where everyone dressed up like characters from her novels.

I wish I liked anything that much. I wish my right leg hadn't been torn up when I wiped out on the bike last night.

Also, I wish people weren't trying to kill me.

I didn't see the movie, but I loved Keira Knightley in **Domino,** where she played a bounty hunter. Very hot.

"What's the damage?" I ask the guy behind the counter, motioning toward the glass case containing the Jane Austen books.

He looks over his glasses at me again. "Volume two has some tearing in the rear flyleaf, and we made some small repairs to a couple of the pages in volume three."

"No. I meant, how much does this cost?"

"Ah. You are looking at a first edition from 1813."

Look, if you don't want to tell me, just say so.

"Sixty thousand," says a man who appears from a door behind the counter. His accent is heavy on the Russian. He is middle-aged, bald, and dressed in a black suit, black shirt, and black tie. His neck is the size of a tree trunk, and his face looks like it was cut out of a rock formation.

"Sixty thousand what?" I ask. "Rubles?"

The man seems amused at my naïveté. "You must not be a collector." He looks at Ellis. "Now, Officer—"

"Detective."

"Yes, Detective. Mr. Kutuzov is not here, obviously. Though I believe he is in the States at the moment, but I cannot tell you this with certainty."

"But you know how to get hold of him," Ellis says. Ellis hands his card over the counter.

Knightley was also good in one of those **Pirates of the Caribbean** movies and one of the **Star Wars** prequels.

The man takes Ellis's card and gives him another card. Ellis takes it and reads it, as do I. It's a card for a lawyer named Edgar Griffin, from Griffin and Weaver.

"That's too bad," says Ellis. "I was hoping to just have a quick chat with Mr. Kutuzov and then move along. But if you're involving lawyers, then maybe we'll have to take him to the police station for questioning. It makes the whole thing more antagonistic."

"Antagonistic." The Russian allows a brief smile. "I thought in America you were not punished for requesting the assistance of counsel."

"You know a lot about our system for a guy who sells used books for a living," I say. It isn't really my place to chime in, but this guy doesn't know that I'm a reporter and not a cop. Maybe Ellis and I can be a team, like on **Castle,** except I'm not a crime novelist and Ellis isn't a hot brunette, last time I looked.

Ellis says, "Tell Mr. Kutuzov, or his lawyer, that if I don't hear from him soon, I'm going to come looking for him again, and it won't be as enjoyable as this visit."

The man stares at Ellis with a flare in his eyes, but he ultimately relents. "As you wish," he says. "I shall pass on your inquiry."

"Please do that."

We're back in the car a minute later. "Well, that didn't take long," says Ellis. "We're barely in the door and the guy's already lawyered up." He looks at me. "It's a start, Ben. We've shaken the tree. Now let's see what falls out."

CHAPTER 46

"Still nothing on Operation Delano?" asks Ashley Brook Clark over the phone. "I haven't pulled out all the stops. You still want me to hold off?"

"Could be dangerous," I say into my cell. I have a limp after the bike wipeout and I'm working on almost no sleep, but it warms me up to talk to a friend and colleague. Ashley Brook's been with me since I started the **Beat** five years ago.

"Danger's my middle name," she says. "Hey, Ben—tell me this much. How did Operation Delano come up?"

"Jonathan Liu mentioned it to me the other day."

"The lobbyist Jonathan Liu? The one they just found dead in his house?"

"That one, yes." By yesterday evening, a few hundred media outlets were reporting the news. Gunshot wound, apparently self-inflicted, according to the reports, but nothing else from the MPD.

"And I got confirmation from one of Diana's best friends, Anne Brennan. She heard Diana mention it once. Delano, not Operation Delano."

"Same difference," says Ashley Brook.

I've never really understood what the phrase **same difference** means. I mean, I get Ashley Brook's meaning, which at the end of the day is the point of communication—to convey a thought—but **same difference** never made sense to me.

Anyway. Back to our regularly scheduled programming.

"So what is this about the Russians?" Ashley Brook asks. "You said when you called that this Delano thing ties into the Russians."

I pass a couple making out on a park bench and experience intense jealousy toward anyone who (a) doesn't have someone trying to kill them and (b) has someone they can make out with on a park bench.

"FDR normalized relations with the Russians," I say. "He officially recognized them and he gave them a lot at Yalta, when he, Churchill, and Stalin were divvying up the spoils after World War II. He caught a lot of heat for that. It's something, at least."

"Not really, boss. It's pretty thin."

"That's why I pay you princely sums to uncover information, Ms. Clark."

"You pay me princely sums? I must not be reading my paycheck right."

Everyone's a comedian.

"Okay, well, I'll look for a Russian angle," she says. "Hey, boss? Are you still living out of a gym bag? A different hotel every night?"

"It beats being dead. By the way, if anyone shows up at the office with a submachine gun, tell them I've moved to Antarctica."

"Will do. I'll tell them you're studying penguin mating habits. But seriously, Ben—be careful, okay?"

"Careful's my middle name."

"I thought Martin was your middle name."

Don't remind me. "I'm off to see Ellis Burk again," I tell her. "We've got a date with Alexander Kutuzov's attorney."

"That should be fruitful. Lawyers are usually very forthcoming and helpful."

"I know. I'm going to brush up on my Latin."

"Okay, well, **stare incolumem.**"

"What does that mean?"

"It's been a while since high school," Ashley Brook says. "But I think it means 'stay alive.'"

CHAPTER 47

Two hours later, Ellis Burk and I are driving to the law firm of Griffin and Weaver, one of those swinging-dick firms with all kinds of connected lawyers and former politicians who represent major players before courts and legislatures and steamroll the rest of us on a daily basis. But that's not why Ellis is troubled. He's been troubled ever since he learned, along with the rest of the world last night, that Jonathan Liu is no longer breathing.

"This is against my better judgment, taking you along," he says.

"We're, like, a team," I say. I mention

Castle to him but he doesn't respond. Most cops I know don't like cop shows. But team or not, I admit I feel more comfortable in the escort of a DC police detective. Who's going to shoot at me while I'm hanging with a cop?

Traffic is light today, late morning. The sky is cloudless and the temperatures will hit one hundred today. The dog days of summer. It makes me think of that giant schnauzer waiting for me back at my town house, probably lifting his leg on my walkway as we speak—

I hear a sound that reminds me of thunder, which makes no sense, and before my brain can register anything the glass on the rear window has shattered, and Ellis lets out a wail and his shoulder is spouting blood and he falls forward, his jaw crashing into the steering wheel, and I start to reach for him but a torrent of gunfire tears across the dashboard and then Ellis pounds his foot on the accelerator and we burst forward, heading into the intersection against the light and cars are screeching to a halt and Ellis is shouting but I can't make out any words. He's using his left hand to steer and we're both crouched down and rocking back and forth with the zigzag of the car and then his gun drops onto the seat cushion and he says, "Use it, use . . . it!" So I pick it up and have no idea how to fire this thing and then the gunfire starts again and glass is shattering everywhere and the body of the car is taking hit after hit **whump-whump-whump** along the passenger side and—

"Are you okay?" I shout.

"Shoot!" Ellis yells.

—and I lift my head up high enough to see out the window just barely and there's a black SUV and I see the muzzle of some machine gun and I point my gun and shoot one, two, three times, blasting out my own window, and then the return fire comes, bullets buzzing over my head, and then something warm sprays onto my neck and hands and I turn and see Ellis's face, or what's left of it—

—and then we veer sharply to the left and something smacks my face and snaps my head back and all I'm thinking, the only thing I'm thinking before everything goes dark, is **Please, not Ellis, please not him, too.**

CHAPTER 48

The paramedic completes her tests on me and announces that I'm going to be okay, whatever that means. I'm seated in the back of an open ambulance in the middle of 12th Street, which has been shut down following the shooting.

"Probably just a concussion from the impact when the air bag deployed, Mr. Casper. You're lucky."

Luckier than my friend Ellis Burk.

"You might want to spend a night in the hospital," she says. "I know these police officers are eager to talk to you, but we can have you put under observation if you'd like—"

"That's okay," I say. "They need to talk to me."

She looks over her shoulder. There are probably a dozen squad cars and some unmarked vehicles as well. "Yeah, it's bad. Y'know, losing one of their own. That's a pretty big deal."

I figured out the pretty-big-deal part all by myself. News vans are lining the police perimeter, and copters are flying overhead. It's not every day there's a shootout at a populated intersection in the middle of the nation's capital, at least on this side of town. It's not every day a cop is murdered.

I close my eyes and try to wish this whole thing away. Ellis was my friend, someone who was trying to help me beyond what his job required. And look what it got him.

"Mr. Casper, Detective Liz Larkin."

I open my eyes. Detective Liz Larkin is my height, over six feet tall, and wider than me. She has a towering presence on a bad day, and judging from her expression, this is one of those days.

"Get down off that ambulance, turn

around, and place your hands behind your back," she says.

I comply. "You're . . . cuffing me?"

"Give the man a prize." She places the cuffs over my wrists about as gently as she would rope a steer.

"I'm under arrest?"

"You're two for two."

"What's the charge?"

"I'll think of something," she says. She leads me to a car, pushes down on my head, and shoves me into the backseat.

CHAPTER 49

Turns out Liz Larkin is not as warm and fuzzy as she appeared at first blush.

I've been in this tiny room at the First District station going on three hours now. My head is ringing and I'm getting incredibly tired from answering the same questions over and over again and repeating my story several times.

I want to help them. I want them to figure out who did this, because Ellis deserves that. But Liz Larkin, I can see, is not treating this conversation similarly. This is no mutual information hunt.

"Let me see if I got all this." Larkin places

her hands on the table in front of me and leans on her arms. She's within a couple feet of me, which I can live with, but I'd really prefer she use a breath mint.

"Your friend Diana Hotchkiss falls from a balcony. There's reason to believe she was pushed. You think maybe it wasn't Diana at all. It was someone else, a body double, because of a missing tattoo above her ankle."

Right. But really, a Tic Tac, a stick of gum—something.

"**Then,**" she continues, "after that mysterious death, someone sabotages your fancy little airplane and you have to crash it—but miraculously survive."

I don't know if I'd go with **miraculous.** I like to think it was good flying—

"Then someone shoots up your cottage on Lake Anna with so many bullet holes it looks like the O.K. Corral—but again, you miraculously survive."

Only because I saw them coming first. It's called the element of surprise—

"Then someone jumps you in an airport bathroom, threatens you, orders you to stop poking your nose around, but for some reason **doesn't** kill you—another miraculous survival."

Yeah, that one doesn't make sense to me yet. They could have killed me but didn't want to—

"And then an associate of Diana Hotchkiss, this highfalutin Chinese lobbyist Jonathan Liu, is found dead in his house from a gunshot wound. You had nothing to do with that, either." She leans into me. "I have all that right?"

Basically.

"And this is all the work of some grand government conspiracy like the ones you see on the History channel? Reaching all the way to the White House itself?"

Close enough.

"Wow." She scratches her head. "Sounds like you've really stumbled onto something big here."

Her dead eyes and sarcastic tone tell me that I haven't sold her yet. I guess I can't really blame her. It's pretty hard even for me to believe.

"You know what, Benjamin? Four hours ago, I wouldn't have given a flying fuck about Diana Hotchkiss or Jonathan Liu because they're the feds' problem. But now all the shit you're in has gotten one of our detectives killed. Someone I've known for over fifteen years. Someone with two daughters at Cornell. So now, Benjamin, now I do give a shit. I give a shit very, very much."

She swears a lot. My father always said that swearing was a sign of laziness. Of course, he was a shit-eating fucking asshole.

Holly Hunter in **Copycat** nailed the female cop role, in my opinion. She didn't try to be something she wasn't. She was courteous and pleasant, but tough when necessary. Anyone who thinks Harry Connick Jr. is just a singer needs to see that flick.

"So now that I give a shit, I want to figure this thing out. You know what we cops do, Ben? When we're trying to figure something out?"

Consult a Ouija board? Flip a coin?

"We start with the easy explanation," she says, answering her own question. "So in that spirit, let me ask you a couple of questions that might make this whole thing a little simpler. Is that okay with you, Ben? I mean, since we're on the same team here and all."

Angie Dickinson was pretty hot in that

old TV show **Police Woman.** Even more so playing the role of the sex-starved wife in that Brian De Palma flick **Dressed to Kill** and that TV mini-series **Pearl.** She was good at playing sex-starved. If she were married to me, she wouldn't be sex-starved.

Calm down and focus, you idiot. This cop is trying to corner you.

"The first question, Ben: Were you in Diana Hotchkiss's apartment around the time she was murdered?"

That one stops me. I show a sudden interest in my fingernails.

"Ah, cat's got your tongue on that one. Okay, Ben, then question number two: Were you in Jonathan Liu's town house in the last forty-eight hours?"

I look away. I can almost feel the walls closing in on me.

"See, I've got a different theory, Benjamin Casper. And it doesn't involve cover-ups and dark alleys and conspiracies. Wanna hear my theory, Ben?"

I need a lawyer. This is exactly what I was afraid of the moment I saw Jonathan Liu dead in his bedroom.

"I'm all ears," I say.

CHAPTER 50

One of my favorite interrogation scenes in a movie is in **L.A. Confidential,** when that detective had two different suspects in different rooms and he could play the audio from one room into the next with the flip of a switch, so whenever one of them said something incriminating, the other would hear it. The best one is **The Usual Suspects,** which was one gigantic interrogation scene. Those are two of my favorite Kevin Spacey flicks, but you have to include **American Beauty** and **Seven** in any serious discussion of his work.

"You seem nervous, Ben," says Larkin.

"Like you got a lot of thoughts rolling around in your head."

You don't know the half of it.

"I can't blame you," she says. "I mean, you have Diana Hotchkiss, a death that looks like a suicide. Then Jonathan Liu, a death that looks like a suicide. And **then** . . ."

I look away while she delivers the punch line.

"Then we have your own mother," Larkin says. "A murder that looked like a suicide. You learned that trick at a young age, didn't you? That's what we call a modus operandi, Benjamin. You skated on a murder charge as a boy, but you never forgot that little trick, did you? You saved it up in case you needed it again—"

"You don't know anything about my life," I say.

"Oh, I know **all** about your life." She picks up a file from the table. "Your father was some distinguished history scholar at American U who specialized in American presidents. You apparently have come to learn quite a bit of presidential trivia yourself, which I guess is your way of, what, bonding with Daddy?"

"Don't talk about my father."

"Your mother, she was killed when you were eight. You walked on the charge because the juvenile court judge said he couldn't rule out suicide. But they found your fingerprints on the gun, which was conveniently placed in your mother's hand afterwards. You killed her and made it look like a suicide, Ben."

"No."

"Then you were basically homebound the next ten years. You had fancy private tutors and a lot of therapy. Then Daddy let you out of the house long enough to get a journalism degree from American U, where he could keep an eye on you. And now, even though you have enough money to never work a day in your life, you run some shitty Internet newspaper that nobody reads, which would be out of business if it weren't for you subsidizing it with your personal fortune."

"We get ten thousand hits a day," I protest.

Larkin drops her hands on the table again, shaking the whole table in the process. "You're going to get ten thousand and **one** hits today if you don't stop interrupting me." She reviews the file again.

"Coworkers and friends describe you as nice and friendly on the surface, but nobody really knows you. **Insular** is the word that keeps coming up. You live in a world of your own. Never a really close friend, never a girlfriend that lasted more than a fling. You're fucked up, Benjamin. You spent the first eighteen years of your life looking out a window, and now that you're outside, you don't have a clue how to operate."

"No."

"But then along comes Diana Hotchkiss. You fall for her. Big-time. She understands you like nobody else ever did, she's easy on the eyes, she fucks you like you've never been fucked—the whole nine yards. Your dream has come true. But then that dream is shattered. You discover she has another guy in her life. A rich lobbyist type. Jonathan Liu. So you have Diana killed. You don't do the dirty work yourself. In fact, you make sure that some people at the street level are chatting with you, so they can remember you later. A good alibi. But you make sure you're there, right? You're a sick fuck who wants to see her body splatter on the sidewalk. But then you get the hell out of there before the police come. You drive away so fast that a patrolman tickets you for erratic driving on Constitution Avenue."

I knew that ticket was going to come back to haunt me.

"You try to create a story with this bullshit about your airplane being sabotaged, you shoot up your own cottage—and then, once you've created this story, you kill Jonathan Liu, too. You do it just like you did with Mommy. Gunshot, staged as a suicide."

"No."

"Then you run to Ellis Burk and tell him your sob story, and to make it look real, you even have your friends shoot at you in Ellis's presence so he can corroborate your story. I mean, you have more money than God, Ben. You can hire whoever you want for whatever you want."

She walks over to me. "The problem is, you killed Detective Burk in the process. And I'm not letting you walk away from that."

"I didn't kill anybody."

"Sure you did, Ben. And you killed Jonathan Liu, too."

"No."

She looks at me like she knows something I don't. I have a feeling I know what that is.

Larkin says, "Why did we find your fingerprint on the computer mouse in Jonathan Liu's bedroom?"

I place my hands flat on the table as the room begins to spin. I should have seen this coming.

We interrupt this program to bring you a breaking report. Benjamin Casper has been set up!

They knew I'd be at Diana's place when they killed her. They knew I'd go looking for Jonathan Liu, so they made sure I found him dead. And they killed him the same way as my mother was killed.

And then I made it easier for them. I made myself visible at Diana's. And I rooted around Jonathan Liu's bedroom and left a print on his computer mouse, of all things.

I've been playing into their hands all along. And I don't even know who "they" are.

Liz Larkin moves in on me, a predator approaching its wounded prey. "It's just a matter of time before I can prove all this," she says to me. "And then I'm going to hand you over to the feds, who'll hit you with a federal murder charge and stick a paralyzing agent through your veins. Your days are numbered, my friend."

Her words echo in a room that shrinks by the second. Whoever they are, they're doing their utmost to kill me. And now, even if I survive, it will just prove that I'm guilty.

They've got me either way.

CHAPTER 51

The bar is dark and hazy, just the way I want it. Just the way I need it. I'm tucked in a corner booth of a swanky lounge, but I'd rather not say which one; I'd rather not say where. For all I know, whoever's chasing me hasn't just tapped into my cell phone—they're reading my thoughts, too.

I mean, they've managed to predict my movements, and they've managed to be in several places at once. And I think there's more than one "they." There's the "they" who have unloaded assault weapons at me on three different occasions and sabotaged my plane. And there's the "they" who accosted me in the Wisconsin airport bathroom, who—as Liz Larkin so eloquently pointed out—could have easily killed me instead of kneeing me in the balls and leaving me with a stern warning.

I take a sip of the Scotch and let the hot, bitter medicine warm my throat. I'm too sleep-deprived to drink very much without passing out, but my nerves are jangling and I need a brief respite. I look around at the crowd in this place—mostly people my age, dressed fashionably, worried about little in the world at the moment except enjoying the soft jazz and getting in someone's pants later—and then look up at the television screen mounted over the bar.

On the screen are President Blake Francis, First Lady Libby Rose Francis, and Bono, the singer from U2. They are behind a podium somewhere, and though the sound is turned down, I imagine they're talking about world debt or world peace or some global assistance initiative. President Francis has never been the most generous president in terms of third-world philanthropy, but it's good optics to share a stage with Bono, and the president has always been about good optics.

Same for his wife, Libby Rose Francis, who seems to relish the spotlight a lot more than she relishes her husband. I always made their marriage as one of convenience; she was a wealthy heiress who wanted to marry a future president, and he was a future president who wanted to be bankrolled by a wealthy heiress. They're affectionate enough in public, and everyone's so plastic on camera that you can never really tell, but I never made them for lovebirds. Ron and Nancy they ain't.

Snowflake, the Secret Service calls her. I don't know why they make their code names public, but they do. The president is Spider. That name kind of suits him. But Snowflake for the First Lady? Well, they have the temperature about right. I'd go with Icicle for a more accurate description.

Woodrow Wilson's wife championed improved urban housing while she was First Lady. Rosalynn Carter made mental health her cause. Nancy Reagan told us to "just say no." Libby Rose Francis's thing is "stay in school." Hard to be against that, but seeing this bejeweled, silver-spoon elitist among inner-city dropouts is like watching Donald Trump milk a cow.

Now Bono, he's a cool one. He's rein-
vented himself musically twenty times
over, fronted probably the best rock band
of my generation, and now tries to feed
the hungry and heal the sick. I wonder if I
could have accomplished what he did. I
think so. All I'd need is a mountain of mu-
sical talent, ambition, and balls. And a pair
of those tinted glasses.

Maybe in the next life. I wonder how
quickly my next life will come. Judging by
the odds, my time in this life is waning.

My cell phone rings. I'm not used to it. I
just bought it today at a convenience store.
It has one hundred minutes on it.

"Sorry I missed your call earlier," says
Ashley Brook Clark. "Caller ID didn't show
up."

"I'm not using my personal cell phone
anymore. That thing's dead to me now."

"I can barely hear you. Your phone's
dead?"

"They've tapped it," I say a bit more
loudly, but trying not to draw attention. "I
can't use it. I'm using a prepaid phone."

"They've tapped your phone? Are you
sure, Ben?"

A waitress passes me who is prettier

than any girl I ever dated in my life. A moment of longing courses through me, then back to the point.

"I'm not sure of anything anymore," I say.

On the TV, Bono and the president raise their clenched fists in triumph. I would love to be so happy about something that I threw my fists into the air in triumph. In fact, screw happy—I'd settle for mildly content right now.

"So how are you doing?" she asks me.

"It's a beautiful day," I say.

"Yeah? Where are you? It sounds like you're in a club. I hear jazz music."

"I'm at a place called Vertigo."

"Don't know it. Where's that? Over on U Street?"

"Where the streets have no name."

"Where the—okay, whatever, you don't want to tell me. How are you doing on your search for Operation Delano?"

"I still haven't found what I'm looking for."

The door to the club opens. An Asian couple enters, young and handsome, looking over the whole place with blank expressions. They could be assassins. Why not? I shrink in my seat.

"I think you're nervous," Ashley Brook says. "You're scared."

"Why do you say that?"

"Because you're quoting U2 song titles to me, Ben. You do things like that when you're nervous. Next thing, you're probably going to tell me which presidents liked jazz."

"Clinton, probably the most," I say. "The leader of the Czech Republic gave him a tenor saxophone as a gift. Otherwise, I'd have to say—"

Then I remember what Detective Liz Larkin said to me about memorizing presidential trivia as a way of bonding with Father, and I shut my mouth. No more of that. I wasn't bonding with Father. Screw him—

The club door opens again, and two men walk in who look like they could play professional basketball, tall and wide and menacing. My stomach does a quick flip, a flurry of **how-did-they-find-me**'s rush through my head, and the ever-imminent sweat breaks out across my forehead before I realize that these two guys are, in fact, professional basketball players for the Wizards.

I take a moment while my heartbeat de-escalates to a human pace. I can't keep this up much longer. I'm flinching at shadows.

"Tell me something good, Ashley Brook," I say.

"Okay, I will," she says. "That busted laptop you dropped off for our techies? They think they can recover the data on there. It's going to take them a few days, but they think they can do it."

She's right. That is good news, the first in a long time.

"Tell them to hurry," I say. "Because I'm running out of days."

CHAPTER 52

Garfield Park is brimming this morning with exuberant children—bouncing around the playground equipment, kicking a soccer ball, or just running around aimlessly. I mix in with the mothers pushing their strollers down the park's central sidewalk, but, as always when I come to check on my town house, I try to stay to the south, by the Southeast Freeway, as much as possible. Anyone watching my house, and hoping to ambush me there, would hang out on the park's north end, by F Street.

Which is where I'm heading right now. A couple of days ago, I rolled the dice and ran up to my town house and grabbed my mail. The entire sixty-second event took a lot out of me, as I felt sure someone was going to open fire on me, and I decided after that to have my mail forwarded to my office.

Still, I feel the need to check on the place. It makes me feel borderline normal. Normal people have homes. Normal people spend a lot of time in them. I have to concede the irony here, though—as Liz Larkin correctly pointed out, I spent most of my childhood locked up in my house, inside looking out, and now I'm forced to stay outside looking in. Maybe life has a way of evening things out, like that **Seinfeld** episode where everything always evened out for Jerry—

Stop. There he is, not ten yards away from me. Oscar the giant schnauzer, with that long gray beard and stump tail, on a long leash held by my neighbor, Mrs. Tooley. I can't prove this, but my theory is that when Satan returns to earth, he'll return in the form of a giant schnauzer. And maybe he already has.

Maybe Father sent him. Maybe Father took a break from his poker game with

Hitler, Stalin, Jeffrey Dahmer, and whoever invented disco to advise Lucifer on the best way to torment me.

I move east of the sidewalk, trying to keep heading toward my town house but away from Oscar. To me, the best **Seinfeld** episode was the one with the library cop, Bookman, who was also the single best supporting character among many good ones. I'd put him slightly above Jacopo Peterman, but it's a close call, admittedly. Am I the only person who thinks the Soup Nazi wasn't as funny as some of the other characters? I mean, there's no bad **Seinfeld** episode, but—

Wait. What's this?

As I approach F Street, I see a few people congregating in the park, looking across the street in the direction of my town house.

Then I see an MPD squad car.

Then the door to my town house opens.

And bounding down the stairs of my walkway, looking like the cat who ate the canary, is none other than Detective Liz Larkin.

CHAPTER 53

I duck behind a tree, as if I have something to hide, as if it's a crime to stand across the street and watch the police search your house.

I open my cell phone and dial Ashley Brook's number.

"Two quick questions," I say to her when she answers. "What's your favorite **Seinfeld** episode, and what does it mean when you say someone looks like the cat who ate the canary?"

"I have a question for you, too," she answers.

"Mine first."

"Okay, well—if you look like the cat who ate the canary, it means you look guilty."

"Isn't that being caught with your hand in the cookie jar?"

"Oh. But the cat isn't supposed to eat the canary, so it feels guilty. Right?"

On the sidewalk just outside my house, Detective Larkin is conferring with two men in sport coats and blue jeans and two uniformed officers.

"I thought it meant you look smug," I say. "Self-satisfied. The cat's happy because it just had a nice meal. It finally caught the canary."

"Hmm. Well, okay, my favorite **Seinfeld** episode? It's a tie."

"You can't have ties."

"I have a tie, Ben. Deal with it. The first is the one with the contest over who was 'master' of their domain; the second is the one where Elaine thought her boyfriend was black and he thought she was Hispanic, but they were both afraid to talk about it; and the third is the one about being gay, where they kept saying 'not that there's anything wrong with that.'"

Fair enough. All of those would make my top ten. She left out the one where Kramer takes the furniture from **The Merv Griffin Show** and starts his own talk show in his apartment. Or the one about "shrinkage," where George emphasized the point by wearing a T-shirt three sizes too small.

Detective Larkin pulls out her cell phone and makes a call. The other four cops head inside my house.

"Now, what's your question?" I ask.

"When was the last time you got any sleep?"

"A week ago."

"You need sleep, Ben. You're acting goofy. I mean, is this why you called me? To ask about **Seinfeld** and some stupid idiom?"

"Is that an idiom or an expression?" I ask.

"Is there a difference?"

"Why are you answering a question with a question?"

"Why are you?"

One of the uniforms comes out of my house carrying my desktop computer. A second one emerges with a banker's box, contents unknown.

"There **was** another reason I called," I say. "Text me the number for Fast Eddie."

"Eddie Volker?"

"The very one."

"Why do you want to talk to Fast Eddie?"

One of the plainclothes detectives pops his head out and calls to Larkin. She hangs up her phone and rushes up the stairs and disappears into my house.

It looks like they found something good. Good for them, I mean. Not so good for me.

"Because I think it's time I finally got a lawyer," I say.

CHAPTER 54

The Hart Senate Office Building is the third building that was constructed to hold United States Senate offices. The building is northeast of the Capitol, adjacent to the Dirksen Senate Office Building along Constitution Avenue, with a view of the Supreme Court Building.

The reception area in the third-floor office is all earth tones. I'm seated in a chair that I'd best describe as sunrise orange—I just made that up, but I like it—while a middle-aged woman busies herself answering the phone and shooting glances at me over her bifocals.

Her intercom buzzes, she picks up a phone, and then she gives me the go-ahead.

Inside the main office, the colors are patriotic. Even the Iowa state flag, standing alongside the Stars and Stripes, fits in with the color scheme, though truth be told the Iowa state flag resembles the French flag more than it does the American flag. Kind of ironic, given that then-congressman Craig Carney was one of the politicians leading the charge to change the phrase **french fries** to **freedom fries** when the French were less than enthusiastic about our invasion of Iraq.

I'm not sure why I'm meeting with the number two man at the CIA in a senator's office. Carney used to be a congressman from Iowa, and he's close with the Iowa senator who occupies this office, but why didn't he just invite me to CIA headquarters?

Carney is handsome, with a square jaw, steel blue eyes, and a full head of dark hair just touched with gray. Some of these politicians, when you get them off camera, let their hair down. I've never seen Craig Carney's hair down. I don't know if he's capable of letting it down. He looks as polished as ever today in his crisp white shirt, navy blue tie with tiny red stars, and cuff links bearing the Stars and Stripes.

Craig Carney is largely credited with helping Blake Francis win the Iowa caucus, which catapulted him from the middle of the pack into front-runner status for the GOP nomination. Carney was even on a short list of candidates for vice president. The president and Carney are very tight, to understate the point.

Deputy Director Carney swivels in his leather chair and invites me to take the seat across from his walnut desk, which doesn't look nearly as comfortable as his own seat. He makes a show of looking at his watch. "My schedule is full today," he informs me.

But he made time for me, I notice. I only called this morning. Usually it takes a week, minimum, to schedule some time like this.

"So you wanted to talk about Operation Sunshine," he says. That's the operation the United States embarked on to give humanitarian relief to the people of Bolivia following a devastating earthquake. That was the excuse I gave for this interview.

He smiles, and so do I.

"I think we both know that's not why I'm here," I say. He wouldn't have dropped everything, and wouldn't have scheduled the meeting away from his office, if the subject were Operation Sunshine.

He reveals nothing but his pearly white teeth. "If there's something else," he says.

"Diana Hotchkiss, Mr. Deputy Director."

Carney nods soberly, turning on the furrowed-brow concerned look that DC politicians learn during their first-week orientation. "She'll be missed."

I almost laugh. He threaded that one just about right.

"Have you spoken with her recently?" I ask.

I just want to see how he reacts. If Craig Carney is capable of sincerity, I've yet to see it. I could see this guy being president one day, and I don't mean that as a compliment.

He cups some almonds out of a dish on the desk and weighs them in his hand while he looks me over. I wonder if the senator who occupies this office knows that Carney is eating his almonds.

"Tell me something, Ben. It's Ben, isn't it?"

That's the kind of thing I hate about this town. Those little put-downs, delivered politely but intended to degrade the other person. This asshole knows very well who I am. If he didn't, I wouldn't be sitting here on such short notice.

"Yes, it's Ben," I say.

"Ben, why would you ask me a provocative question like that?"

"To provoke you."

"Yes, well—I guess that's what reporters do. They shake trees."

That's the same phrase Ellis Burk used.

"Someone who shakes a tree, Ben, needs to be ready for what might fall on him."

"Oh, I'm ready, Mr. Deputy Director. If you had the week I've had, you'd be, too."

Carney takes some time with the almonds in his hand, making me watch him munching them one by one.

"Well," he finally says between bites. "You seem to have some information that I don't. I wish I could help you."

You have to love these politicians. This is another thing they must teach you when you walk through the Capitol doors—how to say all kinds of things without answering the question. So far, this guy hasn't admitted or denied that Diana is alive.

"I think Diana was a spy for the US government," I say. "Probably CIA. And I think she was trying to infiltrate something and she was exposed, compromised, whatever—her cover was blown. So you faked her death to throw the bad guys off the scent. Maybe you were protecting her. Maybe you were protecting classified secrets. I don't know. I don't even really care, if you want to know the truth. **Capital Beat** has never tried to expose classified intelligence information. That's not what we do."

"Thank you," he says. Even when he says **thank you,** it comes out like **fuck you.**

"But here's the thing," I say. "Someone must think that I know what Diana knew, because they're trying to kill me. And someone's trying to frame me for Diana's 'death' and the death of Jonathan Liu, the lobbyist. I might even get blamed for the cop who was murdered in that ambush the other day on Twelfth Street—a good friend of mine, by the way. So now I **do** care, Mr. Carney. And I'll run a wrecking ball through whatever I have to in order to save my life and clear my name."

The deputy director leans back in his leather chair and narrows his eyes. I've just thrown a lot at him. But he doesn't look surprised.

"That all sounds very intriguing," he says. "But I don't see how I could possibly be of assistance to you."

"Oh, you can and you will," I say. "And I'm going to tell you why."

CHAPTER 55

"Oh, please do tell me, Ben." The CIA deputy director seems amused. "I'm waiting with bated breath as to why and how I'll help you—a reporter for some rag that nobody reads, pushing a story that nobody will believe."

I'd really like to smack this douche bag. I'll have to settle for scaring him.

"Mr. Carney," I say. "You remember Gary Condit?"

Typical of his manner, he doesn't move an inch, but the giveaway is a slight twitch of his eye.

"Congressman Condit didn't kill Chandra

Levy," I go on. "All he did was sleep with her. Affairs happen all the time, and they sting you politically, but you almost always recover from them. You hold a nice press conference with your stoic wife at your side, humbly concede your imperfection with vague statements like 'I've made mistakes' or 'I haven't been perfect,' throw in a reference to God and, if necessary, some rehabilitation or therapy—and voilà, you win reelection.

"But Gary Condit, he had the bad luck of having an affair with a woman who wound up dead. So even though he had nothing to do with her death, he was tainted by asso—"

"Do you have a point here, Mr. Casper?"

So now it's **Mr. Casper.** "Oh, I just wonder how it's going to affect your political career when it comes out that you had an affair with a woman who killed herself."

Carney wets his lips. His face reddens, but he's doing his best impression of a mannequin. It's not hard for him. He's had a lot of practice.

"Kind of a catch-22, isn't it, Mr. Carney? I mean, if we're supposed to believe she's dead, then you have to stick with that story, right? So now it's former congressman and current deputy CIA director Craig Carney having an affair with a woman who jumped off a balcony. How do you think you come off in that story? Good? Bad? Ugly?"

(Possible Clint Eastwood mind-scroll here. But I'm a little busy right now.)

Carney's jaw clenches. I know what he's itching to say: **That affair with Diana ended years ago.** Which, according to Diana, is true. But we both know that's just a detail. He'll have to admit to the affair to make that distinction.

"You look like the cat who ate the canary, Mr. Deputy Director."

He blinks his eyes rapidly, digesting that comment. Damn. I think I was right the first time, and Ashley Brook was wrong. I should have gone with the hand-in-the-cookie-jar line. Another lesson to all of you—go with your first instinct.

After a long pause, which I have to put down as some of the best thirty seconds of my entire week, Carney clears his throat and comes forward in his chair.

"Young man," he says evenly, but I detect a tremble in his voice. "Do you have any idea how much trouble you can get in by blackmailing the deputy director of the CIA?"

I shrug my shoulders. "Is it worse than a needle in my arm for murder? Remember, Mr. Carney, you all have done such a good job of fucking with my world that I don't have much to lose."

I get out of my chair and button my sport coat. It's a new one I bought yesterday at J.Crew on M Street, as I continue my nomadic existence. It's a denim job, a more casual look for Benjamin Casper, reporter turned fugitive.

"I have proof of your affair and I'll publish it," I say, framing my hands for the headline. "A conservative, law-and-order, family-values politician, now guarding our central intelligence, caught in steamy affair with top aide who killed herself in despair. Ah, but the police are also looking into the possibility that she didn't jump, that maybe she was **pushed** off that balcony. She was **murdered.** Gee, who might be a suspect? It could take as long as, oh, ten or twelve seconds before every mainstream news outlet in the country is running the story. Are you ready for that kind of publicity? Is your wife?"

I lean over the desk, so we can have a nice eye-to-eye parting. "The words **Operation Delano** might find their way into the story, too. It's already been written, by the way. Killing me won't stop the story."

I straighten up, nod to a visibly shaken Craig Carney, and head for the door.

"You have twenty-four hours, Mr. Deputy Director," I say. "Give me some answers, or you'll be back in Des Moines selling tractors to farmers. And the president will be thinking of someone else as his next CIA director."

CHAPTER 56

When I leave the Hart Building, I run down 1st Street to the Capitol South metro station. I look behind me for any sign of men in black chasing after me, or cars following me, but don't see any. It had been a risk all along, scheduling that meeting with Craig Carney, but I'm hoping my threats held him off for at least a few hours while he ponders his next move.

I spend an hour on the subway, jumping from one train to another, hoping to throw off anyone who might be following me. Everyone is a suspect—the kindly grandmother, the well-dressed young woman who looks like she's headed to an interview, the homeless guy with food in his beard. Trust no one.

In between stops, I find an ATM and withdraw five hundred dollars in cash, then jump on another train before anyone can trace that transaction.

I spend the evening at a deli on 14th Street and look over the notes I've written up for the story on Craig Carney and Diana Hotchkiss. I was bluffing, of course, about having the article written, but I need to finish it now. The story is largely unsubstantiated; I also lied when I said I had proof of Diana's affair with Carney. I don't. I only have Diana's word. In terms of editorial standards, I'd never sign off on this article without more confirmation. But I'm not worried at the moment about journalistic integrity. I'm more concerned with saving my ass.

Will I run this if Craig Carney calls my bluff? I don't know. **Capital Beat** may not be the most popular news website going, but we've never gone with sensationalism. We've never compromised our standards. Am I willing to do so now?

No point in worrying about that yet. Just write it, Ben.

So I crank out a draft, e-mail it to Carney's office and to myself for safekeeping, and close my laptop. I force down a roast beef sandwich, because being sleep-deprived **and** malnourished makes Ben a vulnerable target.

Now it's nearing nine o'clock. The sun has fallen, but my spirits are slightly elevated with the completion of this article. It's a chit. It's something.

Then I pull out my cell phone—my original one, not the prepaid piece of shit I've been using. From my other pocket I pull out the cell battery. I saw in some movie that a cell phone can't be traced if the battery is removed. So now I'm going to put it back in, just to check any messages, then get the hell out of here and move to another part of the capital before any black helicopters can swoop down on me.

When I pop in the battery and check my voice mail, I see four messages. One is from an unknown caller. Two are from George Hotchkiss in Wisconsin.

The last one is from fifteen minutes ago, from Anne Brennan. I punch that message and raise the phone to my ear.

"Ben . . . it's Anne. I—they just—I need

you to come here, Ben. They—they said if I—they said next time they'll kill me— please, I don't know who else to call—"

I jump out of my seat, grab my bag, and head for the door.

CHAPTER 57

"It's Ben," I say to the door. "It's me. Open up."

When Anne opens her door, my heart sinks. Her shirt, a button-down long denim thing, is ripped at the collar, and most of the buttons have been torn off. Her eyes are bloodshot, her eye makeup smeared, her lip bloody. Behind her, the living room looks like a tornado swept through it.

She quickly closes the door behind me and double-locks it.

"Let's sit," I say to her in the calmest voice I can muster, but my heart is shredded and my blood is boiling.

"O—okay," she says, but she collapses to the floor before she can make it to the couch. She bursts into tears, her petite figure shaking uncontrollably. I sit on the floor and take her in my arms, as if I were rocking an infant to sleep. It's a long time before she can speak, and I don't rush her. I keep repeating, "It's okay, I'm here," as if that's any comfort at this moment.

"It was . . . two of them," she says, audibly gulping between sobs. "They said they were from . . . the government and . . . and they just wanted to . . . talk."

"Did they have credentials? Badges?"

She shakes her head.

"You let someone in without—" I cut myself off. The last thing she needs from me is a lecture. I don't know her all that well, but from what I've discerned so far, it seems just like her to be trusting enough to let strangers into her apartment.

"Go ahead," I say. "Tell me what happened."

The story comes out amid sobs and deep breaths. She stumbles around it, but I get the point. They forced their way in. They put a knife to her throat. They ripped off her shirt and pulled down her pants.

"They said, next time—they'd—they'd rape me and then slit my throat," she stammers. "They said if Benjamin Casper doesn't stop poking his nose where it doesn't belong, it will be me who . . . pays."

I hold Anne for a long time, my jaw set in a death lock, my body trembling with rage.

"You want me to stay?" I whisper. "I can sleep on the couch—"

"I want you to stop," she blurts out. "I want all of this to . . . **stop.**"

A door closes in the apartment upstairs. We both jump at the sound. The goons who delivered this message probably won't be back tonight. But maybe they knew I would come.

Anne looks up at me. "I know I don't have a right to ask that. I know Diana was important to you. She was to me, too. But is it worth the cost?"

She's right. It's one thing to risk my own life. I don't really have a choice in that. But I'm endangering people I care about. First Ellis Burk, now Anne—innocent victims, punished for nothing more than listening to me and trying to help me.

"I'll think of something," I tell her, which is about the emptiest promise I could give.

CHAPTER 58

I spend the night at Anne's, sitting up on the couch, dozing off occasionally, but mostly watching the front door and trying to figure a way out of this mess.

In the morning, my head is cloudy, my limbs are shaky, and a permanent dull ache has taken up residence in my stomach. I use my prepaid phone to dial George Hotchkiss, who called my old cell phone twice yesterday but didn't leave a message.

"George, it's Ben Casper. I know you're anxious to learn more about Diana. But I need more—"

"You don't know what I'm going to say," he says, interrupting me. "What I'm going to say is I want you to forget about what you told us. I don't want to make any noise about Diana. I want to let it go."

He wants me to let it go? "George—"

"She's gone, Ben. And the sooner my wife and I accept that, the sooner we can move on with our lives. We've lost two children in the space of a week."

I sigh. I can see his point, of course. But if there was a chance my child were alive, I'd chase that hope like I've never pursued anything in my life. Why wouldn't George Hotchkiss do the same?

Oh. Oh, of course.

"They got to you, didn't they, George? They—"

"Nobody did anything." His voice is rising, as if in panic. "Nobody did anything, you understand? I still have a wife, and I don't want to lose her, too. So I'm not going to ask the government to hand over Diana's body or perform a DNA test or anything else, and I don't authorize you to do those things, either. And I'm telling you that I want you to stop pursuing this. I want you to let this go. Diana is dead, okay? She's **dead.**"

Shit. These guys are smart. They're hitting every pressure point they can find. They got to George and threatened him.

"I **need** you to let this go," George says. "Please, Mr. Casper."

CHAPTER 59

"It's not good, Ben."

Eddie Volker says these words before he says hello. I'm in his law firm after taking the most circuitous route I possibly could to his office. "Not good at all."

Eddie is the **Beat**'s lawyer—the one who represents us in the rare cases when someone tries to sue us for defamation or has some other beef with an article we published. But his principal practice is criminal defense, which is why I had him contact Detective Liz Larkin to discuss my case. I'm here now for a report, and

Eddie's first words aren't what I wanted to hear.

He has the office of a busy lawyer—piles of paper everywhere, the fancy diplomas and honors framed on his wall, the piping hot cup of Starbucks on his desk. He's losing his hair as well as his battle with the bulge these days, but he remains a formidable presence. I feel a small measure of comfort with him on my side.

"As you know, they searched your house. They had a warrant, and it looks fine to me. No basis to quarrel with it. Anyway, what they found wasn't good for us, Ben."

I don't answer. There are plenty of things they could find in my town house that would be embarrassing to me, but I can't imagine what would prove that I killed Diana or Jonathan Liu, especially considering the small detail that I **didn't** kill either of them.

"I made a lot of noise about the First Amendment, that cops can't steal a reporter's notes or work product, threats to run to court to get a protective order. But I didn't see anyone trembling in their boots, Ben. I wouldn't be, either, if I were them."

"Why not?" I ask.

Eddie rearranges some papers on his desk. Avoidance behavior, something you do when you don't want to deliver bad news.

"They found traces of carpet fibers from Diana Hotchkiss's apartment on your shoes."

"So what? I've been in Diana's apartment many times."

"They found traces of carpet fibers from Jonathan Liu's downstairs carpet on another pair of your shoes."

"That's impossible." Since leaving Jonathan Liu's home, I haven't been to mine. I've been on the run.

Eddie gives a curt nod. It's not the first time in Eddie's career that somebody sitting where I'm sitting has denied doing something. It's probably not even the first time today. The words **I didn't do it** have probably echoed off the walls of the office so often that they're embedded in the plaster.

"Ben, they say you killed Jonathan Liu the same way you killed your mother. They say you either snuck up behind him or you subdued him, put a gun against his temple, and pulled the trigger. Then you made it look like a suicide."

I stare at the ceiling. "They have no proof of that. They don't even have proof that I was in his house when he was murdered. A carpet fiber—"

"And your fingerprint on Liu's computer mouse—"

"Okay, fine, both of those might prove I was there at some point, but not when he was killed."

Eddie looks at me like he has more to tell me, like the bad-news express hasn't stopped yet.

"Spit it out," I say to him.

He sighs. "Ben, they found Jonathan Liu's wallet in your bedroom."

"That's bullshit," I say. "That's bullshit!"

"And he used his credit card to buy a plane ticket for himself the evening he was murdered. So anyone who stole his credit card must have done it after that time. Basically, that means they've got you in his apartment right about the coroner's estimated time of death."

I jump out of my chair. "I can't believe

this is happening. They planted Jonathan Liu's wallet and those carpet fibers. They framed me. They fucking framed me!"

"I believe you and I'll fight for you," Eddie says. "But it's very bad. They want you to come in for more questioning. And if I don't deliver you to them by the end of the day, they're going to issue a warrant for your arrest."

I cover my face with my hands and drop my head against the wall. They've finally got me in the corner.

Eddie comes over to me and puts his hand on my shoulder. "It's time to cut your losses, my friend. I'll take you downtown. They'll book you, print you, and I'll see if we can do something about bond."

I let out a bitter chuckle. "Bond for a double murderer? Is there a good chance I'll get bond?"

"Not really, no." Eddie's always told it to me straight. "You're looking at a long time in lockup awaiting trial. But we'll pull out all the stops—"

"I'll never get to trial," I say. "They won't let that happen. If I go inside, I'll never come out."

I take a breath and nod to Eddie.

"I'll be in touch," I say.

"They'll issue the warrant, Ben. They'll come looking for you. It won't be pretty."

Please stop this, Anne said.

Please stop, George Hotchkiss pleaded.

Surrender to the police, Eddie's telling me.

I release my arm from Eddie's hand. "Give me a couple of hours to think about this," I say. "I'll be in touch."

CHAPTER 60

"Deputy Director Carney, please," I say into a new prepaid cell phone I purchased an hour ago.

"May I say who's calling, please?"

"His favorite reporter," I answer. I take a breath and steel myself. **You can do this, Ben. Act confident. Don't act like you're scared out of your mind. Keep the upper hand.**

A moment later: "This is Craig Carney."

"Hello, Mr. Deputy Director. It's twenty-four hours later. You'll recall I set a deadline."

"I do recall that."

"Did you read the article I e-mailed to your office?"

"I read a document that doesn't remotely bear any relation to the truth, Mr. Casper."

"Either way, I snap my fingers and it's online, front and center, a pretty big headline. Should I snap my fingers, Mr. Deputy Director, or do you have something to tell me?"

"I have something to tell you."

"Will I like it?"

"I would if I were you, yes. But not over the phone. Come to my office."

That's about the least surprising thing he could have said.

"Your office? I don't think so. Let me think a second." I take a swig of the bottled water I'm holding. My mouth is dry as a sandbox. My heart is pounding so furiously that I can hardly hear myself speaking.

I take a couple of short breaths. The delay works for me, because he thinks I'm trying to come up with a place to meet. The truth is, I already have one.

"The Washington Monument," I say. "One hour. Stand on the east side and face the Capitol. And Mr. Carney, this is just the two of us, right?"

"Of course."

"Of course," I say, mimicking him. "If it's more than the two of us, I snap my fingers. Know what I mean?"

Carney lets out a sigh. "It will be just the two of us, Mr. Casper."

"Okay. See you there. Wear a Nationals cap."

"Wear a what?"

"A Nationals baseball cap. So I know it's you."

"You'll know it's me."

"Wear a Nationals cap and, come to think of it, have a Nationals pennant. Y'know, those things you wave?"

"Why do I need to do that?"

"Because I'm not going to appear until I see you. And from a distance, I won't recognize you. So wear a Nationals baseball cap and be waving a pennant."

"I don't have either of those things."

"You're one of the most powerful men in the country, Mr. Carney. I'm confident you'll make it happen. Do as I say, or in one hour, we publish the story. Oh, and I also set up a new e-mail address, under a fake name, of course, that is timed to send this article to the **Post,** the **Times,** and about ten other newspapers ninety minutes from now. Unless I stop it, of course."

He doesn't answer. Good. He's letting me call the shots.

"One hour," I say. "And give me your cell number."

He does so. Then I hang up the phone. I wipe the sweat from my forehead, bend over at the waist, and vomit into a bush.

CHAPTER 61

An hour later, I dial the cell number Craig Carney gave me.

"Hello, Mr. Casper," he says when he picks up. "I'm here at the Washington Monument, as you can see. Where are you?"

Where am I? I'm among about five hundred people strolling the west side of the National Mall right now, looking at the many memorials. But he doesn't need to know that. Like pretty much everyone else around here, I have a camera, only I'm not snapping pictures. I'm using it as I would a pair of binoculars, zooming in wherever I need to look, trying not to be too obvious.

"I want you to move to the other side of the monument, Mr. Deputy Director. Come around to the west side and face the Lincoln Memorial."

"Okay, I'll go around to the other side of the monument."

I have a feeling he didn't say that for my benefit. I think he's trying to signal someone—FBI agents, CIA, Capitol Police, whatever—what he's doing. He must be wearing a wire. That's about as surprising as a hot day in August.

"You're not waving the pennant, Mr. Carney. I told you to wave it."

Okay, that wasn't called for or necessary, but give me a break—I'm nervous here. I'm trying to convince myself I have the upper hand. This is high-stakes poker and I've never played anything but solitaire.

"Okay, are you happy now?"

"I'm just kidding. I don't know if you're waving the pennant or not. I'm not on the National Mall right now. Sorry about that. There's been a change of plans."

They say that a lot in movies, when there are ransom drops or other controlled meetings. **There's been a change of plans,** delivered with much more bravado than I can muster right now, when I'm doing my damnedest to keep the tremor out of my voice. Hell, I'm trying not to piss my pants.

I say, "Go to the Foggy Bottom metro station and take the Orange Line to the Landover stop."

"Landover? This is ridiculous."

"Do it or become a national disgrace. The clock is ticking."

I punch off the phone and listen to a tour guide tell me and a dozen other people what each of the pillars on the perimeter of the World War II Memorial represents. Interesting.

Even more interesting? What happens next. Due east, at the Washington Monument, Craig Carney is speaking into his collar. So that confirms he's wired up, and he's obviously telling his people that he's on the move.

Carney starts to head west and north toward the Foggy Bottom station. Several people dressed as tourists suddenly lose interest in the attractions they're supposedly here to view and simultaneously begin to change course. A man in a navy suit and sunglasses near the Korean War

Memorial breaks sharply toward the Washington Monument and trails Carney from a distance. A man in a gray T-shirt and blue jeans at the Lincoln Memorial breaks north into a jog, which means he's either one of Carney's guys or he likes to jog in denim. Two women, one in a blue suit and the other in a brown sundress, strolling east along the reflecting pool, suddenly stop strolling and nonchalantly pivot in the opposite direction. A casually dressed man and woman, who are not more than twenty yards away from me at the World War II Memorial, freeze in their tracks, touch their ears momentarily, and then start following Carney as he passes by on his way to the metro station. A nearby woman who is a dead ringer for Patricia Arquette in **Goodbye Lover** bends over and fixes the strap on her heel. I don't think she's with Carney, but I thought Patricia Arquette was totally hot in that movie.

I dial up Carney again. When he answers, I say, "One more thing, Mr. Carney. I'm going to ask you a question, and if you don't give me a truthful answer, then we're done. The article gets published. Ready for my question?"

He stops and waits a moment before answering. "Ask your question," he says.

"Did you come alone, as I asked?"

He looks around him. He doesn't know if I'm here or not. I told him I'm not, but he can't be sure.

"No, I didn't, Ben. I'm the second-ranking official at the Central Intelligence Agency and I'm meeting with someone who is wanted for two murders and who's trying to extort me. There's no way they're going to let me meet with you without watching my back. But that's all they're doing, Ben. No one's going to arrest you or try to hurt you."

Fair enough. He admitted it. He told the truth. It's a start. There are no guarantees in life.

"Turn around, Mr. Carney. You passed me a couple minutes ago."

"Oh—you're here. Okay. Where are you?"

"The World War II Memorial," I say. "The tour group by the Atlantic arch. I'm the guy in the wheelchair."

CHAPTER 62

When I stand up from my rented wheel-chair, the others in my tour group let out audible gasps. "It's a miracle!" I say. "I can walk!"

I leave them behind and meet Craig Carney, looking resplendent in his dapper three-piece gray suit and crimson tie, the Nationals baseball cap and pennant now discarded. We agree to take a walk along the reflecting pool. He's built up a little perspiration in the scorching heat, which gives me some comfort, because I'm sweating through my clothes right now.

I try to keep my breathing even, but it's

hard. This is what I've been waiting for, but I have a sinking feeling I'm not going to come away a happy customer. And I don't see a whole lot of other options for me out there.

"I know everything there is to know about you, Ben," says Carney. "I know about your childhood. I know about your father and mother. I know that that newspaper of yours is something you do out of love, not because you have trouble paying the bills. It's your baby. And that's why I know that, whatever else, you'd never print a story that you know isn't true. You wouldn't do that to your baby."

"Fear of death can do wonders to your integrity," I note.

"Oh, it doesn't have to come to that." He says it like I'm being overly dramatic. I hope he's right about that. "Y'know, Ben, when my father was in the Senate, he used to have a saying. 'Don't get in front of a ball rolling down a hill.' Pick your battles, in other words. If you can't stop something, don't waste your time trying."

"So he probably wouldn't have been a big fan of, say, Martin Luther King or Susan B. Anthony."

Carney chuckles. "You're equating yourself with a civil rights leader?"

"I'm no hero," I say. "Far from it. But we do have one thing in common. We're both fighting our government. I just didn't realize I was doing so until people started shooting at me and framing me for murder."

We approach the Lincoln Memorial. Gotta love Honest Abe, but I'm not a huge fan of the Greek temple look of this memorial. Still, it's hard not to be awed. I've been here fifty times, and I get chills every time I look up at him.

"The United States government doesn't kill its citizens," says Carney. "If someone's been trying to kill you, it isn't us."

Given that he's wearing a wire, what else is he going to say?

"I never had an affair with Diana Hotchkiss, Ben. If she told you otherwise, then it's one, but not the only, lie she told you."

We turn left—south—around the pool.

"Why didn't you say so, Mr. Deputy Director? This whole thing's been a misunderstanding. My bad. Sorry for your troubles."

Carney doesn't even crack a smile. He's not what you'd call a whimsical guy.

"You're anxious and confused. I don't blame you. You're looking at serious criminal charges. Your life could be over very soon. But you know what, Ben? What you don't realize is how lucky you are."

"Lucky because I know about your affair with Diana."

He lets that comment pass. We bend around the pool again, this time heading east.

"You know much about World War II, Ben?" he asks me.

"Enough, I guess." I saw **Saving Private Ryan** and that HBO series Tom Hanks did. Does that count?

"You know the story about when the Nazis bombed the city of Coventry in England? A lot of people think Churchill knew that bombing raid was coming because British intelligence had intercepted and deciphered the Nazis' coded radio messages. You know about that, Ben?"

"I know that some people think Churchill knew the raid was coming, but he didn't say anything because he was afraid the Nazis would figure out that the Brits had broken their code. So Churchill decided it was better to let one city get leveled to keep this advantage a secret. He let Coventry take a hit for the greater good of winning the war."

"Right. That's right, Ben."

"And I know most people think that story's bullshit."

"Maybe so," he says. "Maybe not." It occurs to me now that I'm talking to a top banana at the CIA, so he may actually know whether that story is fact or fiction. "But surely you see my point, Ben. Sometimes there's a bigger picture. A greater good, as you said."

"Okay, so what does this have to do with Diana? Or me?"

Carney stops and faces me. "It means there are things I'd love to tell you, if I could, that would explain everything to you. But for reasons of national security, I can't."

"Then forgive me if I'm not tracking this," I say. "How does this make me lucky?"

He nods. "Because I want this over," he answers. "So I'm going to make you an offer you can't refuse."

CHAPTER 63

"You'll walk away from all your criminal problems," says Carney. "All criminal investigations are dropped. Diana's death is ruled a suicide. Jonathan Liu's death is a suicide. Any responsibility for that dead police detective? Wiped clean. This little blackmail stunt you've pulled on me—all is forgiven, Ben." He wags a finger at me. "Now, you're not going to find a better deal than that."

I try to maintain a poker face, an air of skepticism. But I can't deny that I've been praying for something like this. A chance to get my life back. To move on. And for

Anne Brennan, and Diana's parents, to do the same. I have more than myself to consider.

"And the people trying to kill me?" I ask.

He stares at me for a long time. I swear I see a trace of a smile, but maybe it's just an optical illusion. If you stare at a wall long enough, it appears to move.

"As I said, Ben, the US government has nothing to do with that."

"Of course not."

"But maybe we know who does. And maybe we can work something out so that problem goes away, too."

I can't keep up this blank expression much longer. I'm not wired for it, as Carney is. So I start walking again, moving toward the Washington Monument along the south side of the reflecting pool. Sweat is dripping into my eyes and running along my cheek. Carney knows that I'm on unfamiliar ground here. I'm in way, way over my head.

"And for all this—for immunity from prosecution and from machine-gun ambushes—I have to do what?" I ask.

"Nothing, Ben. Literally nothing. No more questions. No more investigating. Just let the whole thing go. It's the right thing to do in terms of national security, and you save your life in the process. Everyone wins."

Somehow I don't feel like a winner right now. I'm unsure how to proceed. Every instinct I possess tells me to lap up this deal like a dog, to say yes immediately. This is what Anne wants. This is what George Hotchkiss wants. This is—

This is what I want.

"You're going to say yes," Carney says.

"I am?"

"Yes, you are, Ben. For several reasons. For one, you know if you print that bogus story about me, you'll ruin the reputation of your newspaper. And I'll sue, and I'll win. Because we both know that Diana and I never had an affair.

"And even if you keep up this investigation of yours—and let's pretend you dig up something worth printing—all you'll accomplish is making this country less safe by disclosing tactical advantages we've managed to put in place against our enemies. And **that's** assuming you manage to stay out of jail and you're not under prosecution for two murders. And all **that** assumes that you even manage to stay alive, which, from what I understand, is a very tenuous proposition."

We walk for a moment, and I try to decipher everything this guy is telling me. It sure would be nice to be recording this conversation so I could play it later.

Which is why I'm glad I'm recording this conversation so I can play it later.

"Is Diana alive?" I ask.

Carney smiles. "That's not our deal. Our deal is you don't ask questions."

"Who killed Jonathan Liu?"

"Why, you did, Ben."

"What is Operation Delano?"

He sniffs a laugh. "Enough, Ben. I need your answer. Right here, right now. Do you spend the few remaining days you have left tilting at windmills, or do you get your life back as it was?"

I break away from him to think for a moment. I let my eyes wander over the west end of the National Mall. The Lincoln Memorial was the location of Martin Luther King's "I Have a Dream" speech. Protests against the wars in Vietnam and Iraq, marches for women's and workers' rights— all of them have taken place on the Mall. Every memorial here pays tribute to courageous souls who battled evil forces, some visible and some invisible, to make this country and this world a better place.

I'm no hero. I never have been. I've lived a safe and cautious life. Why should I change course now? Especially when Carney's right—the only thing that pressing forward will do for me is land me in prison or get me killed.

"I need an answer right now," says the deputy director. "Come on, Ben. You know there's only one answer."

"You can wait twenty-four hours," I say. "Don't call me. I'll call you."

CHAPTER 64

The air tonight is mild, as if Mother Nature has given us a brief respite from the stifling heat for this occasion. Idaho Avenue has been closed to traffic from Macomb Street to Newark Street. The sun has set, and the darkness is broken by the light of hundreds of candles held by officers in full dress uniform, civilians, and even children—people who have gathered for the memorial honoring Detective Ellis Montgomery Burk.

There will be a private funeral service later this week. Those were the wishes of Ellis's widow, Delores, and his daughters,

Jody and Shannon. Tonight is the public memorial.

A podium has been set up just outside the police headquarters. A minister has spoken. The Second District commander has spoken. A church choir delivers a touching rendition of "Amazing Grace."

And then it goes quiet, and we hear the voice of Delores Burk.

"Ellis loved this job," she begins. "He loved everything about it. He loved solving problems. He loved helping people. But most of all, he loved all of you. He considered you part of his family, every one of you. He would be glad to see all of you tonight. As am I.

"My husband had a simple saying: 'Have the strength to do it right.' That was just like Ellis, if you knew him. He always broke it down to simple terms. 'Do it right.' There's right and there's wrong in this world, and Ellis always knew where that line was drawn. He never crossed it. He thought that was his duty as a member of the Metropolitan Police Department. He thought that was his duty as a father and husband. He thought that was his duty as a man."

I'm standing on the other side of the barricade. It's not a good idea for me to cut into that crowd. Not because I might be recognized and arrested—though that would be a distinct possibility—but because I might be a distraction on this occasion. And Ellis deserves this memorial.

I'm to blame for this man's death. I reached out for him when I had no other options. And he helped me even though the case was beyond his jurisdiction. He helped me because he thought it was the right thing to do.

Delores Burk is correct. There is such a thing as right and wrong. There is black and white. Washington, DC, is a town that lives in the middle gray. But that doesn't mean I have to.

I owe this to Ellis. I brought him into this fight, and I have to make sure I see it through. If he died in an ultimately noble cause, then his family should know it. If he died as a result of an evil cover-up, they should know that, too.

When the memorial is over, I steer the Triumph onto 39th Street and then head south on Massachusetts Avenue. It will be another long night, another hotel. For a little while there, I really thought my days of running were over.

"Mr. Carney," I say into my cell phone. "I'm not making a deal with you. I'm going to find out what's going on or die trying. So buckle up, Craig. It's going to be a wild ride."

CHAPTER 65

I need to kill some time before my next stop, so I find a bar on 15th Street and nurse a beer and watch CNN on the screen above the bartender. The sound is muted, but the closed-captioning is telling me that the Russians have detained a person they're calling a spy from the neighboring republic of Georgia and are lodging an official protest. The Russians and Georgians had an armed conflict back in 2008, and the fear, apparently, is that fires are rekindling.

I generally favor peace over war as a rule, but if another armed conflict broke out over there, maybe the Russians would call back the guys who are chasing me with machine guns. A guy can dream.

At midnight, I make the short walk to the intersection of 15th Street and Caroline Street. Anne Brennan lives on the ground floor of the three-story brick condo building there, and the lights are on, so I assume she's awake.

I take a good look around first. I don't think anyone's tracking me right now, but they might be watching Anne, hoping to find me. I could be walking into a spiderweb.

But I have no way of knowing. I don't see anyone in the parked cars along 15th Street, and the people strolling along the streets seem to be moving on to other destinations. None of them are wearing signs that say SURVEILLANCE or BAD GUYS, so I have that going for me, but the truth is, if someone is watching Anne Brennan's house right now, I have no way of knowing about it. And I have to talk to Anne in person. So I have to take the risk.

But I don't have to be stupid about it. I head back down Caroline Street, away from Anne's place, and do a wide circle until I'm the next street over and walking through an alley up to the rear of Anne's building. The whole thing is a twenty-minute exercise, but it's worth the peace of mind.

Though Anne lives on the ground floor, there's a ten-foot fence bordering the back of the property, which I could probably climb if I really wanted to. But I don't really want to. So I dial her number on one of the many prepaid phones I have.

"I'm in the alley behind your place," I say. "Can I come in for a minute? Don't turn on any lights near the back of the house that aren't already on. Don't draw attention."

Not five minutes later, she opens the back door and hustles back to the gate to let me in. She seems more nervous than I am. But she looks a lot cuter. She's wearing a pair of sandals and an oversize button-down pajama top that reaches her knees.

Coming in from the rear of her condo, I see her bedroom for the first time and my heart does a little skip. Her kitchen is small but spotless and orderly. She leads me into the living room, where the intruders attacked her the other night.

She sits on a folded leg on the couch and looks at me with those wide chocolate eyes. Wearing that tent of a pajama top,

she looks like a teenager rather than someone in her early thirties. She also looks to
be a nervous wreck, for which I can hardly
blame her.

"I'll be brief," I say. I take her hand, which
she willingly permits. "Anne, I want you to
leave town. I want you to take a vacation.
The airfare and hotel are on me. I can afford it, so don't argue."

"Why do you want—"

"Because I'm not going to let this go, and
I don't want anything to happen to you. I
still don't really know what's going on, but
I know it's something very big and explo-
sive. I can't protect you, Anne."

She thinks for a moment, then places
her free hand over mine. "And who's protecting **you**?" she asks.

"I'll be fine," I say with a confidence I
absolutely do not possess. "A reporter has
some tools at his disposal."

She almost smiles as she looks me over,
appraising me. "That's not very convincing,
Ben. You're not safe, are you?"

"I'm not safe if I sit still, either. I don't have
a choice. You do, Anne. You're not involved
in this. Your only crime is being Diana's
friend."

She looks down at our joined hands. I wonder what it means to her. I wonder what it means to me. I catch a scent of lavender and feel myself, against all good judgment, drawing closer to her on the couch.

Then she draws closer to me.

We draw closer to each other.

This isn't going the way I'd planned.

CHAPTER 66

"It's okay to say enough is enough, Ben." Anne looks up at me. We are so close I feel her breath on my chin. "Whatever you feel like you owe Diana, you don't owe her your life. I don't want to see **you** get hurt, too."

She touches my cheek, and my resistance begins to melt away. No. This is a bad idea. You're endangering her, Ben. Just being here puts her at risk.

She leans into me. Her lips are soft and moist, delicate and cautious. It's the sweetest kiss I've ever received.

"God, you're trembling," she whispers.

Personal foul—illegal contact. Replay first down.

Okay, so we replay it. My mouth parts and our tongues find common ground. My hand slides inside her pajama top and Anne lets out a small gasp that turns into a low moan.

Illegal use of the hands.

Penalty declined; second base. I mean, second down.

She lifts her arms and I pull off her shirt and she tugs at mine and the steam of our desperation and fear and longing ignites something primitive between us. We are not two people whose lives are in danger. We are two people who have nothing but right now, only this moment. She is aggressive and desperate and hungry as her tongue invades my mouth, as she digs her nails into my hair, as she takes my index finger and places it in her mouth, as she arches her back, as she raises her legs and wraps them around me, as she whispers **harder, harder,** into my ear, as she grits her teeth and squeezes her eyes shut and cries out **harder, harder—**

This is wrong this is wrong but I can't stop myself and I don't want to stop, I want to remind myself that I still have a life and I can still feel something for somebody else and if I only have hours or days remaining in this world, I want to spend at least a small fraction of it with something, with someone, who is good, there is still such a thing as goodness in this world—

"Wow." I lie on my back and stare up at the ceiling. I don't know how much time has passed, but I'm guessing more than an hour. We are panting and coming down from the high, and I'm thinking fugitive sex—back to **Seinfeld,** when George was dating that prisoner and he liked the arrangement so he sabotaged her parole hearing—how did that not make my top ten list?

"Maybe our lives should be in danger more often," says Anne, her head resting on my chest.

"Did you used to be a gymnast or something?"

She likes that. Her hair tickles my stomach. My limbs are rubbery, useless. My head is foggy. I've never felt better.

We interrupt this program for a reality check. That thing about our lives being in danger.

"This doesn't change anything," I whisper. "You have to get out of here. You're not safe."

She adjusts herself so that her chin is on my chest, her eyes are on mine.

"I'm not going anywhere. If you're in, then so am I," she says. "So, sweetie, maybe you should buckle up."

CHAPTER 67

I spend the night at Anne's to ensure her safety. Strictly for her protection. No other reason. I mean, there are bad people out there, right? In fact, I might need to come back again tonight to make sure she's still safe.

But this morning, I'm on the move. My calves and triceps and abdominal muscles and neck are sore beyond description. Apparently I've been lacking physical exercise. I also forgot, in the heat of things last night, how much my leg was killing me after I wiped out on the Triumph a few nights back. Luckily, I have this morning to remind me.

In the gym bag that I'm carrying with me everywhere these days, in addition to a few items of clothing and toiletries and my laptop computer, I've been accumulating baseball caps that help shield me from detection by someone who might be, say, scanning the streets for me.

But I know the truth: they're going to find me eventually. Washington, DC, isn't Manhattan. They could just position themselves at various posts and not move an inch, and sooner or later I'll walk into them. So I try to keep my head down and baseball cap on and hope I can figure everything out before they find me.

Now all I have to do is figure out what it is I'm supposed to figure out.

As I'm walking down T Street, I call my trusted colleague Ashley Brook Clark, who is basically running the **Capital Beat** in my absence.

"Any luck on Jonathan Liu's computer?" I ask.

"They're getting there, Ben. I told them it was high priority, but that computer was beat to hell. What did you do, throw it on the ground?"

Something like that.

"One other thing, Ben. A guy came by looking for you. A guy with a real attitude."

"Was he wearing sunglasses and a trench coat, and did he move furtively?"

"None of the above. His name was . . . . here it is . . . Sean Patrick Riley."

"Sean Patrick Riley? What is that—Pakistani? Somalian?"

"I think it's Venezuelan."

"Okay, Sean Patrick Riley," I say. "And what did this Irishman want?"

"He says he's a private investigator."

"And what is he privately investigating?"

"He was very, um—"

"Private?"

"Yes, private with that information. Boy, you're in a good mood, Ben. Did you get laid last night or something?"

She's right, there's been a skip in my step this morning. Maybe things are looking up. Or maybe I just hadn't had sex for a really long time before last night.

"Did this guy give you a bad vibe?" I ask. "I mean, does he seem like a shady bloke?"

"A private investigator? Shady?"

"Okay, shadier than usual. Like, for example, rather than ask me questions, he'd like to put a bullet through my head?"

"No, I didn't get **assassin** from this guy. Chauvinist, maybe. Asshole, definitely. But not assassin. I think he's looking for a missing person."

A missing person.

I reach Vermont Avenue, where a big crowd is gathered at the intersection. I hang back rather than mix in too closely with a bunch of people I don't know.

"As long as he doesn't want to kill me, I'll talk to him," I say. "Give me his number."

CHAPTER 68

I see Sean Patrick Riley seated near the window of the café before he sees me. It's not hard to spot a guy wearing a leprechaun suit and eating Lucky Charms.

Okay, he's more like a middle-aged guy with a full head of reddish-blond hair, a weathered complexion, and a drinker's nose, wearing a button-down oxford-cloth shirt and blue jeans. And no Lucky Charms, as magically delicious as they may be; this afternoon it's a cup of joe.

Yeah, I'm still in a pretty good mood from the sex last night.

We shake hands. "Nice bike," he says.

Okay, there goes my good mood. Normally, that would be a compliment, because normally he'd be talking about my Triumph, which **is** a nice bike. But the Triumph is in a parking garage in the Adams Morgan neighborhood. Now I'm riding a real bike—a bicycle—specifically, a used Rockhopper I picked up at City Bikes. It's more suited to trails than city riding, but I may have to make some acrobatic moves with it one day, and I want something that can handle some quick turns and rough riding.

Anyway, I'm not too happy about it. I already miss my motorcycle. But the Triumph made me visible. With the Rockhopper, plus a helmet and a fluorescent Windbreaker, I look like one of those bike couriers who risk life and limb weaving through traffic all around the capital.

"You're the Ben Casper who runs that newspaper?" he asks.

"I am." Checking out my appearance, he probably thinks I'm a guy who **delivers** newspapers. "And I'm short on time," I say.

He doesn't respond to that. I'm guessing this guy used to be a cop, and judging from his speech patterns, I'm guessing Chicago cop. Last I checked, they have a few Irish people out that way.

They put one of yours in the hospital, you put one of theirs in the morgue! Sean Connery may be Scottish, but he killed as the Irish cop in **The Untouchables.** Killed.

"I was hired by the Jacobs family," he says. "They live in a suburb of Chicago. Their daughter Nina went missing here over a week ago."

Nina . . . Jacobs. I know that—

"Diana's friend," I spit out. I met Nina once at a club. She was tall, like Diana, the same lithe, shapely frame, but not blond like Diana. Nina was a brun—

Oh, shit. Nina was a brunette.

And I'll bet she didn't have a butterfly tattoo above her left ankle.

"Diana . . . Hotchkiss, you mean," Riley says, flipping over a pad of paper.

I take a breath and recall Nina. A beauty in her own right—not the perfect features of Diana's face, but quite attractive. A bit younger than Diana. Up close, you wouldn't confuse one for the other, but from a distance, they might be indistinguishable.

Especially if Nina was wearing Diana's clothes.

And especially if Diana dyed her hair Nina's color, which she did a month ago.

I remember that night at the club, and thinking that Nina looked up to Diana, patterned herself after her. How ironic, in hindsight.

Sean Patrick Riley is looking for a dead woman.

"I'm down to remote acquaintances at this point," says Riley. "I've talked to everyone she knows well, and I'm hitting a dead end. Anyway, she had your business card in her Rolodex. So I'm wondering if you can think of anything that might help me. Any chance you have an idea what might have happened to her?"

Her parents must be in sheer agony right now. I'll help them find justice for their daughter. I won't let this go. I'll tell them everything that happened to their daughter.

But not yet.

"Why don't you tell me what you've put together so far?" I say. "And maybe something will trigger a thought."

CHAPTER 69

"A week before she disappeared," says Sean Patrick Riley, "Nina Jacobs had her mail held at the post office for a seven-day period, and she told the **Washington Post** not to deliver her newspaper for seven days. She also had the lights in her home set on timers. Why would she do all that?

"She'd do that," he continues, answering his own question, "if she were going on vacation for a week, and she didn't want her mail to pile up or her newspapers to accumulate on her front porch. And she'd put her lights on timers so it would look like she was home, not on vacation, to ward off burglars.

"The thing is, Nina didn't go on vacation. She was at work every day. She worked at the Public Face, a PR firm over on Seventeenth Street. She didn't miss a day that week." Riley opens his hands. "So she was in town, but living somewhere else."

"Maybe she was watching a friend's house," I suggest.

"Right. That's the best I can figure. But I don't know whose. She has a ring of three or four friends she spends a lot of time with. I've talked to all of them. They were all in town, and Nina wasn't watching their homes. I've talked to all of them, I should say, except Diana Hotchkiss. Don't know if you heard, but she's dead."

"I heard," I say. "Are you working with the local police on this?"

He lets out a grunt. "The feds," he said. "They've scooped it from the locals. Which means in terms of cooperation, I'm getting a whole lotta nothing."

I don't know what to make of all this. Nina Jacobs was set up. Set up to play the role of Diana Hotchkiss—living at her apartment, wearing her clothes, and ultimately being thrown off a balcony. But set up by whom?

Diana? Was Diana capable of something like that?

"Who in Nina's circle of friends have you spoken to?" I ask.

"Oh, let's see." He flips to another page in his small notepad. "Lucy Arangold, Heather Bilandic, and Anne Brennan."

"What did Anne say?"

He shrugs his shoulders. "Same thing they all said. They didn't know about any house-sitting. I think they figure she just took off somewhere. They said Nina was . . . **impulsive,** I think was the word."

I'm still a little off balance by what I'm hearing. I can't believe that Diana would have allowed her friend Nina to be pushed off a balcony in her place. Maybe the CIA, maybe some rogue government official— but not Diana.

"I need your help," says Riley. "I'm at the end of my string, and you run a newspaper. I'm hoping you'll run a big story on this. Maybe someone will read it and help me out."

"A wee little Internet scribe like **Capital Beat**?"

He plays it straight with me. "Couldn't get interest from the **Post** or the **Times,**" he admits. "I think the feds pooh-poohed it to them, though I can't prove that. Anyway, since you knew the lady, I thought you might be willing."

"I might be," I say.

He stares at me. "What does that mean?"

"It means I'll need your homework," I say. "And it means from now on, Mr. Riley, you and I are a team."

CHAPTER 70

The ride up Massachusetts Avenue is slower than usual, given that I'm on a bicycle, but it feels good to work the lactic acid out of my muscles, which are aching from the workout that Anne put me through last night. The midday sun is cooking me on this bike, but all in all, I've had worse days.

"So . . . Nina Jacobs," says Ashley Brook Clark into the earpiece I've connected to my prepaid cell phone, the fourth I've purchased in a week as a result of my well-founded paranoia. (Is that an oxymoron? Can paranoia really qualify as paranoia if it's well founded?)

Anyway, it's a good thing I have money for all these cell phones and hotel rooms. Which reminds me, I'm low on cash. I need to find an ATM, which, for me, is no small task.

I let out a long sigh. Withdrawing cash from an ATM means I'll be on camera, which means that I can't be wearing my biking outfit lest they'll know it's my disguise. I'm going to have to change back into normal clothes, withdraw the money, get the hell away from that ATM as quickly as possible before the black helicopters drop out of the sky, or whatever's going to happen, and change back into biking clothes.

This is getting old. They're wearing me down. I don't know how Harrison Ford managed to do it in **The Fugitive.** Of course, the technology was way different; it was probably a lot easier back then to hide and stay hidden. Plus it was just a movie, and this is really happening to me.

Tommy Lee Jones was outstanding in that movie and deserved the Oscar he got, but really, that year they should have given out two best supporting actor awards, because John Malkovich was absolutely brilliant as the assassin in **In the Line of Fire.** (Yes, I agree that Ralph Fiennes was great in **Schindler's List,** but Malkovich stole the screen every time he appeared.)

(Why am I putting my thoughts in parentheses? What's next—footnotes? Am I losing my mind?)

"So you want this story on the front page," Ashley Brook says. "And you want a nice big photo of Nina Jacobs, and you want me to mention Sean Patrick Riley's name several times."

"A photo of him, too," I say.

"And why is that? I didn't even like that guy when I met him."

"It makes him safer," I tell her. "If they catch him sniffing around and want to get rid of him, he'll be harder to kill now that he's gotten publicity. He'll be more visible."

"And you think people who are willing to fire machine guns at you in midday, at a busy downtown intersection, care about visibility?"

"I'm doing the best I can here, kid." I stop at the three-way intersection where Idaho Avenue and Massachusetts Avenue meet 39th Street and take a squirt from my water bottle. "If Nina's disappearance becomes big news, then it makes it harder for them to cover it up by killing people or whatever."

"Then why don't you apply that logic to yourself?" she asks me. "You wrote that article about Diana Hotchkiss. Why aren't we publishing that for the same reason? To keep you safe?"

It's a good question. I've already threatened Craig Carney with that very thing, splashing the entire story over the front page of my website—Diana's connection to Carney, Jonathan Liu's murder, Operation Delano, etc. There are two reasons I haven't pulled the trigger yet. One of them Ashley Brook already knows.

"You and your journalistic scruples," she moans.

Well, that's close. I don't have a wife or children and probably never will. **Capital Beat** is my only family. It's the only thing I've ever created. If I print something I can't prove, I deface something I love. And I risk a crippling lawsuit and the loss of the **Beat**'s reputation. We may not be the **Washington Post,** but we are hard-hitting, fair, and fearless, which is more than most news organizations can say these days. So if I go down in flames, I want to know that I've left behind at least one thing that is good in this world. And they can always print the story after my death.

But there's another reason as well.

"I haven't been indicted yet," I say. "They haven't issued a warrant for my arrest yet."

"Okay. So?"

"So—Carney threatened to do that, right? The feds seem to be in control of this situation, and the deputy director basically promised that if I didn't play ball with him, there would be cops serving an arrest warrant any minute. But they aren't. They're keeping their powder dry. So for the moment, I'll do the same."

"I'm not really following the logic," Ashley Brook says.

"I think they're as scared of me as I am of them," I say. "Neither of us wants to pull the trigger, because once we do, the other side will respond in kind."

"It's like the Cold War with us and the Russians," she says. "They didn't nuke us because they knew we'd nuke them. Mutually assured destruction."

Malkovich was mesmerizing in **Dangerous Liaisons** and hilarious as the foulmouthed ex–CIA agent in **Burn after**

Reading. Every time he cussed, I laughed out loud.

The light changes at the intersection from red to green. Traffic starts to move northbound. I start up again on the bike and pedal through the intersection.

"So you must be close to something big," she says.

I pick up the pace on my bike. My destination is only ten minutes away now.

"And if I'm right," I say, "I'm about to get closer."

CHAPTER 71

I sit on a bench outside the Bender Library looking over the Quad, where I spent four years eating my lunch or throwing a Frisbee or playing Hacky Sack between classes. The Quad is sort of the heart of American University's main campus, a rectangular lawn bordered by the library on one end and the Kay Spiritual Life Center on the other. It's crisscrossed with pedestrian walkways and has a seating area in the middle, complete with concrete benches. Some of the main academic buildings are situated along the borders. I haven't been here since, oh, I think it was

2008, when I covered a student demonstration protesting the genocide in Darfur, complete with a mock refugee camp and a "die-in," where all the students lay across the lawn to simulate the mass casualties.

After I've told him my lengthy narrative—the tale of Benjamin Casper over the last two weeks—Professor Bogomolov, seated next to me, puts a frail hand on my shoulder. "A most troubling story," he says.

He should know about troubling stories. Andrei Bogomolov was born in the Soviet city of Leningrad, now Saint Petersburg, where he studied psychiatry and history. But he wanted to live free in the West. So in 1974, while serving as a psychiatrist on a Soviet boat, he jumped ship off the Ivory Coast and swam ashore. The KGB chased him through Ghana, where he reportedly was hidden by Peace Corps volunteers in a camp and later smuggled to the US embassy in Accra, where he was granted political asylum. The whole matter led to an international dustup in the heat of the Cold War period. (Can there be heat during a Cold War?)

Anyway, Andrei came to American University to get a PhD in Russian history and never left. He's been part of the history department ever since. He's one of those professors who likes to sit out on the Quad eating his lunch with the students, enjoying the sunlight on his face and, I suppose, the feeling of freedom as well.

I took one of his classes while I was an undergrad here, but the truth is, I've known Andrei since I was a kid. He and my father were colleagues in the history department for decades. Andrei would come to our house for dinner, always showing up with a present, usually some Russian coin and a story to go along with it.

After Mother's death, he was particularly nice to me. I remember him telling me about harsh winters in Russia, hunger pains in his stomach, a feeling that he had no control over his own destiny, and how his faith in God got him through all of it. **You can suffer anything, Benjamin,** he used to tell me, **if you believe in yourself and God.**

I haven't talked to Andrei in years, probably not since Father's funeral, but I remember him being a man of understatement. After experiencing what he experienced, I guess most things pale in comparison.

"A **most** troubling story," he repeats.

"Operation Delano, Andrei," I say.

He nods. He knew that was the question I was going to ask him, and his reaction tells me I've come to the right place. Ever since I heard the phrase, and then learned about Alexander Kutuzov, I've been thinking about the Russians. If anybody would know about the Russians, it's Andrei.

"Very well," he finally says. "Operation Delano."

CHAPTER **72**

"Let us walk," Andrei says. "They tell me walks are good."

I don't understand the reference and want to ask, but not now. Andrei's always been a man of few words, a reserve probably long instilled in someone who had planned since childhood to defect to the West but had to play along in the Soviet system until the moment presented itself. If he wants me to know about his ailment, he'll tell me.

Andrei pushes his small, withered frame off the bench. He tucks his hands into his slacks—completing the professorial look that his tweed sport coat began—and nods to the wood carving of an eagle in the garden next to us. "I love that bird," he says. "Do you know why, Benjamin?"

The eagle is made from the wood of a hundred-year-old tree that had to be removed from the Quad. One of the classes carved out this beautiful bird as a gift to the university.

"Because it's our national bird?" I guess.

He manages a smile. Andrei was waiting for me here on this bench when I arrived, and seeing him now on his feet, struggling, I'm struck by how ill he appears.

"Because something beautiful came of something dying," he says.

I let him lead, and we walk along the borders of the Quad, past the Mary Graydon Center. I remember meeting there once a week for the Young Democrats of America. Not that I was a Democrat, or, for that matter, a Republican. I joined for the same reason most college guys would join something: because there was a hot girl in the group. I chased after Cassandra Richley for over two years. It was worth the wait.

"Yalta was a time of great uncertainty," says Andrei. He's referring to the Yalta

Conference, where Stalin, Roosevelt, and Churchill gathered to divvy up the spoils after the Nazis went down in flames. "Of course, you have studied this."

"Of course."

"Stalin was truly dealing from a position of strength. He was already occupying many of the countries he wanted to enclose in the Soviet bloc, and he had twice the troops of the Allies. Still, he didn't know if he had Roosevelt's trust. He was rather sure he didn't have Churchill's. He was looking for leverage in the negotiations."

I stop in my tracks. Andrei doesn't seem to notice at first, but then he stops as well and faces me.

"What are you telling me, Andrei?" I say. "Operation Delano was an attempt to gain leverage on FDR?"

Andrei's heavy, tired eyes rise up to mine.

"None of this has been verified," he says. "There is only talk."

"Then tell me about the talk, Andrei."

Andrei breaks eye contact with me and stares off in the distance, as I recall him often doing. Back then he conveyed quiet strength—shoulders back, a broad chest, a defiant chin. Now he is frail, his shoulders curled inward, a stoop to his posture, his skin heavy and ill-fitting on his weathered face, only wisps of white hair covering his head. But those eyes, that glassy stare, haven't changed. Probably no one will ever know what is contained in that stare. Memories, I assume. Memories of things best forgotten.

"The talk," he says, "is that Operation Delano was the Soviets' attempt to blackmail the president of the United States."

CHAPTER 73

"There were always rumors about Roosevelt," says Andrei. "Some of them have since been printed as fact, but in my mind, they remain rumors. Roosevelt was a man of privilege, of course. Some such men . . . did not regard marital vows as solemnly as they might."

I'd read about that. My father had written about Roosevelt, who was believed to have had an affair with his wife's social secretary for years. Eleanor reportedly discovered the affair and offered FDR a divorce. The affair broke off but then rekindled in Roosevelt's last term in office.

And there was another woman, too, so the story goes—FDR's own secretary. Andrei's right—true or false, most of this information has been reported by now.

But it wasn't back then, after World War II ended.

"Stalin wanted to blackmail FDR about his extramarital affairs?" I ask.

We're walking again, past the Battelle-Tompkins Building, where I took many of my undergrad classes. We are moving slowly. It is clearly difficult for Andrei to walk.

Andrei waves a hand. "This Operation Delano may all be fiction, an old wives' tale. All I can say with certainty is, if Stalin got so much out of the negotiations at Yalta because he blackmailed FDR, nobody has ever said so. And much has been said, and written, about Yalta."

Spoken like a true professor, one who demands careful support for every statement before he makes it. He's been full of disclaimers thus far—none of this has been established as fact—but that doesn't mean he doesn't believe it.

"I must sit," says Andrei, and he finds a bench at the Kay center's plaza. "You must forgive a tired old man."

I sit next to him. "I forgive you, old friend. But does this mean the Russians are trying to blackmail President Francis?"

Andrei takes a minute to catch his breath. He lets out a painful cough and apologizes. He's not doing well, that's clear.

"I cannot possibly know such a thing," he says. "Certainly, I know nothing of this president."

I don't, either, but I probably follow the president a lot more closely than Andrei does. Blake Francis and Libby Rose Francis seem about as compatible as Jerry Falwell and Paris Hilton. It's always looked to me more like a marriage of convenience. The president stepping out on Libby? Not a hard swallow at all.

"But you **do** know the Russians," I say. "Why would they want to blackmail Blake Francis?"

Andrei lets out a chuckle, which I mistakenly take as a cough at first.

"Why **wouldn't** they?" he muses. "Having control of the leader of the free world?"

Fair enough. That's probably true.

"But you are correct, Benjamin, that such a thing could not have permanence. Certainly not even a compromised president could allow another powerful country free rein to do whatever it wished. There would have to be limits, surely."

"You mean, like maybe there could be one thing."

He cocks his head to the side. Like I'm getting warm.

"What would be the one thing?" I ask. "What are the Russians trying to do?"

CHAPTER 74

My former professor looks at me as if we have reverted to old roles, like I'm back in undergrad and he's giving me a lesson.

"I have no idea whether the Russians are blackmailing our president, or even attempting to do so," says Andrei. "But I do believe I have a good assessment of Russian leadership these days. So let us assume that there **is** blackmail taking place." He opens his hands. "What is the one thing Russia wants?"

I shrug my shoulders. "Oil? Power?"

Andrei stares at me, blank-faced. I feel like I'm in an episode of that old **Kung Fu** show, where Andrei is blind Master Po and I'm David Carradine. **You disappoint me, Grasshopper. Yet it is not I whom you have failed. It is you. Look within, Grasshopper.**

"Land," I say.

"Land," he says in agreement.

You have done well, Grasshopper.

"And if the Russians wanted land, Benjamin, where would they go?" Andrei wags his finger at me. "History, Benjamin, is the best teacher."

"Afghanistan," I say, but immediately I know I'm wrong. What was true in the 1970s and '80s is no longer true today. Since the breakup of the Soviet Union, a number of independent countries now stand between Russia and Afghanistan—Kazakhstan, Uzbekistan, Turkmenistan, I think, and probably some other hard-to-pronounce names.

"More recent history, Benjamin."

Oh, right. Of course. "Georgia," I say. For years, Russia has been backing independence movements in various republics in Georgia. In 2008, there was an armed conflict between Georgia and two of its would-be breakaway republics in South Ossetia, which most observers saw in reality as a war between Georgia and Russia.

And how quickly I forget what I saw just last night on CNN, before I went over to Anne's place and had mindaltering sex. "The Russians just arrested a Georgian spy in Moscow."

Andrei nods his head. "Supposedly," he says. "Conveniently. Next, expect a terrorist act in a major Russian city that is blamed on the Georgians."

Ah. So the Russians are setting the table for a war with Georgia.

"If Russia really wanted to take Georgia, Benjamin, would it be hard?"

"Militarily? No."

"But diplomatically, Benjamin."

"Diplomatically, yes. Georgia has a relationship with NATO now."

"A problem," he acknowledges. "Tell me this, Benjamin. How much would the American public care if Russia invaded Georgia and overtook it?"

I let out a sigh. "I mean, for some of us who've been around awhile, it would conjure up images of the old Soviet Union. But these days, our military is stretched thin—"

"Just so."

"—and we probably have bigger things to worry about."

"Probably." Andrei nods slowly. "But certainly? Could the Russians be **certain** how we would respond? Remember, Benjamin, NATO is a presence in this conversation. There could be pressure on an American president to resist this aggression. If not by force, then by sanctions, at a minimum."

"So the Russians would want some tools of persuasion at their disposal."

"Just so," says Andrei. "If the United States acquiesces to this aggression, who will challenge Russia?"

"Nobody," I say.

"Certainly nobody of importance," he says. "If the Russians can compromise the president of the United States, they could succeed in their plan."

So the Russians discover that President Francis is having an extramarital affair. They somehow document this. And they have a private chat with the president. They make him a deal. Keep quiet while we invade Georgia, and we keep quiet about these photographs. Or resist us, and you'll be embroiled in a scandal that could cost you a second term in office.

Wow. It's audacious. But so are the Russians.

I take a moment with this. "You think Russia would do all this just so they could take over a tiny neighbor?"

Andrei stares at me, again with a blank face, before a chuckle bursts from his mouth. "Certainly not," he says. "History, Benjamin, history."

I throw up my hands. "Help me out here, Andrei. It's been a long week."

"You are excused, my friend." Andrei pats my knee. "Certainly Georgia would simply be a testing ground for the world's reaction. And a precedent-setting reaction by the United States. This would almost certainly be the beginning, not the end."

My head falls back on my shoulders. The sky is darkening, promising rain. "Tell me you aren't saying what I think you're saying, Andrei."

"Most regrettably, I am," he says. "Oh, Benjamin, I have little doubt that the Russians plan to rebuild the old Soviet bloc, country by country."

CHAPTER 75

I race my bike off American University's campus with adrenaline surging through me. I have to find a cash machine, but I'm not even looking, I'm just riding as my thoughts are running rampant in so many directions, so many questions, so many twists and turns—

But at least I have the main picture. I'm finally there. The Russians dusted off the playbook from the Stalin era, even giving their operation the same name, sentimental softies that they are. Operation Delano is the Russians' plan to blackmail President Blake Francis so he will stand down when Russia starts invading her neighbors. And they've already begun the initial stages of moving toward an invasion of the Republic of Georgia. So—are they blackmailing the president right now? Did their plan work? Or are they still in the process of executing it? Clearly, our government knows about it. So what's going on right now? Is the president going to let all this happen?

And where does Diana fit in? I had her pegged for a CIA spy. So—what? She was trying to stop them, and—but why would someone fake her death, and—

Oh. Oh, shit—

I skid my bike to a halt, almost toppling forward in the process.

No. No, it can't be.

All those evenings Diana spent at the White House, as an aide to the president's close ally Craig Carney. A blackmail scheme. And now the US government desperately wants everyone to believe that Diana's dead. Which means she must be a liability.

Could it be true?

Is Diana the president's mistress?

CHAPTER 76

Lots to think about, but necessities first. I need money.

After getting a considerable distance away from the university campus, I spot an ATM at the intersection of Columbia Road and Euclid Street. But now I have to go through my routine. I head into a Burger King bathroom and change into normal clothes—a button-down shirt and jeans—and then walk over to the ATM. I leave the Rock-hopper a good distance from the walk-up ATM, so the camera won't pick it up. The Russians, or the CIA, are looking for me in civilian clothes, riding a kick-ass motorcycle. No reason to let them know I'm in biking gear on a Rock-hopper.

If Diana is the president's mistress, then what happened on her balcony that night? Did the US government fake her death in an attempt to thwart the blackmail? Does that mean that our government killed Nina Jacobs? There are so many possible permutations. But at least I'm getting closer. Watch out, Mr. Carney, here I come.

At the ATM, I avoid eye contact with the little camera watching me and quickly swipe my card and run through the transaction. Password, withdrawal, checking account, one thousand dollars. I look over both shoulders and don't see anything that raises the hair on my neck.

But when I look back at the ATM screen, the hair rises all the same.

Insufficient funds, the screen tells me.

"Bullshit," I say. I transferred more than ten thousand dollars into checking earlier this week so I could remain liquid.

I run through the whole thing again, password-withdrawal-checking, but this time I go with five hundred dollars. All along, I am cognizant of the ticking clock. Anyone monitoring my account already knows my precise location.

Insufficient funds, it tells me again.

"No. No, no, no." I opt for a new transaction, transferring from savings into checking. This doesn't make sense, but so what, I have plenty in savings—

This transaction is unauthorized.

"Unauthorized?" I yell at the machine. **"Unauthorized?"**

I have to get out of here. I memorize the number it tells me to call and run back to my bike and start pedaling down Columbia to get distance from that ATM. I hook up the earpiece on my prepaid cell phone and dial the number. I get an automated recording.

I terminate the call and focus on getting distance. I take a left on Quarry Road, then a right on Lanier Place. I stop in the middle of a quiet residential area and get off my bike. Standing on the sidewalk, I make the call.

I navigate through the automated commands, my chest heaving, struggling for breath, and finally get a human voice. He thanks me for calling, tells me his name with incomprehensible speed, and asks for my name and account number. I only know the former, so then I have to give him my mother's maiden name (Mapes) before we can finally talk. But the talk is brief. I ask, "Why the hell does my account say insufficient funds? And why can't I transfer from savings to checking?"

The man goes quiet, then he tells me he has to transfer me to "special services," whatever the hell that means, and then there's music, "Train in Vain" by the Clash, which is adding insult to injury because the Clash is one of the best bands of all time and "London Calling" is my all-time favorite song, but all the radio stations play is this cheesy "Train in Vain" and "Rock the Casbah" and WHAT THE FUCK IS TAKING SO LONG—

"Mr. Casper, this is Jay Rowe with special services. How are you doing today?"

"I'm doing pretty fucking poorly, Jay, if you want to know the truth."

"Sir, your account is disabled."

"Disabled? Then undisable it. Able it. Whatever the fuck the word is, do it!"

"We can't, sir."

"It's my money! You can't hold on to it!"

"We can and we must, sir," he says, but by now I get the picture. He's following orders. This isn't a decision my bank made on its own.

"Sir," he says, "your account has been frozen on orders of the United States Department of Homeland Security."

CHAPTER **77**

I hang up the prepaid phone and break it into about twenty-five pieces. I kick the pieces all around the sidewalk and un-leash a torrent of obscenities that would make a trucker blush before I get a grip on myself. I feel like Keanu Reeves in **Speed** after he learned that his partner, Harry, had been blown up by Dennis Hopper. I feel like Dennis Hopper in—shit, I don't know, he gets pissed off in a lot of his movies, so pick one.

Craig Carney has been reluctant to play his trump card—having me indicted and arrested for murder—but he's upping the pressure in other ways. He's eliminated the one advantage I've had, free access to money. I have sixty-two dollars and change in my pocket.

With one of my other prepaid phones, I call Ashley Brook Clark at the **Beat.** I'm trying to keep a cool head, but the waters of panic are rising, and come on, Ashley Brook, answer, answer, ANSWER YOUR—

"Hello?" Ashley Brook says in a rushed voice.

"Ashley Brook, I need your—"

"Ben, thank God it's—"

"—help, I'm in a real jam—"

"—you, everything is going haywire—"

Fuck! I stop talking, so she will, too, and we can have a conversation. It sounds like it's going to be a fun one.

"Ben, everything is going crazy at the office. Payroll is telling me that our bank account has been frozen. The CIA was just here asking me all kinds of questions. They say you're the subject of an espionage investigation and if anyone around here helps you, they will be considered coconspirators. Everyone around here is freaking out—"

"Slow down, Ashley Brook. We can—"

"They took our computers, Ben. They've taken everything. And they're—they're—"

"Ashley Brook—"

"Ben, they've shut down our website!" With these words, Ashley Brook loses her composure, bursting into tears and sobbing over the phone.

No. **No.**

"Have you called Eddie Volker?" I ask.

Through breathless gasps, I think I hear the word **yes.**

Maybe Eddie can think of something. But if the feds are talking about espionage, they're talking about national security. They're talking about the Patriot Act.

They can do pretty much whatever they want to me.

It is over ninety degrees outside today, but I have never felt a greater chill running through my body. They are doing everything in their power to destroy me, and now they're doing something even worse. They are destroying my newspaper, and hurting my employees with it. People who depend on me to put food on the table.

I have to do something. I have to save my paper and the people who've made it so great. But what can I do? Where can I confirm anything I suspect? I can't even separate the good guys from the bad guys, much less turn to any of them for help. And my friends will now be risking a prison sentence for so much as loaning me five bucks or answering a question. I can't jeopardize any of them. But take them out of the equation, and who do I have left? I don't even have a newspaper anymore.

I'm out of money, resources, and friends.

And probably time.

I can only think of one other thing. I take a breath and hope against hope.

"What about Jonathan Liu's computer?" I ask. If there is any place where I can find proof of what's going on—not supposition, but proof—it will be on that computer.

Ashley Brook is quiet for a long time.

"They took it," she says.

CHAPTER 78

Eddie Volker parks his Mercedes sedan in the parking garage below his law office. The place is hot and sticky but also dark and private, so it's not a bad place to wait for him when he comes off the elevator past seven o'clock tonight after a day's work.

I show my hands when I step out from between the cars. As anyone would, he stops, retreats, and assesses, but then he relaxes when he sees it's me.

"You're gonna give me a heart attack, Ben." He loosens the collar on his dress shirt and takes a couple of breaths.

"Can we talk in your car?" I ask.

Eddie joins me in his Mercedes. The passenger side is full of napkins and food wrappers and unpaid bills. It looks like the interior of my car, which I hardly ever drive.

"You need to know everything, Eddie," I say. "Before we decide what to do, you need the full picture."

I give it to him in fifteen minutes. It's a lot to digest, going back to when someone jumped off Diana's balcony to now. But he already knows much of this, and say what you want about Eddie's personal habits and clientele, he has a sharp mind.

He lets out a nervous giggle. "I've had all kinds of clients," he says. "But you may have won the prize for stepping into shit."

"So what the hell do I do, Ed—"

"First things first, Ben. Right now, if you go online to the **Beat,** it says the website is under repair and maintenance and will be back soon. It's an agreement I worked out with Justice. So okay, it's not ideal. You'll lose advertising revenue and readers, sure. But it's not fatal. Nothing about the DOJ shutting you down, nothing about espionage or anything like that. The paper's reputation is intact."

"For now," I say.

"For now," he acknowledges. "If I were you, I'd focus on solving your personal problems first. Which are considerable, I'll grant you." He drums his fingers on the steering wheel. "So . . . the president is having an affair and the Russians know about it. They're blackmailing him so he'll keep quiet while they start rolling their tanks through the old Soviet bloc countries?"

"Basically, yeah."

"And Diana Hotchkiss is the president's mistress."

"That's my guess. It makes sense."

"And the US government has made it a point to tell the world that Diana, not some stand-in, is dead."

"Yeah. The president said it in a press conference. The MPD is saying it. They've even coerced Diana's family into saying it. So the Russians are supposed to believe Diana's dead. I guess this is how the CIA thinks they'll thwart the blackmail. If there's no 'she' in the **he said she said,** then the president can deny the affair and nobody can contradict him."

Eddie takes all this in. Then he turns and looks at me.

"So if our government has taken care of

the problem by faking Diana's death, why are they still afraid of you, Ben?"

"Because I'm not accepting that Diana's dead."

He shrugs. "Yeah, but so what? You're just some reporter without proof. The president will deny it, Diana's parents will deny it, and that will be the end of the discussion."

I give that some thought.

"So I ask again," says Eddie. "Why does the US government consider you a threat?"

It's a good question. The right question. If I were trying to cover up an affair, the first thing I'd want to do is remove the mistress from the equation. They've done that. They've made everyone believe Diana is dead. So what else could—

Oh. Oh, of course.

By George, I think I've got it.

But all things considered, I better keep the thought to myself for now.

"Eddie, I have to run, but listen. I wouldn't ask—but I need some cash."

"Cash?" Eddie thinks about that. "I'm . . . not sure I can help you, Ben."

"Right, I understand—you can't assist me in any way. I don't want you to go to prison. I was just thinking, if you had some pocket money on you, that kind of thing. I'm not suggesting you write me a check or anything."

Eddie is quiet for a while. "I suppose when I'm taking my keys out to start my car, some money could fall out of my pocket that I wouldn't notice."

"That could happen, sure."

"It wouldn't be more than a couple hundred bucks."

"It would be a couple hundred bucks more than I have."

Eddie gets out of the car. As silly as we both find it, he actually takes the cash out of his money clip and drops it to the cement floor. "Oops," he says.

I don't pick it up right away. I'll wait until he drives out of here. Might as well play along with the charade. He can truthfully say he never handed me money.

But he did hand me an idea. I think I know what the US government is afraid of. And I have an idea how I can confirm it.

CHAPTER 79

Suddenly finding myself forced to economize, I stay at the cheapest hotel I can find. You know it's a cheap hotel when the bathroom's down the hall. When "air-conditioning" consists of waving your hand in front of your face. When you can hear the guy in the next room rolling over in bed. When "room service" means they loan you a flyswatter. When the telephone is in the lobby instead of on the nightstand. When there **isn't** a nightstand.

But I've seen the sun rise another day. That in itself is a major victory.

With the few remaining minutes on one

of my three remaining prepaid phones, I make the call and set up an appointment. They tell me I'll have to wait until after lunch, so I have some time to kill. I should probably hide in the hotel room, but it's so crappy that I think I'll take my chances on the open streets.

Or at least in a coffee shop, where I pull my baseball cap low and nurse a small coffee and pick at a blueberry muffin. I grab a **Post** that someone left on the next table over and go to the headlines. I've missed being a reporter and vastly prefer it to fugitive life. The pay's better and nobody tries to kill you.

"Shit!" I yell when I see the lead story above the fold: RUSSIAN LEADER ESCAPES ASSASSIN'S BULLET.

I quickly whip through the article. Russian prime minister Yuri Mereyedev narrowly escaped assassination last night when a man opened fire on him while he was speaking at a rally outside Moscow. Russian police captured a man who is believed to have ties to—surprise, surprise—the Georgian secret police. The US State Department is said to be "closely monitoring" the situation.

I throw down the newspaper. Andrei Bogomolov anticipated this very thing. A terrorist attack, he predicted, that would be blamed on the Republic of Georgia. This is close enough. Certainly close enough for provocation's sake.

Russia is moving closer to an invasion of her southern neighbor. The plan to reconstruct the old Soviet empire is already under way.

CHAPTER 80

I lock my bike to a parking meter, visit a fast-food bathroom so I can change into some presentable clothes, and enter the building a block away. I show my press credentials at the sign-in and the next thing I know, I'm in a plush waiting room. It reminds me of my visit to Jonathan Liu's offices. It didn't turn out so well for Jonathan. Let's see how this turns out for Edgar Griffin.

"Mr. Griffin will see you," says an elderly woman who doesn't think much of my appearance. Apparently one of the principals at the law firm of Griffin and Weaver isn't accustomed to people of my ilk crawling in.

"Yes, Senator, I agree." Edgar Griffin is speaking into a headset while waving me into his lavishly appointed office. This is corporate chic at its chicest, if that's a word. It probably isn't. Anyway, this office is the size of a tennis court. It has a wall full of fancy books, another wall full of diplomas and framed photographs of Mr. Griffin, Esquire, interacting with important people, and a floor-to-ceiling window overlooking K Street. The decor is walnut and brass. Money and power. And helping people with money and power get more money and more power.

Mr. Griffin, Esquire, is wearing a striped shirt, a power-red tie with a tie clip, silk braces over his shoulders, and gold cuff links. His hair is full and greased. He has a thin, narrow face and neatly trimmed eyebrows.

"Senator, I couldn't have said it better," he says into his headset with a laugh.

I'll bet you anything there isn't anybody on the other end of the line. He just wants me to see his importance. That's why I'm here, after all—at least in his mind. I called earlier today and said I was a reporter doing a piece on the "top ten movers and shakers in the capital," and he was going to be numero uno, with his mug plastered on the front page of our humble website.

Suddenly he found that he could spare a half hour in his busy schedule.

"Edgar Griffin," he says to me, removing his headset.

"Ben Casper." We shake hands. I make sure he can see my press credentials sticking out of the pocket of my sport coat. I hope they will distract him from its myriad wrinkles, given that said sport coat has been balled up in my gym bag for several days.

"There was going to be a photographer?" he says.

"There was. There will be," I say. "We'll try to schedule something for tomorrow."

"Fine. Just talk to Cheryl."

I look around the office. "Wow," I say. "You've done quite well for yourself. I've done my homework, Ed, and I've gotta say, when I ask around about the powerful people in this city, your name comes up a lot."

"Edgar," he says.

Are we reintroducing ourselves?

"Ben," I say.

"No. I mean—you called me Ed. It's Edgar."

"Sorry. I have a lawyer named Ed. Actually, it's Eddie. Eddie Volker. You know him?"

He wrinkles his nose. Apparently, Mr. **Edgar** Griffin of Griffin and Weaver doesn't know Eddie Volker, a lawyer several notches below him on the elitism ladder who defends criminals and helps journalists.

"I knew an Edward Verrill in Cambridge. Not Vogel, I don't think."

Annnnnd **there.** It took him less than five minutes to tell me he went to Harvard Law School.

"That's a family name, isn't it?" I ask. "Edgar."

"Yes, it is."

I nod. "And that law degree from Harvard? I'll bet you weren't the first in your family, were you?"

Edgar seems slightly offended. "My father attended as well."

Okay, he didn't **go** to Harvard. He **attended** it.

"Grandpa, too?" I venture.

Now he **is** offended. "My grandfather as well, yes."

So he basically just had to make sure he didn't wet his pants at the interview. He was in before he submitted his application. But better I don't say that to him. Not yet, anyway. Maybe on the way out.

I raise my hand, a sign of peace. "It's my resentment showing. I tried for Harvard and didn't get in."

That's not true. I didn't apply to Harvard. In fact, I didn't even apply to American University. My dad just informed me one day that my days of private tutors were over and that I was going to American the following fall. But I've made Edgar feel just a little bit more superior than he already felt. If that's possible.

"So, Edgar, you've managed to build up quite a list of clients," I say, looking over a sheet of paper that does not contain a list of anything whatsoever. In fact, it's blank. "Ah, Alexander Kutuzov, I see here. The billionaire?"

Now we're back in Edgar's comfort zone. "Alex has been wonderful to work with."

That's one way superior people try to act more superior—using famous people's nicknames to show their familiarity. **Yeah, I was having lunch with Jenny Lopez**

the other day, and who was sitting at the next table but Bobby De Niro and Marty Scorsese.

"Here in the States," he says (people refer to the United States as "the States" when they want you to know they're world travelers), "we've helped Alex with licensing and some related litigation over his soccer franchise."

I point to the same piece of paper that has absolutely nothing on it. If this guy didn't have his head so far up his ass, he might notice that.

"I see here you helped Mr. Kutuzov with the negotiations on that oil pipeline in Russia. The one that feeds oil to Russia's neighbors."

Actually, it was Griffin and Weaver's London office that handled it, but I'll bet all my frozen assets that he's going to take credit for it.

I certainly hope he does.

"Could we chat about that for a minute?" I ask.

CHAPTER 81

Edgar Griffin, Esquire, rests his hands on his stomach and forms a temple with his hands. "A sensitive negotiation, to be sure, that oil pipeline. The Russian government can be difficult. But we've managed to put together a very lucrative arrangement that benefits both sides. We think Alex will have a profitable partnership with the Russian government."

"We're talking about a billion-dollar deal?" I ask, like I'm impressed.

"Easily. Tens of billions, ultimately."

"Wow. I can't even imagine how much pressure that must be, to negotiate something like that. You're an awfully impressive guy, Mr. Griffin."

He seems to agree. We both take a moment to admire him.

"Just out of curiosity," I say, leaning forward. "I mean, this stuff is way, way over my head, but—just wondering. This recent development, with Georgia and Russia starting to bicker again. What happens with something like that? Like, what if war breaks out and Russia cuts off its oil supply to Georgia?"

He nods and tosses a hand. "There are standard force majeure clauses."

"Wow," I say. "Latin."

Now that it's clear that we're on the same page about how impressive he is, Edgar has loosened up considerably. "Actually," he says with a chuckle, "as long as this is off the record—this is just on background, agreed?"

"Agreed," I say. **On background** means I won't print it or attribute it to him. But Kutuzov's contract with the Russians is a matter of public record anyway. I found it online, albeit in Russian. Either way, this guy's ego is way too large to prevent him from giving me information.

Edgar says, "Not only is Alex's obligation to supply oil terminated in the event of war, but Alex would be compensated handsomely for the interruption."

"He'd be paid for **not** supplying oil?"

"Correct." Edgar is beaming. "He's guaranteed the same amount of profit, but he doesn't have to go to the expense of actually pumping the oil."

"Or he could pump it and sell it to somebody else," I note. "Double the profit."

"Exactly."

"Wow," I say for the third time. "You served your client well. You really **are** a top lawyer. I hope Mr. Kutuzov paid you well."

Edgar cocks his head, then winks at me and says, "He did."

"And I suppose if Russia installed a puppet regime in Georgia, that regime could even agree to pay higher oil prices to Alex. I mean, hypothetically."

He thinks about that. "Well—I hadn't considered that."

But your client Alex sure did.

"Well," I say, "that explains why Kutuzov went along with the side deal."

Mr. Edgar Griffin, Esquire, shifts ever so slightly in his seat. "Excuse me?"

"Excuse you?"

"A side deal, you said? I'm not aware of any side deal."

He probably isn't. No reason the feisty billionaire would share that kind of information with his lawyer in **the States.**

"Oh, sure," I say. "His side deal to help Russia blackmail the US government while Russia invades the Republic of Georgia. No wonder Kutuzov's willing to help. He'll make a fortune."

The lawyer draws back and reappraises the situation. The temperature has dropped in the room.

"Y'know," I say, "I'm glad we could reschedule this, Eduardo. You don't know this, but I was planning on joining you in your meeting with Detective Ellis Burk a few days ago. For some reason, we had to cancel . . . oh, now I remember." I snap my fingers. "Someone ambushed us with machine-gun fire on our way here. Don't you just hate it when that happens? My friend, Detective Burk, was killed, by the way."

I shrug. "Anyway, E-Dog, I just need you to deliver a message to your good friend Alex. Think you can handle that, sport?"

Edgar is still at a loss for words. He's a lawyer, so he can put up a stoic front, but there's something cooking beneath his collar.

It took me a while, but eventually I figured it out. My own lawyer, Eddie-not-Edgar Volker, asked me a simple question—if Diana is out of the picture, why is the US government still afraid of me?—and it all became clear to me. I know why the CIA is threatened by me. It's the same reason, I assume, that the Russians want to kill me.

I pick one of Edgar's business cards off his desk and scribble a place, a time, and a few other instructions on the back. "Tell your valuable client, Mr. Kutuzov, to meet me here tonight," I say. "And I want to know how to reach him. So get a cell number for Kutuzov, and when I call you at five tonight, you'll give it to me."

Edgar still looks like he swallowed a bug. "Why . . . would he meet you?" he manages.

I lean over the walnut table and accidentally, or maybe not so accidentally, spill his cup of Starbucks. But Edgar never takes his eyes off me.

"Because I have a copy of the video," I say. "And I'm selling it to the highest bidder."

CHAPTER 82

I walk down Half Street and check my watch. It's 6:45 on the nose. When I reach the intersection with N Street, I look over to the red awning just east of the center field gate at Nationals Park. Over the will call window, an electronic billboard advertises GRAND SLAM PLAN—BUY 4 GAMES, GET 1 FREE! Okay, guys, sure, now that you've finally put together a decent squad. Hell, it only took you eight seasons after bringing the franchise here from Montreal.

I kid because I care. I like the Nats, and I like the development of the Capitol Riverfront district by the Navy Yard since they arrived. Hell, I love having a hometown team to root for. I'm just saying, let's get more consistency from that starting rotation and some left-handed hitting coming off the bench.

And now we join, already in progress, the reason I came here.

There he is, below the electronic sign, standing next to the will call window, dressed as I requested—in an orange Windbreaker. Maybe a little over the top, but I've never seen Alexander Kutuzov in person, and I wanted him to stand out from all the other fans heading into the Nationals' 7:05 start against the Braves.

He's a tall man, athletic, and very well manicured. He seems perfectly at ease this evening, probably because he's a man of such mind-boggling wealth, or possibly because of his various hoodlums positioned—let's see . . . two of them by the team store, two of them looking down on their boss from the second story of the parking garage, and others, presumably, who have done a better job of blending into the crowd. He's probably got a whole army here. If they all bought tickets, the Nats could double their attendance tonight.

Me? I'm in disguise. I'm wearing a red Nationals T-shirt, under which I've added a fat belt that I picked up from a costume shop and that adds about thirty pounds to my frame. Oh, and they also sold me a wig that makes me bald on top and gives me bushy hair on the sides. Plus fake eyeglasses.

Maybe not the most convincing disguise under close scrutiny, but I'm not expecting any close scrutiny. In fact, my work here is done. I jump in a cab outside the stadium that has just been vacated by a pack of drunken college kids. The smell of stale beer lingers in the cab, but I don't care. I put my head against the back headrest and listen to the cabdriver talk on his cell phone in some language I don't understand.

Amazing how such a simple task has left me sweating through this T-shirt. But so far, so good. Alex Kutuzov dropped everything and flew out here, on six hours' notice, to meet me. So I must be doing something right.

I pull out my prepaid cell phone and dial

the number that Edgar Griffin gave me for
Alex Kutuzov. I called Alex an hour ago.
That was a short call. This one might be
longer.

Let's see if I can avoid screwing it up.

CHAPTER 83

Alexander Kutuzov answers my call on the second ring. "Hello?" he says.

"Alex, I see you made it. Welcome to Nationals Park."

He pauses. "Thank you, Mr. Casper." His English is precisely delivered, the thick Russian accent notwithstanding. "Where are you?"

"Did you come alone, Alex, as I asked?"

"Of course."

Of course **not.** But it doesn't matter. I'm more than a mile away now, in a cab. "Did you bring what I asked, Alex?"

"I did." He's being cautious over a cell

phone, as I'd expect him to be. He won't say what it is, but I told him to bring a baseball glove and to stuff ten thousand dollars in cash into the finger holes of the glove. And to write my name on the glove.

"Turn it in at the lost and found at the guest services office. It's right by you at the center field gate."

After another pause, he says, "Then I will not be meeting you tonight?"

"We need trust," I say. "If the glove is in the lost and found, we'll have trust."

And I'll have some spending money.

"This arrangement is unacceptable," he says.

"Well, okay, Alex, if that's how you want it. I have another buyer."

Yet another pause. Face-to-face, Kutuzov probably gets far with piercing stares and long silences. It's not as effective over a phone, but it still works for him, I hate to admit.

"And what assurances do I have, Mr. Casper, that I will receive the only copy? How do I know you will not give another copy to your superiors, once I give you the money?"

My **superiors**? Who does he think my "superiors" are?

"You have only my word," I say. "But you do have that."

Another pause, but this time it's so long that I begin to think he hung up on me. I consider asking him what he means by my "superiors," but better I stay as mysterious to him as possible.

"Mr. Casper," he says. "You are . . . living in fear, yes?"

Very much so, but I was beginning to feel like I had the upper hand. This guy's confidence is making me second-guess myself.

"Do I sound afraid, Alex?" I say.

"Yes, you do. You sound very afraid. You sound like a man who is trying very hard to act as if he is not. But I can hear it in your voice. I am . . . accustomed to recognizing such things."

I'll bet he is. "I think you're the one who's afraid, Alex."

"Do I sound afraid, Mr. Casper?"

I wish he did, but he doesn't. Not the least bit.

"You went to a lot of trouble getting here on short notice, Alex."

"Oh, I do not deny that I want the item you have. And I will pay you handsomely for it. But do not mistake that for fear, Mr. Casper. And it is critical that you and I understand each other on one particular point."

"Please, Alex, I'm all ears." I'm trying to keep up my bravado, but this guy's a serious customer. I'm just a goofy reporter.

"Until you give me what I want," he says, "you should remain in fear. Nothing has changed."

"Your goons will still come looking for me? Is that what you're telling me?"

He doesn't answer. He doesn't want to admit something like that over the phone, I assume. But that's what he means. Until my copy of the video is in his hands, I still have a target on my back.

Boy, I wish I actually **had** a copy of that video.

"And Mr. Casper, if I learn that another copy has fallen into the hands of your superiors and you have played me for the fool, then believe me when I say I will not be pleased."

"Fair enough, Alex. We understand each other."

"You will find the glove at the lost and found," he finally says. "And I shall look forward to hearing from you, Mr. Casper."

"Sounds like a plan, Alex."

"But do not test my patience," he says.

I was really hoping that this conversation would end with me feeling good and him feeling worried. But he doesn't sound worried. And I don't feel so good.

"And until you deliver that item to me," he adds, "you should sleep with your eyes open."

CHAPTER 84

Another restful night of sleep on a mattress about as thick as a piece of cardboard and only slightly less comfortable than sandpaper. I only had to wait about an hour to use the toilet and shower down the hall. I didn't mind standing in line with my towel and toothbrush next to a mangy guy who kept asking me if I had any hemorrhoid cream (I didn't), laxatives (nope), dental floss (sorry), or hemorrhoid cream (still no). I was just glad I got to use the bathroom before he did.

Now I'm back at the National Mall—maybe not the most creative choice, but I like it because there are so many people around and I'm close to the metro, where I can hop aboard and go in any number of directions on a moment's notice. Even if they triangulate the call and figure out where I am, I'll be long gone before they can get here.

I dial the number and assume—hope—he'll answer, that he wants me to call.

"Hello, this is Craig Carney," he says.

I glance around me but don't see anyone pivoting in my direction or brandishing a firearm.

"Mr. Deputy Director!" I say into the phone. "It's your old friend. How are you today?"

Nobody ever uses the word **brandish** unless it's in connection with a weapon. Why is it you can brandish a sword or a revolver but not, say, a set of keys you just found in the couch cushions? I would brandish keys.

"I might ask you the same question, Benjamin. Sounds like you've fallen on hard times. Have you come to your senses yet?"

I do another once-over of the National Mall. Nothing that makes my spidey sense tingle. I'd hate to have webs shoot out of my wrists, but having that spidey sense to detect danger would be awesome.

"I haven't lost my sense, Mr. Deputy Director. Maybe my dollars, but not my sense."

He chuckles. "I gave you a chance, Ben. Remember that. And I'll give you another one, but your options are growing more limited. I'm not sure I can keep you out of prison anymore. But you can avoid the death penalty and get your assets back."

I shake my head, trying not to let him plant fear in the pit of my stomach. I was just starting to get my groove back yesterday. Alex Kutuzov may have shaken me a little bit, but he **did** come halfway around the world to meet me at Nationals Park, and, according to my friend who works security for the Nationals, there **was** a baseball glove bearing my name at the lost and found last night. So at least I have confirmation of the video.

I clear my throat before breaking the news to Craig Carney.

"Mr. Carney," I say, "I have the video."

If we were talking in person, I'd **brandish** the video, which I would have just taken out of my coat pocket. (I mean, if I actually had the video.)

Carney pauses a beat. He's too polished to shout out **Holy shit!** or moan or cry, but even a smooth operator like the deputy director has to take a moment for this turn of events.

"Video?" he asks.

"Yes, sir. The video. The video that is bringing our federal government to its knees? Does that ring a bell?"

I'm enjoying this, I admit. But I have to be cognizant of the time. This is like in the movies when there's a call from a fugitive, and on the law enforcement side, guys are scrambling to run the trace, and one guy is separating his hands in the air to indicate the call should be strrrrrretched out, and then another guy whispers, **He's somewhere in the city,** and finally they get a precise location, someone draws a circle on a map, and everyone bolts from their seats.

In **Mission: Impossible,** they needed thirty seconds to locate Tom Cruise, but he knew that and hung up after twenty-nine. That always seemed unrealistic to me. Wearing totally lifelike masks of other people's faces, sure, but a thirty-second phone trace? No way.

Anyway, back to reality, where the deputy director of the CIA is about to play dumb.

"I don't know of any video, Benjamin. You'll have to be more specific."

Surprise! Still, my heartbeat skips up a notch, and I start pacing near the World War II Memorial. "Don't bullshit me, Mr. Deputy Director. We both know there's a video of the president and his mistress. And I have a copy."

He doesn't answer right away, but now that I've given him the detail, he's probably shitting his pants.

"Son, I don't know what game you're trying to play, but as usual, you're in over your head. There's no video of the president and some 'mistress,' because there **isn't** any mistress. The president is faithful to his wife."

He doesn't sound like someone who's shitting his pants.

I pause, but he doesn't elaborate. He's not being defensive. I don't detect the slightest tremor in his voice, not a single indication that he is ceding the upper hand to me. If anything, he's showing me the **back** of his hand.

"You're good, Mr. Deputy Director. But I'm not buying your act."

"Then publish the video, Ben. Play it on the evening news. Give it to one of your reporter friends. Be my guest."

Now **I'm** the one shitting my pants.

I stare at my phone. What is he doing? I didn't expect him to come out and admit the existence of the video, especially over the phone, but he's not even trying to placate me. He's not asking me what I want or where we can meet.

He's telling me to go fuck myself.

I terminate the call and start running to the metro station. That conversation, to say the least, did not go as planned.

Is there a blackmail video or not?

CHAPTER 85

I'm missing something . . . I'm missing something . . .

I get off the Red Line at the Van Ness stop, unlock my Rockhopper from one of the bike racks, then change back into biking gear in a fast-food bathroom. I do these actions robotically while my brain tries to unscramble this mess.

I thought I had this thing figured out. I thought there was a video. When I mentioned it to Alex Kutuzov, he jumped to attention. But Carney all but yawned. He actually dared me to publish it. I wouldn't trust him as far as I could throw him, and

I'm sure he can bluff with the best of them, but if there's a video . . . he wouldn't have acted that way. I must be missing something.

I dial Sean Patrick Riley, my Irish comrade, for an update. I'd given him a homework assignment and tried to convey to him the urgency of the matter. Let's hope the lad came through.

"I've got something," he says. "You were right, Ben. I checked Nina's e-mail account first thing when I started this job, but I didn't conduct a forensic examination. It turns out there are a couple of e-mails that were erased by a hacker."

"E-mails they didn't want anyone to see."

"E-mails they didn't want anyone to see."

"And those e-mails are good?" I ask.

"Those e-mails are good."

This guy's repeating everything I say. Is Aaron Sorkin scripting this?

"When can we meet?" he asks.

Well, let's see. I've got a manicure later today, then I was going to take in a show; tomorrow I have Pilates, and then I'm meeting some friends for brunch, and I've been meaning to organize my sock drawer . . .

"When can we meet?" I say, exasperated. "How about right freakin' now, Sean!"

We make our arrangements. I'd rather not say what they are. I'm superstitious like that. In the movies, whenever the actors spell out for you what the plan is, you know the plan is going to fail or at least hit a serious road bump. If they just say to each other, **Okay, here's the plan,** but then the scene fades out without telling you the details, you know the plan is going to succeed. Check it out sometime. I know of only one exception to this rule: in **A Few Good Men,** Tom Cruise revealed that he was planning on coaxing Jack Nicholson into admitting he ordered the code red, and then the plan worked. (Coincidentally, that was an Aaron Sorkin script.)

Sorry, I'm starting to ramble again. It's my nerves jangling about. Just when I thought I was on to something with the idea of the blackmail tape, just when I saw a way out, I'm back at square one, with Craig Carney all but laughing at me.

I jump on my bike and pedal down Connecticut Avenue, cognizant of the fact that the last time I went this way I nearly killed myself and smashed Jonathan Liu's computer.

I stay to the right on Connecticut, as most of the cars on the road take the traffic tunnel. I reach Dupont Circle, which has an interior park area surrounded by a roundabout with several exits. In the park area inside the roundabout, people are lounging on the benches or catching a late lunch. I remember visiting Rome once and just sitting with a baguette and block of cheese and watching the kamikaze drivers merge from four lanes to one and honk at one another and narrowly avoid death. It was better than watching the Indy 500 on television.

One guy sitting in the park is staring intently into traffic and then looks at me and gets off the bench and keeps following me with his eyes. **What the hell, buddy, you never saw someone ride a bike before?**

The sound of the horn jolts me. Some asshole thinks he should be able to hang a right on Massachusetts without yielding to me, the cyclist. I hit the brakes hard and come to a stop. Before he executes his turn, the driver lowers his passenger window and curses at me, threatening to squash me like a bug.

Get in line, pal. There are entire governments that want me dead.

I look to my left, back at the park area. The guy who was watching traffic isn't standing by the bench anymore. He's moved to the sidewalk, closer to me.

And he's looking right at me, peering at me. Like you'd stare at a guy you thought you recognized but couldn't place.

His eyes widen. He's placed me, all right.

He raises a radio to his mouth and shouts something out. I don't recognize the language.

But it sure sounds like Russian.

CHAPTER 86

I don't know what's Russian for **I found him! I found him!** but whatever it is, I'm pretty sure that's what this guy is screaming into his radio.

I start pedaling from a dead stop, following along Dupont Circle, on the run like Matt Damon in one of the **Bourne** movies, except he had a motorcycle. The guy is tracking me, staying on the park's inner sidewalk but moving around its perimeter to see where I'm going to turn off. I pump my legs with every ounce of power I can muster, weaving between cars and drawing some objections from angry horns. I take the right on the roundabout at 19th Street and look back over my shoulder. The guy sees me, and he's shouting into his radio and pointing in my direction, too.

I put my head down and pump those legs, maneuvering around a giant Pepsi truck and screaming at a couple crossing the street to get out of my way. Then I hear some shouting behind me and the sound of a car engine in full throttle. I glance behind me and see a black SUV closing the gap quickly. I have a head start, but I'm going maybe twenty miles an hour and the SUV's doing about fifty and counting. This is not a fair fight. They have a car and automatic weapons. I have a bicycle and a winning personality.

In ten seconds, tops, they'll reach me, and they'll shoot me full of holes.

Matt Damon would figure out something. He'd ride the bicycle backward or jump in the car with the bad guys.

But I have a trick or two, a couple of advantages. One, I know this town better than they do.

I skid into a hard right turn and head down Sunderland Place, a narrow street with cars parked on both sides and, helpfully, a UPS truck unloading near the intersection with 19th. An oncoming Mercedes honks its horn and I veer to my right and hop up onto the sidewalk just as I hear the black SUV's tires skid forcefully at the intersection of 19th and Sunderland behind me. I'm pedaling like crazy and blowing out air and listening, listening, as the SUV guns forward again but then meets a serious horn objection from the driver of the Mercedes, who is probably wondering why this SUV is traveling west down a one-way eastbound street.

That's advantage number two: my bike can go places their car can't.

The extended horn tells me the Mercedes driver isn't planning on putting his car in reverse, not when he's the one going in the right direction on the one-way street and there's not enough room for the SUV to get around it. I keep my head down low, but I doubt they'll try to shoot at me from this far away. I sneak a look back and see the SUV whip backward onto 19th and then head south, out of my view.

So I'm totally safe, right? Like in the slasher flicks when the woman hears the noise upstairs but checks every room and doesn't find anyone, then relaxes and thinks, **I guess it was nothing!** only to find the man in the hockey mask with the ice pick standing behind her.

The Russians, speeding south on 19th, are almost certain to turn right on N Street and take it over to 20th and make another right, so they can head back up north to look for me. It won't take them long . . .

I hit 20th, part of a three-way intersection with New Hampshire Avenue, a street that cuts diagonally across. I maneuver through the intersection, drawing some car horns, and take the hard left on New Hampshire as I hear braking and squealing tires to my left. The Russians' SUV is swerving around other cars, almost at the three-way intersection. They see me. I know they see me.

In a close call, I choose **The Departed** over **Good Will Hunting,** but both are top five Matt Damon movies **okay stop, Ben—**

I hop onto the sidewalk on New Hampshire, my head down, and pedal with everything I have. Chaos behind me at the three-way intersection, horns honking, people shouting, metal crunching. New

Hampshire is another one-way street, so once more, the Russians will have to drive the wrong way down a one-way street to catch me. There's a lot of traffic passing me and I hope it poses enough of an obstacle that it buys me some time.

Because now I have an idea. Matt Damon would think this is cool.

I pass Firefly on the right. I went there once with Diana, blue-cheese dates and the mini pot roast, she talked the waiter into bringing a couple of beer-battered pickles, even though neither of us ordered the burger, Diana could do things like that—

Focus, Ben.

I have a prepaid phone in my pocket and I pull it out with some difficulty, and the earpiece is still attached and I shove it into my ear and dial furiously, a phone call that might save my life—

Rat-a-tat-tat and they're shooting at me, and the building behind me absorbs the gunfire, bullets hitting brick, and dammit ANSWER THE PHONE, ANSWER—

I can hear them behind me, the SUV's engine gunning southwest toward me, there's no way I can outrace them, but if I can just buy some time, if I can just get to Ward Place—

The Informant! showed Damon's growth as an actor—

The phone picks up and I shout into my earpiece, completely out of breath, but I repeat the same words over and over again, **Twenty-Second, southbound**—

And then two magical words that will wake them up, two radioactive words I shout over and over and over—

A woman is racing with her stroller to get out of the line of fire and I narrowly avoid her and pedal as hard as my legs can go, but they're coming up behind me, I can hear them, they're maneuvering around oncoming traffic and everyone has dived to the pavement for cover and I hear more gunfire, bullets pelting a parked FedEx truck, **thump-thump-thump,** and then I skid into a right turn at Ward Place, a tiny, narrow street—

Ward, don't you think you were a little hard on the Beaver last night?

—and I pump-pump-pump those legs, and moments later, the SUV brakes hard and skids near that turn, and I forgot all about **The Talented Mr. Ripley**—

Ward Place is another one-way street, eastbound, which means once again they'll have to travel against oncoming traffic. But there isn't any traffic on Ward Place.

Other than their desire to follow the rules of the road and maintain a spotless driving record, the Russians have nothing stopping them from speeding down this street and closing the gap in a matter of seconds.

CHAPTER 87

Ward Place is a short, narrow connecting street, so I'm maybe halfway down before the SUV rights itself and motors down toward me. From the north sidewalk, I jump the curb onto the street and then hop onto the curb on the south side. Their guy with the machine gun is on the right, on the passenger side, so he won't have an angle on me from that direction, he'll have to switch sides, any time I can buy is precious—

Must have the precious, they stole it from us, sneaky little hobbitses.

—Come on, 22nd, come on, 22nd, come on—

Chunks of brick explode off the building over my head, they don't have a good angle but it's not going to stop them, someone is shouting and WHERE THE HELL IS THE CAR TRAFFIC, nothing's stopping these guys, every second they're closer, closer, closer, **Closer** is one of my favorites, Natalie Portman in a pink wig in a strip club—

—**Focus, dumbshit**—

—Jessica Alba in **Sin City**—

—and now the machine-gun fire is nonstop, splintering buildings and smashing car windows and pummeling metal—

—**Closer, please**, Hannibal Lecter to Clarice—

Clo-ser!

And I swerve left into the final bend on Ward Place as bullets ricochet off the columns on the corner building. The SUV can't turn as nimbly and smashes into a parked car, costing them a few seconds, I'll take any seconds I can get, because 22nd is just up here—

I make the left turn onto 22nd, heading south down a northbound one-way street. I ride under a hotel awning, upsetting a concierge and some arriving guests, as I hear tires screeching and horns honking and—**smash**—metal crunching, and I dare to look back and, yes, the SUV has collided with an oncoming car as it turned onto 22nd, but it will right itself soon enough and refocus, like that creepy Terminator who got blown to pieces but then re-formed—

Have you seen this boy?

Pandemonium on a busy street, the asshole in the black SUV going the wrong way, every car letting him know it with their horns, but ultimately, no driver wants to play bumper cars, and they'll get out of his way.

Time, I need time, where is it, where is it, I'm on 22nd, where the fuck is it—

My legs are burning, sweat fills my eyes, horns are honking, and tires are squealing as the SUV stops and starts, stops and starts, weaves around oncoming traffic, but I can hear them, I can hear them, and now all the cars seem to get it, and they're pulling over to get out of the way of the asshole SUV, like the Red Sea parting, so now I have Charlton Heston as Moses in my head, this better not be the last image in my brain before I die—

They have a clear path to me, the engine guns forward as they close the gap, only seconds now, only seconds—

Bullets spraying buildings and cars and windows, people ducking for cover, where is it, where is it, where the fuck—

As I reach the intersection with M Street, gigantic green military trucks converge from both directions on 22nd, cutting off the intersection, followed by black sedans and some MPD squad cars. A helicopter appears overhead, seemingly out of nowhere.

Finally.

I skid into a left turn onto M Street, out of the line of fire, as I hear another set of tires skidding—the SUV's, as it approaches the intersection. I ride behind the barricade to stay safe and watch.

The SUV has stopped about fifteen, twenty yards short of the barricade at M Street. Behind it, another set of cars, sirens blaring, is speeding down 22nd to form a back end to the barricade.

I stand over my bike, panting with relief. The Russians are surrounded.

People on the streets scurry for cover. Soldiers in full combat gear jump out of the trucks and aim their weapons at the black SUV. MPD police officers draw their weapons and do the same. Everyone is shouting at the Russians.

Turn off your engine! Drop your weapons! Place your hands on your head and exit the vehicle!

(And from now on, be nice to Ben Casper!)

Nobody's approaching the vehicle. Not yet. Everyone is standing their ground. The helicopter looms overhead, maybe fifty feet or so in the air.

The police are directing bystanders to clear out, forcing cars to the south of the barricade to U-turn and get some distance. I get pushed away, too, but about a block down, I climb onto the roof of a parked car so I can watch. I think I've earned that right.

Several agents in plain clothes have joined the fray, talking into radios and, like everyone else, aiming their weapons at the bad guys. These guys are Secret Service. They're here courtesy of the two magical words I used in my 911 call.

White House. I told the operator the car was headed for the White House. It tends to get the government's attention.

The SUV remains idling in the middle of 22nd Street. Government agents continue to shout orders at the Russians, but so far, no movement in the SUV.

A standoff.

Every minute that passes brings additional law enforcement vehicles to the scene. There's got to be twenty of them by now.

"Party's over, guys," I say to myself. "Give it up."

And then the black SUV bursts into a ball of orange flame, an internal combustion so powerful that the doors, the roof, everything blows apart. The last things I see, before the force of the blast topples me from the roof of the parked car, are the green military trucks flying backward, bodies hurtling through the air, glass sailing in every direction.

And then I hit the pavement hard, facedown, followed closely by the **clang** of metal crashing to the ground and the unforgettable **whump** of human bodies landing in the street.

CHAPTER 88

I open my eyes. I don't know how long I was out. I raise my head and think, **This is what mass chaos looks like.**

People are scattering. Everyone is shouting. Sirens are blaring. Multiple helicopters are overhead now. Fighter jets are patrolling the skies. Fire and rescue trucks are arriving.

Bodies lie everywhere. I'm too far away from the epicenter to have a good sense of the number of casualties, but some of the bodies, thank God, are moving. Others are prone.

The air is thick with the smell of fire, gasoline, smoke. Of death.

I get to my feet on wobbly legs. I'm in one piece. I shake my head and shards of glass fall out of my hair. The street is littered with broken glass.

I start toward the wreckage, to offer any help I could possibly provide, but police officers are already pushing people away from the scene and setting up blockades.

There's nothing I can do. Not here, anyway.

I look up at the sky, at the cloud of black smoke hovering above the spot where the Russians' SUV once sat. The thugs inside that vehicle were blown to pieces, no doubt. And that, clearly, was the point of this overkill. This wasn't just a suicide, a cyanide pill crushed between the teeth to avoid interrogation by the enemy. No, these assassins didn't just want to avoid capture.

They wanted to avoid **identification.**

The Russians, and Alexander Kutuzov, have covered their tracks well.

CHAPTER 89

Two hours pass. I watch helplessly from the police barricade as emergency medics treat patients feverishly, as they haul some others away silently, with less urgency. Buildings adjacent to the explosion have suffered damage—broken windows and collapsed storefronts.

There's no reason for me to stay. I'm not providing any help. I'm not solving any problems. But maybe it's time I did.

I get on my bike and pedal away from the pandemonium. Rescue vehicles are speeding past me in both directions. I pray that they will succeed in their mission. But contrary to the hope that strangles my heart, that burns through my chest, I know that innocent people have died back there. More deaths attributable to me. I brought the Russians to that barricade. I caused that barricade.

I find the house easily, burned into my memory. There were many visits over the years, but one in particular sticks out, less than a month after Mother died. It was just a simple lunch out on Andrei's back patio, sausages and kebabs on the grill. It was the first time, other than Mother's funeral, that I had smelled fresh air since her death.

I remember standing by the garden, counting the petals on these beautiful flowers in a kaleidoscope of colors, wondering how something so vibrant and beautiful could exist in a world that was so cold and dark. I remember him coming up behind me and putting a hand on my shoulder. At first I thought it was Father, but of course Father would never have laid a tender hand on me like that. Father didn't like physical contact.

Anyway, there I was by the garden, and he came over and smiled at me and looked over his shoulder, to be sure that Father was a good distance away. Then he said to me, **If you ever feel that you're in danger, you can call me, Benjamin. I will help you.**

But what did an eight-year-old kid know about danger? Your parents tell you something and you accept it. Your father tells you that your mother killed herself and you say, **Yes, Father.** He tells you not to talk to the police and you say, **Yes, Father.** He tells you he'll protect you and you say, **Yes, Father.** You don't listen to what is rumbling inside you, those wicked, incomprehensible fears. You don't tell yourself that your father killed your mother and, for good measure, set you up as the fall guy just in case.

I carry my bike up the steps and ring the doorbell. I don't know if he's home, but if he is, it will take him a while to answer.

He finally does. "Benjamin," he says. He always called me by my full name.

"Andrei," I say. "I think it's time we had another talk."

CHAPTER 90

Professor Andrei Bogomolov leads me through his house toward his back patio. But I stop in the den and watch the television, which of course is covering nothing but the events I just witnessed firsthand. An aerial view of the scene shows a black crater where the Russians' SUV once rested. Rescue vehicles are everywhere, and bodies are being lifted on gurneys. Too early for a casualty estimate. The fact that this event took place about eight blocks from 1600 Pennsylvania Avenue, after a 911 call from an anonymous cell phone warned of an attack on the White

House, seems to be occupying the thoughts of the reporters and commentators more than anything else.

"Come," Andrei urges me. "That story isn't going anywhere. Let us sit outside."

We pass the kitchen, where bottles of pills are lined up on the counter, where an IV drip rests in the corner. Cancer would be my guess, but it's Andrei's decision whether to tell me. I need to know a lot of things from Andrei right now, but that isn't one of them.

"I should assume that what I was watching on television involves you in some manner?" he says to me, as he carefully settles into a cheap lawn chair on the brick patio. He has a small yard back here—it seemed huge when I was a kid—and a garden of flowers and plants that are precisely arranged in rows and columns.

"Why don't we stop talking about assumptions and predictions," I say. "And why don't we start talking about what you know."

Andrei looks up at me, then blinks away the eye contact and looks over his garden.

"Tell me that story again," I say. "The one about how you were a psychiatrist on a Soviet ship, you jumped in the water off the Ivory Coast, and swam ashore. Then the Peace Corps volunteers hid you from the KGB and smuggled you to the American embassy in Ghana. Tell me that one again, Andrei. Because when I was a kid, I thought it was the most inspirational story a man could tell."

His expression softens. "And you now doubt this story?"

"Cut the shit, Andrei. Okay? You've done a remarkably accurate job of predicting what the Russians are up to. 'Expect a terrorist act soon'? 'The Russians are rebuilding the Soviet bloc'? You nailed it. All of it. So let's stop pretending it was just a lucky guess."

He doesn't answer. Not verbally, at least. But his eyes dance as he considers what I've said.

"You're CIA," I say to him. "You're a spy."

A soft smile plays on his lips. **I've taught you well, Grasshopper.**

"I'm a patriot," he answers. "I was a patriot to this country before I even lived here."

Considering it fresh as an adult, it all

makes perfect sense. An officer and psychiatrist in the Soviet military probably learned a lot of dirt. A lot of secrets. Andrei was working for us. He was passing secrets to the CIA. And then something must have happened. Maybe the Soviets were growing suspicious. Or maybe Andrei had served out the terms of his agreement with us and wanted the prize—freedom. So the CIA set it up so he could defect. Maybe he really did jump off the ship off the Ivory Coast, but I'll bet the rest of the story is bullshit. It was coordinated. The CIA had someone waiting to whisk him away to the United States.

"Listen, good for you, Professor. But fast-forward to the present, and it sounds like you still have your ear to the ground. You still hear things. You know a lot more about what's going on than you're letting on. And it's time you told me."

Andrei always has been, and in whatever time he has left always will be, a man of discretion. He will reveal only a fraction of what he's feeling and thinking. But I think he expected this visit from me. I think he wanted this visit.

"Sit, Benjamin," he says, motioning to the lawn chair next to him.

I pick it up and hurl it into the yard. Then I stand directly in front of my old friend.

"What's on the video, Andrei?" I ask.

CHAPTER 91

Professor Bogomolov looks up at me with tired eyes.

"I honestly don't know what is contained on that video," he says. "It is a carefully guarded piece of information to which I am not privy. You could probably count on one hand the number of people in our government who know what is on that video."

"But there **is** a video."

He nods. "Yes, there is a video."

"And the Russians have it."

"Yes."

"And they're blackmailing our president."

He sighs. "So it appears."

"But it's not a sex tape of the president with Diana?"

Andrei shakes his head. "I am told it is not. I am told that it is worse than that. I am told that it contains highly sensitive content."

Worse? **Worse** than a sex tape of the president and his girlfriend?

"Why did you 'predict' all this stuff about the Russians, Andrei? Why did you tell me about their plans?"

Again, Andrei cranes his head upward, with some difficulty. He seems surprised that I don't know the answer, as if it's obvious. "I told you because I'm a patriot, Benjamin. I'm a patriot with every fiber of my being. A patriot does what is best for his country, not what is best for its leader."

True enough. Spoken like someone who grew up in a totalitarian regime.

"So you think this is personal to the president. Not classified information, like nuclear codes or photos of undercover spies, but something personal."

Andrei lifts his bony shoulders. "That is my suspicion," he says. "And if I knew that to be true—if I knew what it was, and it was just something embarrassing to the president, I would tell you. In fact, if I knew that, I would tell every newspaper in the world. I would do whatever I could to make that information public, to release the United States from this blackmail scheme. Even if it landed me in prison.

"But I **don't** know, Benjamin. So if I went to the newspapers, I could not speak with any specificity. I would be easily discredited. You can imagine the government's response—'A sick old man who is hallucinating, senile,' this sort of nonsense."

He's right about that. Our government is good at plausible deniability. And at smearing anyone who gets in its way.

"The best I could do, Benjamin, was to arm you with some information and hope that you would be able to learn more than I could."

"Me? Why me?"

With a frail hand, Andrei reaches out and grabs my wrist. "You are far more talented than you've ever given yourself credit for, Benjamin. You've had to overcome challenges that would have broken most people. You are resourceful and determined and, in my judgment, brilliant. You've found some way to bury the demons of your childhood and find some measure of—I don't know if it's happiness. But some equilibrium. You've managed to avoid the Russians' attempts to kill you, figure out the existence of the video, and strike fear into the heart of the Oval Office."

I squat down so that I'm facing Andrei face-to-face.

"Why did they kill Jonathan Liu?" I ask.

Andrei playfully slaps my cheek. "My friend, surely you do not need me to solve that riddle."

I think about it for a second. "The Chinese," I say. "The Chinese. They don't want the Russians to rebuild the Soviet empire. If the Russians take over the former satellites, especially Kazakhstan, they'll be a threat to China." I look at Andrei. "The Chinese know what the Russians are up to, don't they?"

"I suspect they do," he says.

"Sure. Of course. They want a copy of the video, too. But not to blackmail the United States. They want to make it **public.** They want to stop the Russians from blackmailing us, so we'll stand up to Russia's aggression on behalf of NATO."

And **that** explains why the Russians

killed Jonathan Liu. They can't let the Chinese get that video. Their extortion doesn't work if the video becomes public.

"And why **me**?" I ask. "Why have they been trying to kill **me** ever since Diana disappeared? Why do they think I, of all people, would have a copy of the video?"

Andrei breaks eye contact, lost in thought. He seems troubled. He seems not to know the answer. But trying to read Andrei is like trying to solve a Rubik's cube.

Yesterday, I told Alexander Kutuzov I had a copy of the video. But they'd been trying to kill me for a week before that. They've thought that all along. I only told them something they already believed.

"Either the Russians think you have the tape," Andrei says, "or they think you're trying to get hold of it."

That makes sense. Either way, I'm a threat to the Russians.

Which means there's only one way I can end this.

"I have to figure out what's on that video and make it public," I say. "It's the only way to stop the Russians."

"And the only way to save yourself," he adds.

That would be nice, too.

I get out of my crouch and sit down flat on the porch. The sun is falling, and with it the temperature. In a few weeks the colors will change, and the air will turn brisk.

"So what's worse than a sex tape of the president?" I ask.

CHAPTER 92

I leave Andrei's house tied up in knots. I've now confirmed that there's a video, which is crucial. But I've also confirmed that it's not a sex tape of the president and his mistress, which is just as significant. And that means I screwed up this morning, when I tried to bluff Craig Carney. And it's going to cost me.

Carney's smart, very smart. When I told him I had a copy of the video, he challenged me. He asked me what was on the video. And I gave the wrong answer. So now he knows I'm bluffing.

The video, I now see, has been my chit

all along. Carney's been pressuring me in every way imaginable—threats of prosecution, threats against Anne, shutting down my website, and freezing my assets—but he hasn't gone all the way and let the local cops arrest me yet. Of course not. Because he was afraid I had a copy of the video and I'd make it public. He was never sure if I had that video.

But now he knows I don't.

I've been playing checkers while the CIA has been playing chess. And now we're at checkmate. Craig Carney has no fear of me now.

I call my lawyer, Eddie Volker. I assume he's been trying to reach me but doesn't know how.

"Ben, I've been trying to reach you," he says when he answers. "I've got some bad news."

I take a long breath and look to the sky. "The Metropolitan Police Department has issued a warrant for my arrest," I say.

"Yeah, that's right. How did you know?"

"Let me guess," I say. "It was issued about, oh, ten thirty or so this morning."

"That's right. How did you know that?"

Because I got off the phone with Carney about ten fifteen this morning. He wasted no time, I see. As soon as he realized I didn't have the video, he pulled the trigger. He took the leash off of Detective Liz Larkin.

"You have to turn yourself in," says Eddie. "Every cop in this town is hunting for you. You're a cop killer to them, Ben. You don't stand a chance."

CHAPTER 93

Having missed my planned meeting with Sean Patrick Riley, I call him to reschedule. We agree to meet at a bar and grill on Rhode Island Avenue. This better be good, because I'm living on borrowed time now. It's one thing to hide from a handful of Russians who are positioned around the capital hoping to spot me. It's another to be on the radar of every MPD cop who patrols the capital on foot or by car.

Riley's already sitting in the dining area munching on some chicken wings when I arrive. (God, that looks great—eating pub food and having a few beers, as though you don't have a care in the world.) Like most restaurants, this one seems to be full of people in a relatively festive mood, albeit tempered somewhat by the events of this afternoon. The networks have been covering the explosion on 22nd Street nonstop since it happened, and most people are calling it an aborted terrorist attack on the White House.

"Think it was the Muslims?" Sean asks me when I join him in the booth. That's the big question everyone's asking—who were these guys in the SUV? The knee-jerk reaction is that they were Islamic terrorists from Asia or Africa, but eyewitness accounts make them for Caucasian, which cuts against the idea of Islamic radicals, though it doesn't exclude the possibility.

No one will ever know the answer to that question, because with the amount of explosives they detonated, the Russians' bodies are in hundreds of pieces.

"Let's do this, Sean," I say.

Riley brandishes a piece of paper. (I'm not in the mood for a debate. I say you can brandish paper.) "An e-mail that Nina Jacobs received. Dated August fourth. This is the week before Nina had her mail and newspaper stopped."

I look at the paper Riley hands me:

From: "Diana M. Hotchkiss" <ladydiana @intercast.com>
To: "Nina Jacobs" <jacobsnina@metoo .com>
Just checking in!

Hey, Kiddo . . . just touching base. All set for next week? It's a really big favor and IOU big! Please feel free to eat whatever in the fridge, use the landline, wear ANY of my shoes, and of course don't forget to feed Cinnamon!

xxoo

Di (p.s. I know this all seems kind of weird but will explain later!)

"Bizarre," says Riley. "I mean, Diana Hotchkiss is the suicide, the one who jumped off her balcony. From this, it sure looks like Nina was house-sitting for her."

Yeah, it sure does. I figured that some way, somehow, somebody got Nina into Diana's apartment and got her to dress in Diana's clothes. What I didn't know was who. Who set up Nina? Who talked her into doing this, suspecting—or maybe even **knowing**—that it would get Nina killed?

And now I know. It was Diana. Diana set up her friend Nina.

So I guess I didn't know Diana at all. All that time I spent with her, and it turns out she was a fraud, a complete mystery to me.

"I have a theory," says Riley. "Want to hear it?"

CHAPTER 94

I try to maintain an even keel, keep my composure, as it dawns on me what I have now learned about Diana. It's almost incomprehensible that she'd set up her friend Nina like that.

Maybe she didn't. Maybe someone else sent this e-mail from her account. I don't know. But this can't be. I couldn't have been **that** wrong about Diana—

"So do you want to hear my theory or not?" asks Sean Patrick Riley.

I left Diana's apartment just before ten, as she had requested of me over the phone earlier that day. But I just barely

made that deadline, having been a bit dis-
tracted by Diana's lingerie and sex toys.
Nina Jacobs must have gotten off the elevator and walked into the apartment only
minutes, if not seconds, after I scooted out
the fire escape.

And someone—our government, the
Russians, the Chinese, take your pick—
pushed Nina off the balcony only minutes
later.

"Sean," I say.

"It's a crazy theory," Sean says.

"No, I—"

"Maybe it wasn't Diana Hotchkiss who
fell from that balcony. Maybe it was **Nina.**
Maybe Diana Hotchkiss set up Nina to be
there so—"

"Sean, listen to me. Listen to me carefully. Go home."

He draws back. "Come again?"

"Go back to Chicago. You've done your
part. This is enormously helpful. This proves
what I've thought all along."

"What have you thought all along?" he
demands. "What the fuck is this about?"

I sigh. "This is about an SUV detonating
today. This is about a conspiracy and
cover-up all the way to the Oval Office."

Sean Patrick Riley watches me for a long time before he speaks. "The fuck it is."

"No foolin', Sean. Diana was in the middle of something big. SUVs-exploding-in-the-capital big. Poor Nina was an unknowing pawn in a high-stakes game. I think Nina is lying in a morgue with a tag on her toe that says 'Diana Hotchkiss.' And as much as I don't want to believe it, the evidence you just gave me doesn't lie. She was wearing Diana's clothes and staying in her house. She was pretending to be Diana, Sean. She was set up. And you've just helped me prove it."

It takes him a while, but even a skeptical ex-cop like him can't deny the e-mails he himself found. E-mails that were carefully deleted, that couldn't even be discovered in the e-mail program's trash. E-mails that were deleted by a pro, and that could only be discovered by a fellow expert that Sean hired to conduct a forensic examination of Nina's computer.

"So that's why you wanted me to do the forensic review of her computer," he mumbles. "You figured there might be something like this on here."

Right. Hooray for me. "People will kill you

for knowing this," I say. "So go back to Chicago. In a couple of days, this will all be over, one way or the other. If I don't survive this, then run with what you know. You can wait that long, can't you? Nina's not going to get any deader."

He argues the point. I don't know if I've convinced him or not. But I do know that I have to get out of here, separate myself from him, and keep on the move.

CHAPTER 95

I leave Sean at the table and pass through the bar on my way out. I stop to take a gander at the bar's television to get the latest updates. It's the only thing the networks are covering.

The news reports are saying at least six are dead from the blast and dozens injured. Four cops and two Secret Service agents, their faces plastered one by one on the television screen, killed in the line of duty. That makes seven law enforcement officials dead, including Ellis Burk. Add in Jonathan Liu, Diana's brother, Randy, and Nina Jacobs, and we're at an even ten.

When is it going to stop?

I fish into my gym bag for one of my prepaid phones. I get it out and start to dial when my eyes wander back up to the screen.

Breaking News, the screen says, and I brace myself for yet more casualties from the explosion today.

But it's not about the SUV. It's not about what happened in the capital today. It's breaking news on the international front.

Take a guess.

Threatened by the discovery of a Georgian spy in their country, and days later by an attempt on the Russian prime minister's life by a Georgian operative, the Russians have begun amassing thousands of troops and tanks on their border with Georgia.

The UN is convening an emergency session of the Security Council. China's ambassador to the UN is calling for multilateral talks and urging NATO to join in.

Then President Blake Francis is on the screen, standing next to his wife, the wooden princess Libby Rose, in what looks like a taped recording from earlier today in the Rose Garden. The sound is muted but the closed-captioning is on.

Our president is talking about Russia's right of self-defense, and how NATO must proceed with caution in the face of Georgia's provocation. Russia, like any other country, he says, cannot be asked to sit idly by when threatened.

"Shit," I say to nobody. It's happening. The Russians are moving forward, and we're lying down and letting it happen. Once we let the first country fall, it will be harder and harder to justify stopping their continued aggression.

I'm running out of time.

I walk outside and dial Anne Brennan on my cell. The next twenty-four hours are crucial for the Russians. Once they invade the first country, there may be no turning back for the United States. And the Russians know that. They'll be desperate to stop me. SUVs shooting up the capital are probably out now, after today. But finding someone I care about and threatening her? Very much **in.** I don't think they know about Anne, but I can't count on what I **think.**

And I admit, I just want to hear her voice. I could use a bit of comfort right now. I can smell her hair whenever I inhale. If circumstances were different, if I could even spend one more night with her—

The phone picks up before one full ring. Weird.

"Hello, yes, hello?" Anne says in a hurried, startled voice.

"Anne, it's Ben."

"Oh—oh, Ben. You're—you're not **here,** are you?"

My spidey sense kicks up. Something in her voice, in her reaction upon hearing **my** voice. And how she answered so quickly. She was expecting someone else. And she sounds worried that I might be showing up at her place.

I decide to play this safe. "No, I'm staying in Maryland tonight," I say.

"Oh, okay." She takes a breath. A breath of . . . relief? What's going on? Why doesn't she want me to come to her house?

"You okay, Anne?"

"Oh, yeah. I'm . . . I'm fine. I'm . . . I was just dozing off. I'm tired. I need sleep."

She was tired, but she answered the phone before one full ring? She doesn't sound tired. Not one bit. She sounds nervous. Is someone there with her?

"Well, no problem," I say. "Get some sleep. I'll call you tomorrow."

"Okay. Good. Tomorrow would be great, thanks."

I punch out my phone and a wave of fear passes through me. She didn't want me to come over. And she didn't want to say why.

Anne's in danger.

I rush back into the restaurant. Sean Patrick Riley has just ordered another Budweiser. He looks up and appraises me as though I'm about to kiss him.

"You sure you want in on this?" I say.

He wipes his mouth with a napkin. "I went from twenty years on the force on the south side of Chicago to chasing around cheating husbands. I could stand a little excitement."

"I need help, Sean. This could be dangerous. This isn't a joke. You got a gun?"

"Course I do."

"You got cameras? Zoom lenses, that sort of thing?"

"In my car."

"Where's your car?"

He throws down his napkin. "Right outside."

"Then giddyap, cowboy," I say. "I need you ten minutes ago."

CHAPTER 96

Anne's place is a straight shot up 15th Street, only about half a mile or so. We reach the intersection with T Street in the time it would take me to unlock the chain on my Rock-hopper.

Sean pulls over on the west side of the street. This is all residential housing around here, so we got lucky with the spot.

He hands me an earbud. "Stick this in your ear."

Check. Like Jennifer Garner in that old **Alias** show.

"Now put this around your neck."

"What is this?"

"It's a Bluetooth loop. You ever sync a Bluetooth up to your cell phone? Same thing, but put the loop over your head like you're wearing a necklace and run the cord under your shirt."

I do what Sean says. He hooks himself up the same way. He's excited about this. This is fun for him. I wish it were for me.

"Now hook the plug into your cell phone. I'll do it, too. Then we can talk."

I look over at Sean. "Remind me never to piss you off."

He checks his revolver. "Sorry I don't have a spare gun."

I wouldn't know how to use it, anyway. I'd probably shoot my dick off.

"I'm going to scout the place first," I say.

"I'm the one with the gun, sport. I'll go."

But I'm the one with the guilty conscience. Enough people have died for something that's my problem. If I can help it, I'm going to be in the line of fire before him.

"I'm going." I push open the door and step outside. Sean calls my cell phone and we do a test. We're hooked up.

"Hey," he says to me before I shut the door. "When I was a cop, we had a saying. 'Don't get dead.'"

I look at him, waiting for more. "That's it? 'Don't get dead'?"

"That's it."

"Good advice, Sean." And I'm on the move toward Anne's house. I cut around the block to come up through the alley.

Alias is my favorite of Jennifer Garner's roles, though she was excellent in **Juno.** Didn't love **Daredevil** other than the motorcycle, but she was smokin' as Elektra.

When I'm halfway there, Sean's voice comes through my ear. "You said she answered real quick, like? And she sounded like she was expecting someone else?"

"Right," I say as I jog toward the alley leading to Anne's back door and fence.

I approach the back alley cautiously, my heart in my throat, moving as silently as I possibly can, walking on tiptoes and stopping after every single step to listen.

I can see her place right now . . .

Can anyone see me?

I jump at the sight of movement in the back of Anne's apartment, the kitchen. Can't make out the features, just a figure quickly passing by the shade over the window. Was it Anne? But if she were being held by somebody in there, she wouldn't be walking around freely.

I move a few more steps. I'm hiding behind someone's garage now. It's the last structure between me and the fence at the rear of Anne's building, about ten yards away.

Garner played slutty pretty damn well in the **Arthur** remake. I love it when actresses decide to branch out and play slutty. See Jennifer Aniston in **Horrible Bosses**—

Focus, you moron. Once I move past this garage, I'm exposed, out in the open. The lighting isn't great back here, but it's good enough. If anyone's looking, they'll see me.

Here goes nothing.

I step out from behind the garage and tiptoe toward the fence, feeling as visible as a neon sign. If they're looking, I'm a goner, so my money has to be on them not keeping a vigilant watch. They shouldn't be expecting me, after all. I told Anne over the phone that I was miles away in Maryland.

I walk along the brick wall on the side of

her building. Anne has a window in her bedroom. The shade is drawn, but there's no light behind it. That room is dark.

I silently creep forward. There is light coming from the front of the house. The shade on the window isn't drawn. If I stand on the balls of my feet, I might be able to see in. But will **they** see **me**?

Only one way to find out. I slowly rise from my crouch.

"So that sounds more like she's waiting to hear from someone."

I jump at Sean's voice in my ear. I'm not used to this spy stuff.

"You almost gave me a heart attack!" I whisper.

"I'm saying, it sounds like she's waiting for someone, either for a call—"

"Or for someone to drop by in person. Good point. Watch for cars, okay? Any car would have to travel north up Fifteenth, past you. Got your camera ready?"

"Oh, yeah."

I take another breath. I stand up slowly, raise up on my tiptoes—

"She's by the window."

I jump back down. "Jesus, Sean. **What?**"

"She's by the front window, looking out

over Fifteenth. I'm out of my car and I got an angle with my zoom lens. The lady's looking out the window. She's waiting for someone, Ben. Believe me. She's looking down the street. She's waiting for a car."

Then so will I. But not here in the alley. Too conspicuous.

I do a crab walk forward a few steps toward 15th Street, so I can see the front yard of the building next door to Anne's without revealing myself to Anne. As I remembered, there's shrubbery bordering the small parcel of grass in front of that apartment building. Most of the buildings around here have some kind of small grassy lawn, and most of them put up some shrubbery or garden on it. There isn't a whole lot of cascading acreage here in the U Street Corridor, so any plot of grass, no matter how tiny, usually gets dolled up.

That shrubbery isn't much, but it's about three feet high, which should be enough. If someone's really looking for me, they might spot me. It's a risk. But hey, I left risky back in the dust long ago. I've been walking a tightrope for days.

"Tell me when she's not standing by the front window," I say. "I'm going to stake out a spot, but she'll see me from the front window."

A pause, but not a very long one.

"Go. Go fast. She's pacing around, and she'll be back at the window soon."

I dart from my position and almost dive behind the shrubbery next door. I must have looked ridiculous doing so. And I probably look ridiculous now.

"Nice swan dive," says Sean.

But I made it.

Now let's see who comes a-callin' on Anne Brennan.

CHAPTER 97

Several cars pass by on 15th. Each time, Sean signals me. Each time, my pulse ratchets up. Each time, the car keeps going—false alarm.

The winner of the surprisingly-good-at-slutty thing is Glenn Close—not on any-one's list of supermodels, but **Dangerous Liaisons** and **Fatal Attraction**? Seriously. I think it's her cheekbones.

"Maybe she's just waiting for friends to hit the clubs," says Sean in my earbud.

"No, this is no social call. She was too nervous," I say into the grass. I'm still face-down, afraid to move lest I attract Anne's attention. But I'm obscured behind the shrubbery, I think, and, more important, I'm north of her and she's looking south, waiting for some car to arrive from the only direction it could travel on this one-way street.

Anne Hathaway should try slutty. She's done sexy but not slut—

"Coming your way, coming your way. A black sedan. It's moving slowly."

Okay, focus, Ben. A black sedan. Maybe a government vehicle.

Maybe a billionaire's vehicle.

"She sees it, too. She's grabbing her purse. Now she's heading for the door."

I rise slowly, sitting on my knees, using my hands to part the shrubs and get a look at the street. "Tell me if I'm sticking up over the hedge," I say.

"You're good, you're still hidden."

"Use that camera, Sean. Snap everything you can. I'm not sure I'll have a view."

"Will do."

The good news for me is that this parcel of grass where I'm hiding is elevated, raised off the sidewalk, so I can see over the car parked outside Anne's building.

I see the black sedan pull up by Anne's building. I listen to the hum of an engine idling. There's absolutely no reason why anyone in that sedan would be looking in my direction, and according to Sean they wouldn't be able to see me anyway, but none of that stops my heartbeat from kicking into full throttle.

I hear Anne's front door open, then the **clack** of her shoes bounding down the small set of stairs.

The sedan's rear passenger door opens and, as I'd hoped, the overhead dome light comes on, bathing the interior of the vehicle in light. A man in a dark suit gets out and frisks Anne before she gets in the car. Then she almost dives into the backseat, greeting the person sitting back there with a full-on, passionate kiss.

Anne Brennan is kissing someone, and it's not me.

"Jesus Christ, is that who I think it is?" Sean cries.

The guy in the dark suit closes the rear door and gets in the front passenger seat. A moment later, the interior light evaporates and the car is dark again.

"Should I follow the car?" Sean asks.

I let out a breath, my chest burning. "No," I say.

The car drives off briskly. I release the shrubs.

And my brain releases a flurry of thoughts.

Operation Delano . . . worse than a sex tape of the president . . . Delano . . .

Shit. Of course. I've been so stupid.

"Ben, did you see inside that car? Is that who I think—"

"Yes," I say, falling down to my haunches. "That's who you think it is."

CHAPTER 98

Sean Patrick Riley and I sit in his rental car outside my fleabag hotel. It's been three hours since we left Anne Brennan's house. Three hours for me to process what I saw in the back of that sedan.

And three hours to figure out what to do next.

"You're sure about this plan?" Sean asks me.

I sigh. "No, but I can't think of any other. I have to do something."

"No, you don't," Sean says. "Who put you in charge of saving the world? If I were you, I'd get as much money as I could out of that Russian billionaire, cut whatever deal you need to cut with the feds, and move to some island. But that's just me."

The guy makes a good point.

"And this whole plan of yours depends on the video," Sean says.

"Right. Now that I know what's on it, I can make this plan work."

He grunts with disapproval. "You mean now that you **think** you know what's on the video, you **think** you can make this plan work."

That's a bit more accurate, yes.

"I mean, you're just making an educated guess, Ben. And if you're wrong, you're basically fucked."

"Just worry about your phone call," I say, changing the subject. "You're sure you have the phone number?"

He groans. "I do. I've already read it back to you."

He's not used to someone giving him directions. That's probably one of the reasons he stopped being a cop and became his own boss as a private eye.

"And you'll use an untraceable phone," I say.

He waves me off. "Yes. Yes, already.

Don't worry, Ben. I'm capable of making one damn phone call."

I nod. We are quiet for a moment. At least Sean seems to be enjoying the excitement. Me, I have acid burning a hole in my stomach.

"If your plan doesn't work," Sean informs me, "you're done. They'll arrest you and bury you in a hole. You can make all kinds of wild accusations, but you won't be able to prove them."

All that is true, of course.

"And that assumes you survive, the odds of which are fifty-fifty at best, in my opinion."

Never tell me the odds, Han Solo said in **Star Wars** as he navigated around the oncoming asteroids.

"Then my plan better work," I say.

CHAPTER 99

I stretch my arms to release some nervous tension. I'm in my boxers, staring at a stained wall in my dingy hotel room, holding in my hand a cell phone that Sean Patrick Riley gave me last night, about to make a phone call that could change everything.

The calm before the storm. Rocky, looking into the mirror before he entered the ring against Apollo Creed. Tom Cruise, before he cross-examined Jack Nicholson at the court-martial. Mikey in **Swingers**, before he summoned the courage to call that girl from the bar, Nikki, which ended in Mikey leaving her seven or eight voice mails in a row, each one more disastrous than the previous one, before she picked up and told him to drop dead.

Okay, maybe that last one is less inspirational. But notice there are no presidents in there. Not since Detective Liz Larkin said that I learned all that presidential trivia as a way of bonding with Father. That isn't true. I just thought it was interesting information. I wasn't bonding with Father. Screw him. I don't need him. I've done just fine without him. I'm never going to recite another piece of presidential trivia as long as I live. No more poems they liked or shoes they wore or dogs they owned.

Never again. Write it down. The only president I'm going to worry about is the one occupying the White House right now, who has breached his oath of office and is fucking with my world.

I haven't slept, in case you hadn't noticed. I gave up trying last night about four in the morning, and, unable to leave this hotel—with police all over the capital hunting me—I have done nothing but pace the floor in this tiny, dirty room for hours on end. It's probably a good rehearsal for federal prison, which, if this call doesn't go well, is probably the best outcome I can expect. The worst is a coffin.

Game on, Ben. Don't fuck this up.

I pick up the prepaid phone. I dial the number and place the phone to my ear.

One ring. Two. My empty stomach churns on adrenaline. My hand can hardly hold the phone.

Don't screw this up . . . don't be like Mikey—

"Hello." The word is delivered in an icy, flat tone, dripping, of course, with the thick accent.

I take one deep breath. "Mr. Kutuzov, it's Ben Casper."

"Ah, Mr. Casper." **Meester Kahsper.**

"We have some business to discuss," I say.

"Do we, now? I must tell you, Mr. Casper, that I am having my doubts about you. When you first contacted me, I assumed that you had come into possession of a very important item. Now I am not so sure."

"Well, you should be sure, Alex. I have the video. And I have a digital file rigged to be e-mailed to every news outlet in North America if anything happens to me."

"I see," he says with amusement coloring his tone. Like he doesn't believe me.

"I want twenty million dollars wired to a specific account, Alex. And when I receive it, you have my assurance that the video will remain confidential."

Kutuzov clucks his tongue. "No, no, Mr. Casper. I think not. My friend, I know you are trying to find this video. But I now believe that you have been unable to obtain it. I believe you were—bluffing, as you Americans say? You were bluffing me previously."

That's true. I was. And I'm bluffing now, too.

"I'm not bluffing now," I say.

"Then tell me what is on the video," he says. "Prove to me that you have a copy."

That's basically the same thing Craig Carney said to me yesterday, and I failed the test. I hope I pass this time. Because if I don't, I have no way out.

"It's a sex video of Diana Hotchkiss with the First Lady, Libby Rose Francis," I say.

And I hold my breath. This is the moment. Right or wrong. Live or die. It sure would be nice if I actually had that damn video file.

Kutuzov releases a sigh.

"Give me your account number," he says, sounding like he's lost a little bit of the confidence in his voice.

CHAPTER 100

I pace the room another half hour. My legs are unsteady and my limbs are tingling with dread.

Give me your account number, Kutuzov said.

So this time, I guessed right about the video. The clues were there for me all along. Operation Delano. I was right that the original Operation Delano was a plan to blackmail President Franklin Delano Roosevelt. But I was wrong about the reason.

I forgot about his wife, Eleanor. The rumors, to this day, are unconfirmed, but in many circles it's accepted as fact that

Eleanor Roosevelt was a lesbian. Stalin must have heard those rumors, too. He was trying to dig up proof that FDR's wife was gay so he could use it as leverage at the Yalta summit—as blackmail.

In the 1940s, that would probably be damaging information.

(For the record, this doesn't count against my moratorium on presidential trivia.)

Anyway, fast-forward almost seventy years, and it's Operation Delano 2.0. The Russians get proof that Libby Rose Francis has a girlfriend named Diana Hotchkiss. In this day, would it be a damaging political scandal for the president to admit that his wife is a lesbian? Haven't we come further than that as a nation?

Apparently, President Francis doesn't want to be the test case.

And who knows what's on that video? If it's graphic sex—I pause here to recall all Diana's sex toys in her bedroom closet—it would be enough to scare any politician. That, I assume, is the straw that broke the camel's back from the president's point of view. He couldn't survive a video making its way around the Internet of his wife doing kinky things with another woman.

I jump at the sound of a loud rap on my door. My pulse explodes into a pounding throb. **Who even knows I'm here?** I search for a means of escape—

Suddenly there came a tapping, as of someone gently rapping, rapping at my chamber door.

There isn't a window in this place, nowhere to hide—

" 'Tis some visitor," I muttered, "tapping at my chamber door; only this, and nothing more"—

"It's Sean!" he calls out. "It's Sean, Ben."

I put my hands on my knees and wait for my breathing to resume. Deep breaths, Ben. Deep breaths.

"Hey," he says when I let him in. He takes a moment to appraise me. "What were you saying just now?"

"I wasn't saying anything."

"Something—it sounded like that Edgar Allan Poe poem. 'The Raven.'"

I take a breath. "I said that out loud?"

"You did." He puts a hand on my shoulder. "Did you sleep last night?"

"Not a wink." I close and lock the door behind him. "You've got an untraceable phone to make your call?"

"Yes. For God's sake, how many times are you going to ask me?"

"That's a big help to me, Sean. Really."

"Think nothing of it." Sean takes a look around my fleabag hotel room and probably thinks, well, nothing of it.

"So?" he asks. "Did you guess right about the video?"

"Yep."

"Jesus. A sex video of Diana Hotchkiss and the First Lady?"

I nod my head.

"And you figured it out just by what you saw last night in that car?"

"I should have figured it out long ago," I say. "But yeah, last night did it for me. And your photos from your zoom lens are even better than the view I had."

He nods with pride. "Yeah, I got a nice, tight shot of that kiss. That was no friends' kiss, either."

He pulls a copy of that photo out of his bag. He showed it to me on his camera last night, but it's the first time I've seen a printout of the photo.

A close-up photo of Anne Brennan, sitting inside the black sedan, planting a passionate, urgent kiss on Diana Hotchkiss.

He's right—it's no kiss between friends. It's a kiss of two women who desperately miss each other. A kiss of two women in love.

Oh, Diana. I guess you'll never stop surprising me.

The photo is enough of a close-up that you can't see a whole lot more than their faces, but I saw a flash of orange when I peeked into the car last night, and Sean's photo shows a bit of Diana's clothing as well. And what seals the deal is the glint of steel on her wrist as her hand tenderly caresses Anne's face during the kiss.

Diana was in handcuffs and an orange prison jumpsuit.

Diana wasn't a spy working for the United States. Diana was a traitor. She secretly recorded a sexual romp with the First Lady and was selling it to the highest bidder. My guess is she was working with the Russians initially, but then got greedy and invited the Chinese in, too. Or maybe she was working with both all along, but didn't tell one about the other. Who knows?

The details don't really matter. What matters now is that I have to deal with it, and if I don't do it right, I'll either go to prison for life or be fitted for a coffin.

"What do you need from me now?" Sean asks.

I snap out of my funk. "I just want you to make that phone call."

"Nothing else?"

"Only this and nothing more," I say.

He doesn't know whether to laugh or frown. "You sure you're okay?"

"I don't want you anywhere near the National Mall today, Sean. If this doesn't work out, I'm either dead or under arrest. And you'll be charged as an accessory."

He makes a face. Telling him to stay away from excitement is like telling Kim Kardashian to stay away from a camera.

"All you've done so far is investigate the disappearance of Nina Jacobs," I say. "Nobody can prosecute you for that. If you help me now, you could spend the rest of your life in prison. Or get killed in the crossfire."

I walk over to the door and open it. Enough innocent people have died. If I'm next, so be it. But not Sean.

"Go," I say.

He finally relents. As he passes me on his way out, he flicks the back of his wrist against my chest. "Hey," he says.

"I know," I respond. "Don't get dead."

CHAPTER 101

This ends here.

I always wanted to say something dramatic like that. But guess what? When it's really happening, it ain't so fun.

The sky is a sheet of powder blue this afternoon, bright and serene. I'm dressed in slacks and a button-down shirt I purchased earlier today. My forehead is greasy with sweat, and my shirt is stuck to my chest.

The crowd on the National Mall is swollen today. Could be that it's nearing the end of summer and people are getting in their vacations before school starts in September.

Or maybe there are more "tourists" than usual because some of them aren't tourists at all. I don't kid myself. There are probably dozens of them stationed throughout the Mall, standing at the various memorials, watching my every move, communicating with one another, ready to pull the trigger the moment they see a simple hand gesture or hear a signal uttered into a mouthpiece. I probably have twenty targets on my chest.

And I'm making it easy. I'm standing still, about twenty yards from the Lincoln Memorial, looking over the Mall. This is my favorite place in the capital—it's an inspiration, a tribute to the courage that so many people exhibited in defense of this country and of individual freedoms. This might be the last time I ever see it.

I walk up to the memorial. But I don't see Honest Abe today. A blue tarp has been pulled down over his statue, along with a sign apologizing for the repair work that needs to be done and promising to have the memorial ready soon. It will be a disappointment to sightseers, but there are plenty of other things to see around here.

So I sit alone, halfway up the stairs of the memorial, looking over the reflecting pool and the Washington Monument while parents corral children and snap photos, while sightseers move from one memorial honoring heroic people to another.

Once upon a midday humid, while I
    pondered weak and stupid
Over motives of these gentlemen so
    adversarial,
I sat quietly frustrated as I nervously
    awaited
For a visitor to meet me at this grand
    memorial,
An inquisitor to greet me at this proud
    memorial—
Only this, and nothing more.

Well, a little more than that. The caller I'm awaiting, over whom I'm ruminating, has been long deliberating how to put me at death's door. So after careful preparation, I'll assess the situation, and I'll pray my presentation leads to peace and not to war.

"Hello, Mr. Kutuzov," I say to the smartly dressed man climbing the stairs.

And if I'm wrong, I'm nothing more.

CHAPTER 102

"Hello, Mr. Casper," says Alexander Kutuzov in that rich, textured accent. Up close and personal, he is rougher around the edges than I would have expected. He's dressed in casual billionaire attire—a tailored yellow silk shirt with the cuffs rolled up, trousers, and a thousand-dollar haircut. But his skin is pockmarked and leathery; his nose looks like it's taken a few hits; his forearms are scarred. He has amassed a fortune of more than twenty billion dollars, but he fought some battles getting there.

"You're right on time," I say. "You're a very reliable fellow."

A couple walks up to the monument and looks beyond us, wearing disappointed expressions. The National Mall has all sorts of great things to see, but surely one of their top choices was the statue of Honest Abe, now hidden behind a blue tarp.

"You have chosen a wise location," he says. "Public enough to give you a feeling of safety. And yet private enough, what with the rehabilitation work on Mr. Lincoln, so that nobody is present to overhear our conversation."

Actually, I just wanted a spot where there wouldn't be innocent bystanders.

That and it's close to my next appointment, if I ever make it out of here alive.

"Or perhaps not," he says.

A jolt passes through me. "I don't get your meaning."

He turns and looks at me.

"Are you recording this conversation, Mr. Casper?" he asks.

I try to manage a chuckle, as though I'm amused. It comes out more like I'm clearing my throat. "Why would I record this?

I'm breaking the law by making this deal with you. I could go to prison."

"True," he says. "Still, indulge me and let me check you for a recording device."

"A sign of good faith?" I ask. "Cooperation?"

"You could think of it that way."

"Maybe I'm not feeling cooperative," I say.

Kutuzov gives me an icy smile. "Victor," he says.

Before I can ask him what he means, or who the hell Victor is, I hear a **thwip** pierce the air and the stair immediately below where I'm sitting explodes. I jump up and tumble over to my side. Kutuzov enjoys a good laugh at my expense.

I look back at the place the bullet landed. An inch or two to either side and one of my feet would have been blown off. An inch or two higher and I'd be singing with the Vienna Boys' Choir.

I look around the Mall. I have no idea where that bullet came from. But the sharpshooter's marksmanship is unquestionable. Kutuzov has made his point.

Kutuzov, who has remained as still as a statue this entire time, turns and winks at me. "Perhaps now you are feeling cooperative?"

I nod my head and get to my feet, the adrenaline dump now catching up with me. My heart is pounding, and I'm standing here wondering if I've bitten off more than I can chew. To which the answer is, **Absolutely.**

"You win," I say, raising my trembling hands. "Check me for a wire."

He nods in the direction of the reflecting pool, where a large gentleman suddenly moves toward us.

"My associate will check you," Kutuzov says as he gets up and walks away.

My pulse rockets in my throat. "Where are **you** going?" I ask.

He doesn't answer. He just winks at me and bounds down the stairs.

And his "associate" walks up the steps toward me.

I love you, Mother, I whisper, in case they are the last words I ever speak. But he's not going to kill me, right? Kutuzov wouldn't have come here personally if they were just going to kill me. Right?

He would've just had his sharpshooter, Victor, kill me.

Right?

The man walks up to me and reaches inside his jacket. I hold my breath and savor it. I've come to enjoy breathing. I'd like to keep doing it.

He removes a long wand from his jacket. "Please raise your arms," he says in a thick accent. He reminds me of Drago from **Rocky IV,** only he's not as handsome. But he has a similar sense of humor. I'm waiting for him to say, **I must break you.**

I stand up. He runs the wand over me, with no sound coming back. No hits. No signal coming off me. Then he pats me down for a microphone. I feel like I'm going through airport security in Leningrad. He leaves no corner of my body unchecked. He even checks my prepaid cell phone, which I have turned off. He can search and probe all he wants. He's not going to find anything.

Because I'm not recording this.

He walks past me up the stairs. I turn and watch him as he pulls back the blue tarp covering the monument and checks behind it.

Once he's finished back there, he walks back down the stairs, passing me without comment, and gives a curt nod to Alex Kutuzov. Kutuzov then comes back up the stairs and rejoins me.

"Thank you," he says. "You are quite right. You'd have no sound reason for recording this. But you can understand my concern. I must . . . exercise discretion."

I say, "Of course," like I'm cool. But I'm not. I shouldn't have come here.

"Now," says Kutuzov, "we talk business."

CHAPTER 103

"You are nervous," says Alexander Kutuzov. "You are shaking."

I wish I had a good comeback. That's what Bruce Willis would do. He'd squint and arch his eyebrows and say something icy smooth. "Icy smooth" would be a good slogan for mint gum. I wish I had some gum right now, because it calms me down. You always seem more at ease when you're chewing gum.

"I understand the local police are pursuing you with great urgency," Kutuzov says.

"Yeah, I'm pretty much out of friends," I say.

"Well, you have one now." Kutuzov turns to me. "Miss Diana, she warned me that she had stowed away the video for her reporter friend as a measure of insurance. We looked ourselves and could not find it. We knew you were looking for it, too. And so, Benjamin, you were my adversary. And I took measures to . . . prevent you from obtaining it."

"'Measures,'" I say, mimicking him. "You mean like firing machine guns at me? Are those the 'measures' you mean, Alex? The ones that killed my friend Ellis Burk and six other law enforcement officers?"

He pats my leg. "You are upset. I understand. And if it helps, I apologize. But we must put such matters in the past. You have won, Benjamin. You have found the video despite my efforts to stop you. For this, I congratulate you."

Somehow, the praise doesn't seem so sincere coming from this guy.

"So now, Benjamin, we move on to better times. I want you to be happy, my friend. Happy and wealthy. I trust you have confirmed the wire transfer to the account you specified? Twenty million dollars?"

"Yes," I say. "It will certainly help my quest for happiness."

"Indeed it will. You are being rewarded handsomely to keep this video confidential."

I rub my hands together and try to sound authoritative. When I get nervous, my voice tends to go up an octave, which is pretty much the opposite of cool. "You understand what I said before, Alex. If anything happens to me, if a bullet accidentally finds its way into my skull, that video goes viral. It gets released to every media outlet in North America."

"I do understand that," he says. "You were very clear on the phone this morning. You are very clear now. If I kill you, the video becomes public."

Yeah, but I wanted to say it again. It's what will keep me alive.

"But **you** understand," says Kutuzov, "that if you have second thoughts about our agreement and decide to release this video, you will die a painful death."

I shrug. "Maybe. Maybe not." If I were chewing gum, I'd blow a bubble right now. That would look cool.

I turn toward Kutuzov, who grabs my shirt with one hand and tugs me close to him. I've hit a nerve with him, obviously.

"Listen to me, my little friend. Do not mistake what has happened in the past for the future. You were in hiding, and we lacked adequate time to prepare, and still you only narrowly escaped us. Those bullets that killed your friend the detective were within inches of you, yes? And never again will you have a barricade of police and Secret Service agents saving you. Had they not arrived yesterday, you would have been dead within seconds. Do not mistake what I can do."

Kutuzov releases my shirt with a push. This, and no other reason, is why we are meeting face-to-face. Kutuzov could have wired my money with the tap of a keystroke and flown back to Russia. But he wanted to deliver this message personally. He wants me to live in mortal fear of him.

"That's a helluva way to talk to a friend," I manage.

Kutuzov looks me up and down. "Do you require another reminder from Victor?"

I show my palms, like **stop.** "No, no. You made your point."

After a moment, Kutuzov shows me another cold smile. "Very well, then, Benjamin. If I kill you, you release the video. If you release the tape, I kill you. Mutually assured destruction, yes?"

A term from the Cold War. How appropriate.

Kutuzov claps his hands. "You have heard my warning and I trust you understand its sincerity. So now we are done. Yes?"

Kutuzov offers his hand to me. I don't care what Victor does with his next bullet, I'm not shaking this asshole's hand.

"No," I say.

I just have one thing left to say to him. It's what Robert De Niro said to Dennis Farina at the end of **Midnight Run.** If these are the last words I ever utter—and they might be—I might as well go out quoting one of my all-time favorites.

"There's something I've always wanted to say to you," I tell Kutuzov. "You're under arrest."

CHAPTER 104

Alex Kutuzov's smile evaporates. He jumps to his feet. His mind is racing. He can't reconcile his disbelief with my confidence.

"It's real," I say. "You should say something."

Jay Mohr's line to Tom Cruise in **Jerry Maguire** when he fired him at lunch. Now I'm feeling better.

"You just confessed to being behind the deaths of those cops," I say. "I'm no lawyer, but I'm pretty sure that's a crime in America."

Kutuzov's eyes race over me. "You did not record this conversation," he says, panicking. "We checked. We took every precaution."

"That's true," I concede. "I didn't record this."

"Then it is simply your word against mine."

"It's really just **your** words, Alex."

Kutuzov removes a small handgun from the pocket of his pants. I didn't even know he had it. He points it at me and starts speaking furiously in Russian.

"Sorry, I don't speak Russian," I say, but he's not talking to me.

"Explain this!" he shouts at me. "Or I'll kill you now."

"You shoot me," I say, "and you're liable to lose a lot of those humanitarian awards." Chevy Chase to Joe Don Baker in **Fletch.** This is like a buffet for me.

"**Nyet!**" he shouts, again not to me. But I know a little Russian. His name is Andrei Bogomolov.

"Explain what you say," Kutuzov says to me, sweating now, his hand trembling as he approaches me with the gun aimed at my head.

"I didn't record this," I say again. "But **you** did, Alex."

His eyes widen. He knows I'm right. He's been wearing a wire so his entire team, including the sharpshooter, Victor, can listen in. That's why he had to walk away when his goon checked me for a recording device. The detector would have gone off because of **Alex's** wire, which is probably tucked under his shirt and taped to his chest.

"You've been sending an electronic signal to your people all around the National Mall," I explain. "The Metropolitan Police Department intercepted that signal, Alex. Everything you've said to me is on tape now. Amazing, the technology law enforcement has."

"You're bluffing," he spits, trying to show disdain but unable to hide his growing fear. "These are all lies!"

He's talking to me, but he's really talking to his team listening in. They aren't loyal to him; they're loyal to the Russian government. And Alexander Kutuzov needs to convince them that he hasn't just become a very big liability—a man who is about to be arrested by the DC police, a desperate man who would confess to Operation Delano in order to save himself from the death penalty for killing DC cops.

And then I hear the sweetest sound, the melodious song I've been eagerly awaiting.

The sound of police sirens. Metropolitan Police squad cars racing to the National Mall.

"Here they come," I say. "They recorded the entire thing and now they're here to arrest you. You better start thinking about that deal you're going to cut." I raise my voice for that last comment to make sure his team hears it.

"Lies!" Kutuzov shouts. "The police are after **you,** not me."

"Okay, fine, Alex. Let's both sit here and see which one of us they arrest."

He stares at me. I stare at him. For a glorious moment, it seems that time has stood still.

But it hasn't, and with each passing moment, those sirens get louder.

"Quite the pickle you're in," I note. "You think the cops will take the death penalty off the table if you tell them about Operation Delano?"

And then something happens. Kutuzov touches the earpiece in his left ear and shouts, **"Nyet!"** as the goon by the reflecting pool breaks into a full sprint to the south.

A number of other people on the National Mall—the rest of the Russian team—scatter in various directions. Somebody, somewhere, is ordering the team to disperse.

Kutuzov, in full panic now, waves his pistol around and unleashes a flurry of appeals in Russian. I assume he's telling his team that I'm lying, that I'm bluffing. And he would be correct. The DC cops aren't working with me. They didn't record anything. The only reason they're speeding toward us is an anonymous call that Detective Liz Larkin just received from an untraceable phone used by a crusty Irishman and former Chicago cop informing her that wanted fugitive Benjamin Casper could be found at the Lincoln Memorial. They're coming here to arrest me.

But Kutuzov doesn't know that. And neither does his team. They have to make a decision and make it fast, because those sirens are getting louder.

"I will kill him!" Kutuzov shouts toward the Mall, and I assume he means me, but before he can turn in my direction, another crisp sound pierces the air, another **thwip.** The back of Kutuzov's head explodes and his eye vomits blood. His knees buckle and his body rocks back and forth before he falls, face-first, down the stairs of the Lincoln Memorial, bouncing two or three steps before coming to a rest.

The sirens are upon us now, the sounds of the police vehicles crunching over the grass. I squat down next to Alex Kutuzov's lifeless body.

"That's for Ellis Burk," I say to him. Then I turn and run.

CHAPTER 105

I run with every ounce of my remaining strength to the south, where I find my Triumph parked on Independence Avenue. I can hear the police behind me, but I don't know what they're doing. They've found a man bleeding out on the steps of the Lincoln Memorial and, for all they know, it's the guy they were coming to arrest—me. I hope that will make them pause for at least a minute or two.

I'll take any delay I can get. I hop on the Triumph, look to my left, and see uniformed officers pointing at me and shouting. The police vehicles won't be far behind. I kick the Triumph to life and bolt onto Independence heading east, navigating between cars under the blanket of the overhanging trees, the joggers and walkers to the north and south paying me little attention on a beautiful summer afternoon. I'd love to check my watch for the time, but there's nothing I can do about it now. I tried to time things out as best I could, but if I didn't, it's too late to fix it now.

I hear the sirens behind me as I race the Triumph onto the Kutz Bridge, which carries me over the Tidal Basin. They're probably wondering where I'm going so they can roadblock me up ahead. (Is **roadblock** a verb? It should be.) Anyway, I have many options, but at the fork with Maine Avenue, I stay left on Independence.

They're not far behind now, but at the intersection ahead, I skid into a sudden left turn onto 15th Street—sudden for them, though it was always my plan. I draw some horns but complete the turn and hope I've left a mess behind me.

Any delay doesn't last long. The cars in the opposite lane of 15th, southbound, pull over, and one of the squad cars catches up to me and pulls up alongside me, like when Chevy Chase was being chased in **Fletch** and he said, **Hey, Fred, how's the herpes?** but I don't think these cops would appreciate the humor and I have no intention of having a conversation, so—

I jump the curb, jump the tiny chain-linked gateway, and drive onto the pedestrian walkway, which is, thankfully, empty, and then cut onto the park grass to shortcut a right turn onto Madison Drive. (**Shortcut** might not be a verb, either.) The cops can't follow my route by car, and Madison is one-way going west, so they'll have to travel against the grain to chase me—just like when I was riding that bicycle, only this time, I have a little more horsepower propelling me.

It's a short jaunt on Madison, avoiding cars coming directly toward me and unhappy to see me, before I hit 14th Street, but I'm not going to bother with a turn at that congested intersection. Instead I turn left early, jumping the curb again and heading north up the sidewalk, the Smithsonian looming across the street from me. They've got a new exhibit featuring photographs of

Union generals from the Civil War I've been meaning to check out. Maybe now's not the right time.

I hear sirens behind me, the squealing of tires, and I look back and see a squad car bearing down on me on the sidewalk. I have just enough of a lead to beat it to the next intersection, which is all I need.

I see a lull in traffic and jump the curb, cross the street, and hop onto the opposite sidewalk. I skid to a stop at the intersection, jump off my Triumph, and break into a headlong sprint.

Running to my own funeral, I'm afraid. But I'm out of options. And if this is the end, I'm going out on my terms.

CHAPTER 106

The Mellon Auditorium, part of the Federal Triangle on Constitution Avenue, is a magnificent neoclassical structure built in the 1930s that served as the site for FDR's reinstatement of the draft, the signing of the NATO treaty in the 1940s, and the signing of the NAFTA treaty in the mid-'90s. This afternoon, it's the location for an awards ceremony hosted by the Boy Scouts of America.

I cross Constitution on foot and rush up the stairs, brandishing—yes, brandishing—my press credentials to the dark-suited man at the gate. He waves me past and I walk through a metal detector unscathed. I jog through the lobby and head toward the auditorium as I hear a ruckus behind me, shouting from outside. Cops, I assume, having spotted me entering the building. The man who just let me pass—a member of the Secret Service—is probably just beginning to realize that the cops might be talking about me.

I slow my pace as I approach the two Secret Service agents manning the door, keeping those press credentials out for them to see.

"Hi, Ben Casper, **Capital Beat,**" I say. "I'm running late."

The agent looks over the list to find my name. He won't find it.

I turn back to look at the commotion as the cops reach the door.

"Oh, my God—does that guy have a **gun**?" I say to the agents, motioning back behind me to the front door.

The Secret Service agent blocking the auditorium door reaches into his jacket and takes a single step forward. I quickly push him aside and burst through the door into the huge, gilded auditorium.

"Alabama! Alabama!" the agent behind

me cries out, which must be the current code word for "emergency."

Inside, it's all blue and red—the American flag, the Boy Scouts' crest, the series of tables set up for a crowd of thousands, and the president and other dignitaries on the stage at the far end. The president's authoritative voice echoes throughout the chamber.

I'm in full sprint mode. Secret Service agents from every corner of the room descend upon me. The president stops his address as agents to each side of him grab him and pull him down. I run down the center aisle as far as I think I can get and start shouting.

"Mr. President!" I yell out. "The Russian government is blackmailing you into letting them invade Georgia! The Russians are blackmailing you and the American people deserve to know!" The first agent to reach me tries to bulldoze me, but I juke him and miss the brunt of his tackle. I fall to the floor but keep my head up and shout, "I'm Ben Casper of **Capital Beat**! I have proof the Russians are blackmailing the president! I have proof and the government knows it!"

And then they pile on, one black-suited G-man after another, and I'm at the bottom of a rugby scrum. The entire room is in chaos, people jumping from their seats, somebody from the government taking the mike and appealing for calm. I can't even see the stage in the front of the auditorium now, though I assume the president is no longer there. He's probably not in the room at all.

"I have proof!" I shout. "I have proof and the president knows it!"

And then, before you can say **My name is Ben Casper, and my life is over,** the agents lift me off the ground and carry me horizontally out of the room. I keep shouting out the same phrases, "I'm Ben Casper" and "I have proof," not so much for the scoutmasters in the room but for the reporters, most of whom know me and presumably have some level of respect for me—at least enough to allow me to dominate the headlines on this event. At least enough to make them ask questions. At least enough to make it difficult for the US government to sweep this all under the rug.

And that, in the end, is the best I can do. I don't have the video, but I can accuse the administration publicly and hope it's enough to stop what's going on. It's too late to stop what's going to happen to me.

My name is Ben Casper, and my life is over.

CHAPTER **107**

Once upon an evening late,
　　having signed away my fate,
I reluctantly await my ruthless
　　punishment's arrival.
I have sorely taxed the patience
　　of the governmental agents;
I have severed my relations with
　　those holding my survival
In their hands, for I depend on two
　　conditions, truth and honor—
Only that, and nothing more.

The room is nothing but gray walls, a
table, and two chairs. I was placed in here

by two members of the Secret Service who didn't say a word to me and pushed me through the door before locking it closed.

It's chilly in here, but otherwise I'm comfortable—relaxed in a way that's reminiscent of the way I felt at the end of final exams (though I don't recall any final exams where people shot at me). I can't change anything now. All the running and hiding and searching and strategizing is over. I did it. There's no taking back what I said. I've given up all leverage with Craig Carney. He is free to bring the full weight of the federal government down on me.

But I got a few things in return. I got payback against a Russian billionaire and justice for Ellis Burk. I got twenty millions dollars that, unbeknownst to said billionaire, was wired into an account for families of law enforcement officers killed in the line of duty. And I stopped the Russians from controlling our foreign policy.

I've sat in here for three hours. During that time I've made some hard decisions. The first is that Ben Affleck has now fully redeemed himself for the whole J.Lo-**Gigli** disaster, especially after **The Town,** which is one of my favorite movies. The second is that Andrew Dice Clay, however piggish he may be, is really not a bad actor.

The third is that I'd really prefer not to go to prison, but there's not much I can do to prevent that now.

A large African American man enters the room, closing the door behind him. He is Ronald Hamilton, the top Secret Service agent protecting the president.

He cocks his head and gives me a scolding look. "Have you totally lost your mind?"

"Hi, Ham," I say. "Sorry about that. If it's any consolation, your agents acted professionally and decisively."

"That's no consolation. You're in a lot of trouble, son."

"You don't know the half of it, Ham."

I wish I had a cool nickname like Ham. The only thing that came from Ben was Benji, like that annoying dog. I could handle T-Bone, which is what George Costanza wanted. But not Koko, which is what he got instead.

"You mind telling me what the hell you were shouting about in there?" he asks.

Actually, I do mind. Ham's a good egg—

mental note, possible future pun—and there's no need to draw him into this mess.

"Ham, how long have we known each other?"

He cocks his head. "Maybe four years?"

"You ever know me to be crazy? Off my rocker?"

On second thought, I'm not sure I want to hear his answer.

"What's your point?" he asks.

"My point is I had a good reason for doing what I did. I want to talk to the president, Ham."

"No," he snaps. "It doesn't work that way."

"Well, then it will work **this** way. You give the president this message for me. I only said 'blackmail' in there. I didn't say what the blackmail was. I could have, but I didn't. So you tell the president, unless he wants me to talk to the press the first chance I get and reveal what the blackmail was, he and I need to have a chat."

Hamilton shakes his head. "Ben—"

"That's it, Ham. Give him that message. It will be off the record, if that helps. But I'll only talk to the president or to the reporters, the first chance I get."

I get out of my chair and walk to the

corner of the room, turning my back to him. After a moment, Ham gets out of his chair and leaves the room.

Another hour passes. In some ways it's agonizing, the slow crawl of time in this barren room, but considering what I've been dealing with over the last ten days, this is like a stroll along the beach. I don't have to make any more decisions.

The door opens again. I turn.

It's CIA deputy director Craig Carney. And he doesn't look happy. But he doesn't really look angry so much, either.

Scared is a better word.

He approaches me, getting so close to me that he could almost kiss me. Like Judge Reinhold, the close talker in that **Seinfeld** episode.

"There's still a chance to salvage this," he says to me. "I'm going to give you that chance. You've been under a lot of strain. You're wanted for murder. People close to you have died. You're under considerable stress. Everyone would understand that. You're sorry for your irresponsible comments, and you need to check into a rehab institute for some much-needed rest and therapy. You will disavow what you've said."

"No," I say.

"And if you don't, I'll destroy you. I'll put this entire thing on you, Casper. We'll charge you with treason and ship you to Guantanamo Bay. I'll put you in a cell with some towel-head whose life's ambition will be to castrate you. And that's to say nothing of the local charges for murder. You'll spend a decade in agony. You'll be begging for that day to come when we strap you to a gurney and stick a needle in your arm."

I look away from him and try to block out what he's saying, but even with my brain's considerable ability to wander to bizarre and irrelevant places, it isn't easy. This is essentially what he's threatened all along.

"Oh, and that's just the start," Carney continues, speaking so quietly he's almost whispering. "I'll destroy everything and everyone you care about. Ashley Brook Clark? Dead. Diana's friend Anne Brennan? Dead. I'll do it. I have resources you couldn't dream about. It's your choice. Turn this car around right now. Right here."

His eyes are boring through me. His cheeks are red with passion.

I clear my throat. "Since you put it that way," I say.

"So we're agreed?"

A noise at the door. The knob turning. Craig Carney's eyes search mine.

And behind him, in walks the president of the United States.

CHAPTER 108

"Mr. President," says Craig Carney. "Sir, I think we have this all cleared up."

The president, dressed in a suit and tie, his eyes squinting, focuses on me. "Hello, Ben," he says.

"Hello, Mr. President."

The president looks around the room, unimpressed. "Apparently, you wanted my attention. And now you have it."

"Mr. President," says Carney. "I think Ben here will tell you that he's been under a lot of strain, and he's made some statements that he regrets. He's willing to publicly disavow those statements."

President Francis looks at me for confirmation.

"That depends," I say.

"Mr. President, I have this under control," says Carney. "You don't have to listen to any of this, sir. I'll take care of this."

And then it comes to me, like the parting of the seas—no, wait, that was Moses, that wasn't really a revelation so much as a miracle from God—let's try this again.

And then it comes to me, like a shot of sunshine piercing a dark cloud—that works—a glimmer of hope for me. I hadn't really given this thought serious consideration. It might have been floating around the recesses of my brain, but it never got my full attention. How stupid I've been. How utterly naive I've been this whole time.

"Your wife," I say to the president.

"That's enough!" Carney shouts at me. "Mr. President, really—"

"What **about** my wife?" says the president, approaching me, fire in his eyes.

Carney raises his hands as though he were a referee separating boxers. "This man is a traitor and a murderer, Mr. President. I promise you I have this under—"

"What about my wife?" the president repeats.

"Mr. President—"

"Goddamn it, Craig, that's enough. I want to hear what this man has to say."

Carney goes silent, but he turns to me. His face is a shiny crimson and his eyes are trying to tell me something. They're telling me to keep my mouth shut.

"Your wife was having an affair with Diana Hotchkiss," I blurt out. "Diana made a video of a sexual encounter with the First Lady and sold it to the Russians. They're hanging it over your head so you'll stand down while they invade Georgia and then every other former satellite, country by country, until they've rebuilt their Soviet empire."

The president's mouth opens and he steps back. His skin has gone pale, his eyes vacant.

That was my glimmer of hope. I can't believe it never occurred to me before now.

The president didn't know about any of this. He didn't know about the video. He didn't know the Russians were blackmailing the United States government.

"Craig," he says. "What is he talking about?"

"Nothing," says Carney. "This is preposterous."

"If it's preposterous," I say, "then why did Carney lie to you about Diana Hotchkiss being dead? She's alive, Mr. President. You eulogized her at the White House press briefing. I was there. But she's not dead."

"Diana?" The president looks at me, then at his CIA deputy director, his old, faithful friend. "Diana is . . . alive?"

"This is ridiculous, Mr. President," says Carney.

"I'll bet Carney was the one who told you she was dead," I say to the president. "I'll bet he was the one who asked you to mention her at the press conference. He wanted the Russians to think they had succeeded in killing her."

The president's eyes glaze over. He's thinking back to that day. And he's remembering it exactly as I'm saying. I can feel it.

"Mr. President, I can prove this. I have date-stamped photos of Diana from last night, handcuffed inside a government car. Even better, you can order a DNA test on the body in the morgue. That woman isn't Diana Hotchkiss. It's Nina Jacobs, of Downers Grove, Illinois. A DNA test will prove it. And I have e-mails that show that Diana set up this poor woman to be at her house at the time she was pushed off the balcony."

"This man is a killer and a traitor, sir," Carney says. "There's no reason for you to listen to any of this. This man was trying to blackmail us. Now he's trying to turn it around—"

"Is it true, Craig?" asks the president. "Is Diana still alive?"

"Mr. President—"

"Is. She. **Alive?**" The president's face is changing colors.

Carney struggles to find words. But has no answer. He silently bows his head.

"It's a . . . complicated situation," he finally says.

"Christ almighty," the president whispers. He runs a hand over his face. "Christ almighty. What have you done, Craig?"

"And I'll bet it's Craig Carney who's been pushing you to lay low on the Russia-Georgia dispute," I say quickly, not wanting to lose my momentum. "He's cut a deal with the Russians behind your back, Mr. President. They think they're blackmailing you, Mr. President, and you don't even know it."

"Mr. President," Carney pleads.

"Mr. Carney," says the president, his jaw clenched. "I want you to walk out of this room right now, stand out in the hallway, and talk to no one until I come out. Is that clear?"

For such a bright guy, the deputy director seems to have trouble following what I thought was a very clear command.

"Leave us," says the president. "I want to hear what Ben has to say."

CHAPTER 109

"The Russians approached Carney because he was the perfect choice," I say. "He was CIA and he was one of your best friends. He was the perfect person to covertly deliver the message to you. But Carney didn't deliver that message. He kept it to himself and some small team of thugs over at the CIA, who probably didn't even know the details. He didn't tell you, Mr. President, because he knew that no matter how embarrassing that video would be, no matter how politically damaging, you would never sell out your country."

The president, customarily a commanding presence in any room, the hunter-gatherer sort, has wilted. He is ashen and uncertain, his hand against a wall. This is a lot for him. He's considering the damage to his administration and his reelection campaign. He's thinking of his wife. And he's thinking that he has been betrayed by one of his closest and most trusted friends. What I don't know is the order in which he's prioritizing these things.

"Carney knew the video, if it ever got out, would ruin you politically, sir. Which would ruin **him** politically. He wants to be CIA director. So he made the decision all by himself."

The president pinches the bridge of his nose, seemingly addressing a massive headache. "The explosion near the White House the other day?" he asks.

"That was the Russians, chasing me," I say. "They were trying to kill me before I could find a copy of the video." I watch him for a moment. "Let me guess. Carney took over that investigation, didn't he? He probably told you it was al-Qaeda or something."

The president doesn't answer. He doesn't have to.

"And do you have this . . . video?" he asks, saying the last word as though he's just swallowed a bitter pill.

"No, I don't," I say. This might not make the top ten list of smartest moves I've ever made. Every bit of leverage I've been able to maintain in this sordid affair has come about because of that video. And now I'm willingly giving up that chit. But I'm not going to lie to the leader of the free world. I'm done bluffing. I'm going to stick with the truth for a while and see where that gets me.

"Mr. President, I don't care about your personal life. Or the First Lady's. If I wanted to expose it, I could have done so today in front of the national press. All I said was 'blackmail.' I didn't say what the blackmail was."

He turns and looks at me. "You could have come directly to me," he says. "You didn't have to confront me publicly."

"Yes, I did. Until just now, I didn't know that Carney was running this operation solo. I thought you were part of this. And I had to stop what was happening."

The president rights himself and brushes his suit jacket. This will not go down as one of his better days.

"You're a reporter," he says. "And you're telling me you won't say anything about my wife?"

"That's what I'm telling you. The public doesn't need to know about her personal life. Not unless it affects your foreign policy strategy."

The president breaks eye contact with me and nods. "So if that strategy were to change, and we were to oppose a Russian invasion?"

"No, no." I wave him off. "I'm not making a deal with you, Mr. President. Just tell me you're going to do what you think is best for our country. That's all I care about."

The president takes a deep breath and sizes me up. "You're not really helping your bargaining position here, son."

"That's because I'm not bargaining. I did what I had to do. Now I'll deal with the fallout."

The president starts with a comment but thinks better of it. I think, somewhere in that look he gives me, he is thanking me. Then he shakes his head, exasperated, and leaves the room.

CHAPTER 110

Midway through his address to the White House press corps, President Francis takes a moment and appears to review his notes. But I don't think he's really reviewing those notes. He is mourning the loss of a friend who betrayed him.

"I should emphasize that the reason I am accepting the resignation of Deputy Director Carney today is that he failed to inform either the CIA director or me of the existence of this entire matter. It was a direct breach of protocol, and it was not in the best interests of this nation. But I must also emphasize that I do not believe that

Mr. Carney broke the law. He should have told me what was happening, yes, but otherwise Mr. Carney did his best to thwart the extortion and keep classified national security information from public disclosure. And he appears to have succeeded in that endeavor."

The president, looking uncharacteristically shaky, clears his throat and continues. "I have spoken with Prime Minister Mereyedev, who has once again assured me that Mr. Kutuzov was acting alone in his attempt to shape US policy regarding the Russia-Georgia dispute in an effort to bolster his oil company's profits. He has assured me that Russia was not, at any time, aware of what Mr. Kutuzov was doing and that Russia condemns his actions."

Yeah, right. But that's the song both countries are singing. I would have liked to have been a part of the conversation between President Francis and the Russian prime minister. Once I made the public allegation of blackmail, it became very difficult for the Russians to use that video. It put a spotlight on everything that was happening over there and on our country's response to it.

And you can be sure that President Francis let it be known that, after everything that had transpired, the United States government would not look kindly on a Russian invasion of its tiny neighbor Georgia. I imagine sanctions and possible military action made their way into the conversation.

By the way, I have a theory that Alex Kutuzov was getting more than money out of this deal. I'll bet a bottle of Stolichnaya that he was promised something big, like maybe being named the next prime minister of the Soviet empire he was helping to re-create. But I guess we'll never know that, either.

"Ladies and gentlemen, this happened on my watch, and I take full responsibility for it," says the president. "I'm embarrassed. But rest assured that I have corrected the problem and it will not happen again. And finally, I would like to personally thank a reporter in this room today, Benjamin Casper, for his diligent investigation of this matter. Without Ben, the outcome of this affair would have been very different."

Aw . . . I'm blushing over here. I've come out okay in all this. Craig Carney has given a full statement for the record, implicating Alexander Kutuzov in the attacks on me that resulted in the deaths of the cops and Secret Service agents. He has also fingered Kutuzov in the murder of Jonathan Liu and in the murder of Nina Jacobs—even though the Russian thugs were sent there to kill Diana. I'm not really sure how that all played out, but I figure that Carney somehow got wind that the Russians were about to kill Diana and made Diana arrange for Nina to be an unwitting stand-in.

The president, I'm told, insisted on this full disclosure from Carney. He did it, more than anything, for my benefit, to spare me any hassle from the local police. Maybe he did it for all the right reasons, but my guess is he's trying to keep me happy. No matter how many times I assure him I will keep the secret about his wife, he must not be totally convinced.

"Now I'd be happy to answer any questions. Yes, Jane?"

"Mr. President, what is the effect of Diana Hotchkiss's guilty plea? Will the classified information remain confidential?"

"Yes, it will," the president says. "Ms. Hotchkiss will be spared the death penalty and a trial on charges of treason in exchange for her guilty plea and her agreement not to divulge the information. Yes, Don?"

"Mr. President, we understand that as a CIA liaison, Diana Hotchkiss spent a good deal of time in the White House, particularly with the First Lady. What has been the First Lady's reaction to these developments?"

The president pauses a beat. I swear that his eyes shoot in my direction for a nanosecond. "My wife is devastated," he says. "It is true that she had a personal friendship with Ms. Hotchkiss. She was very upset to learn of Ms. Hotchkiss's conduct. Yes, Dean?"

"Mr. President, there are reports that you will issue a presidential pardon to Craig Carney if the special prosecutor charges him with a crime. Is that a possibility, sir, and have you made such an agreement with Mr. Carney?"

I was wondering that myself. The attorney general appointed a special prosecutor to look into Carney's behavior. Did Carney make a veiled threat to the president? Did he say that if he were forced to defend himself in a criminal trial, he might reveal what was on the video? Probably. But we may never know for sure. Or we might have to wait until twenty or thirty years from now, when people are at the ends of their careers and looking to write their bestselling memoirs.

Nixon fired the special prosecutor in the Watergate investigation after—

No. Stop. No more presidential trivia!

The president wags a finger. "I'm not going to comment on an ongoing investigation the special prosecutor is conducting. All I can say is that I haven't made any 'deal' with Mr. Carney or anyone else." The president waves a hand. "Thank you, all."

The president steps down. For the first time, I see the First Lady, Libby Rose Francis, lurking in the corner. She looks back over the press corps as the president moves away from the podium. We make eye contact. She looks less frosty than usual, probably humbled by recent events. She doesn't wave to me or mouth any words to me, but her expression eases and she nods her head in acknowledgment.

I don't know what her life must be like. She is the First Lady, after all, so by most measures she's doing pretty damn well. But she's living a lie, and probably has done so her entire life. I can't imagine what that does to a person.

Maybe these events will provoke something within her, will lead her to publicly out herself. Or maybe that video will surface some way, somehow, in the Wild, Wild West that is the Internet. I don't know. And I don't really care.

I just want to go home.

CHAPTER 111

Anne Brennan walks down the steps of her condo and looks up at the sky. It is promising rain. She begins to head north, then she catches my eye across the street. She stops and looks at me, unsure of how to respond. A casual wave wouldn't fit the occasion.

I cross the street and stop short of her.

"They made me do it," she says.

"I know." I sigh. "You were in love with Diana."

She nods. Her eyes well up with tears. "They said if I helped them keep tabs on you, they'd go easier on Diana. And they'd let me see her."

That's about what I figured.

"When I first came to you," she says, "I wasn't doing it for them. I didn't even know Diana was alive. I really wanted your help. But they saw me with you, and then they sunk their claws in me. They told me Diana was in custody and that how well she'd be treated depended on how much I helped them."

None of this is surprising. I take it in without comment. There's really nothing for me to say to her, which makes me wonder why I've come here at all. I guess I just wanted to see her one more time.

She searches my face for something other than bitterness. I'm not sure what she finds.

"That night we had," she says. "That wasn't part of the plan. It just happened. I was . . . kind of a mess at that point. And you're such a good guy. Anyway, I don't regret it. I hope you don't, either."

But everything else was a lie. That night she called and said she'd been attacked and threatened. Her fear of being prosecuted. All of it was a lie, orchestrated by the feds to get me to stand down.

"They're never going to let her out of

prison," she says, speaking the words as though she hopes they aren't true.

But they **are** true. Diana will spend the rest of her life behind bars.

Anne's lucky she didn't get pinched, too. After all, she was Diana's lover. Didn't she know Diana was blackmailing the US government? Apparently not—or at least the feds don't think so.

My guess is she didn't know. But who am I to judge? This lady fooled me twenty times over.

"You got caught in a tough situation," I say. "No hard feelings. Move on with your life, Anne." I consider a hug, or extending my hand, but nothing makes sense. It will probably be a long time, in fact, before any of this fully makes sense to me.

So I just walk away as warm rain drops on my shoulders.

CHAPTER 112

I thought I was prepared for what I would see when I turned the corner, when the guard pointed to the chair and told me I had thirty minutes and that my conversation would be monitored. But I'm not.

Diana Hotchkiss is dressed in a shapeless orange jumpsuit, as I knew she'd be. Her once silky hair is now a flat mop on her head. Her face is pale, void of any color from makeup or the sun. All this I expected.

What I didn't expect was her eyes, looking at me through steel bars, hooded and dark and glassy, revealing nothing. She is neither happy nor sad to see me. There is no hope in her expression, no life whatsoever. All emotion has been washed away. Diana is utterly and irrevocably broken.

I shrug my shoulders, unsure of where to possibly begin.

"Were we even friends?" I ask. "Was anything real?"

I hate myself for asking. I don't want to care about the answer. But I do.

Diana is standing, leaning her back against the wall in her solitary cell, so that I see her in profile. She chews a fingernail that, from the looks of it, has been reduced to a nub already.

"Everybody plays everybody," she says. "Everybody lies to themselves and others. Everybody uses everybody else."

That's what she needs to tell herself. What she did was wrong, but it was just a variation on what everybody else does. A pretty big variation, though. She was helping another country blackmail the United States of America.

"So why am I here, Diana? Why did you ask me to come?"

She takes a moment before answering. "I wanted to apologize," she says. "I'm sorry I ever got you mixed up with this. I didn't mean for you, or Nina, or Randy—"

With that, her expression breaks, her composure crumbles, and she is sobbing into her hand. Her cheeks have probably absorbed countless tears over the last weeks, as her life disintegrated before her eyes. I don't know what she expected to happen. Did she really think this was going to have a happy ending?

Probably not. They'll probably teach a course on her at Quantico, a case study in self-destructive behavior.

I feel myself pitying her, but then a sudden anger emerges. "What you did to Nina Jacobs was unconscionable," I say. "Unforgivable."

Diana's sobbing escalates to uncontrollable spasms, overcome by the magnitude of her disgrace, her shame, her lack of a future—take your pick. She slides to the floor and cries for the better part of ten minutes.

When it finally abates, she says through her hand, "The week that Nina stayed at my apartment . . . was the week that . . . everything happened."

"The week you gave the video of you

and the First Lady to the Russians," I say. "And the week they showed it to Craig Carney."

"Yes." She takes a deep breath. "I wanted a head start. I knew Kutuzov's people were keeping tabs on me. I wanted them to think I was staying at my apartment."

"So as they watched your apartment from a distance, they'd see someone who looked like you and wore your clothes going in and out of your apartment, sleeping there, feeding the cat—and they'd think you were still around town. When in fact you had left the country. Someplace warm, I assume. Someplace without an extradition treaty with the United States."

She nods again. The CIA probably used its considerable resources to relocate her and decided that they didn't care one bit about an extradition treaty. I picture an acquisition team dropping out of a black helicopter, arresting her on a beach or something, and then whisking her back to Quantico.

"And why call me to install the surveillance?" I ask. "You just felt like embroiling me in an international conspiracy? Misery loves company?"

"Because you were the only person I could trust," she says.

I don't respond. Inside, I am fighting the temptation to believe what she's saying. She's fooled me enough for one lifetime.

"I realized the Russians might try to kill me once they had the video and I was no longer any use to them," she explains. "And if they tried to kill me, I wanted them on video inside my apartment." Diana looks up at me. "Ben, I swear to you, I didn't know they'd move so quickly. Nina was going to leave the next day. I didn't think they'd come after me that night. I . . . I didn't want her to die. I didn't. I swear."

I don't know if I believe her or not. But either way, she was being awfully reckless with someone else's life.

"And who covered up Nina's death?" I ask. "The CIA?"

She looks at me like the answer's obvious. "Of course. By then they knew everything. They might have even known that the Russians were coming for me. They made a decision that they wanted everyone to believe I was dead."

And it worked. For a while, at least. Until I got curious.

But now it's over. Diana checked her morals at the door, made an admittedly bold and daring attempt at scoring a huge payday, and lost as badly as someone can lose. Now she will spend the rest of her life in a cell.

I loved this woman. You can't just turn off that kind of feeling. But I loved a person who didn't exist. I loved someone Diana was pretending to be. Maybe the signs were there, but I refused to see them. Maybe I didn't **want** to see them.

The guard approaches and tells me that my time's up. I take a deep breath and look at Diana.

I place my hand gently on the bars of the cell and look at Diana one last time. "There's still good in your life," I say. "It's going to be harder to find it. But it's there, Diana. Don't stop looking for it."

Then I walk away, wondering if I should start taking some of my own advice.

CHAPTER 113

Professor Andrei Bogomolov doesn't answer the door when I ring the bell. Instead, a nurse leads me back into his den, where Andrei is lying on a hospital bed positioned against a wall.

Andrei looks twenty times worse than the last time I saw him, only a week ago. The hideous disease that ails him is rapidly winning the fight. Wisps of hair atop his head stand in various directions. His eyes are black and vacant.

The hospital bed wasn't here the last time I came. Or at least he didn't let me see it. It tells me that the end is near for him, and that he wants to die at home, not in a hospital.

He tries to smile, but even that small feat seems to cause pain. I take his hand in mine and squeeze it gently.

"Hello, old friend," I say.

"You are . . . a hero," he manages. **You've done well, Grasshopper.**

"All in a week's work." I'm trying to lighten the mood, but it falls flat.

I look out the window to the garden, recalling that barbecue only weeks after Mother died. **If you ever feel that you're in danger,** Andrei had said to me, **you can call me, Benjamin. I will help you.**

"You have come here . . . for a reason," he whispers.

"I came to see my good friend." I smile at him.

Andrei winces, and then a coughing attack ensues. I pick up a washcloth at his bedside and wipe his mouth when it's over.

"You don't have to say anything you don't want to say," I tell him.

"Yes, I . . . do," he manages. "It is . . . long past . . . time. A subject . . . I've debated . . . many times. Many . . ."

His eyes close. He drifts off to sleep. The

pain medication from the IV drip, probably, or maybe just general weakness. After a few minutes, he snaps awake, his eyes unfocused, and he takes a moment to orient himself before he looks at me again.

"Why did my father kill my mother?" I ask.

The question and, probably, the memories it invokes cause him pain, and his mouth contorts briefly. "This is not . . . something . . . that we could confirm . . . at the time. But now . . . now we believe . . . we know . . . the answer."

"Why did my father kill my mother, Andrei?"

Andrei takes a deep breath.

"He didn't," he says.

I draw back, as if zapped by electricity.

"His . . . employer did," says Andrei. "Your father . . . tried to . . . prevent it."

His **employer.** Father's employer? He doesn't mean American University.

"So there was a reason the CIA put you at American U," I say. "You were spying on my father."

Andrei closes his eyes and nods. "It is . . . true."

"Who did Father spy for?" I ask. "The Russians?"

Andrei's eyes open again. "China," he says. "We believe . . . that your mother . . . discovered this . . . and they . . . the Chinese—"

"The Chinese killed my mother because they thought she was going to blow Father's cover," I say, everything crystallizing now.

"Just so," he whispers. "Just so."

I release his hand and back away from his bed. "And . . . why . . . **why** . . . why the hell . . . did Father frame me for—"

Out of nowhere, my throat closes up and I completely lose my composure. The tears almost jump from my eyes down my cheeks, and my chest starts to heave. I stay that way for God knows how long, whimpering like a child and crying like I don't remember ever crying, struggling for oxygen and seizing up, trembling and screaming in choked wails, everything buried deep within me now pouring out—

Father was a spy? And that's why Mother was so despondent all that time? She found out that her husband was a traitor. She didn't know what to do.

When it's over, when I've wiped my face

and my nose and caught my breath again, I look over at Andrei. He opens a hand to me. I return to his bedside and hold it.

"My good . . . Benjamin," he whispers. "If the . . . truth . . . came out . . . they said . . . they would kill . . . they would kill you next."

"Father was **protecting** me?" I say the words as though they're poison on my tongue.

"Your father came home . . . and found her dead. The Chinese told him . . . they could not . . . be implicated . . . nor could . . . he. You were . . . the only choice. Benjamin . . . your father . . . took every . . . step . . . to ensure your acquittal."

No matter how my mind is spinning right now, no matter what avalanche of memories besieges me right now, even I would concede that point. I had the best lawyers and I did, after all, beat the charges.

"Is this why I never went to school? Is this why I had private tutors and hardly ever left home until college?"

Andrei nods. "He feared . . . for your . . . safety."

Everything is upside down. Every belief I held about him—wrong.

"Years later," says Andrei, "we finally . . . caught your father. It was . . . too embarrassing to publicly . . . reveal. He cooperated and . . . was placed . . ."

"Under house arrest," I say. He was placed under house arrest at his cabin. That's why he stayed there and never let me come, all those years, until he died. He didn't want me to know.

"A traitor, yes," says Andrei. "But a traitor who . . . loved his son."

No. No. This is too much. Overload. System failure.

I hear myself speak but I don't know what I said, and then I'm pacing around his den, and then the air outside is somehow cold, stinging my skin, up is down, down is up, someone else is inhabiting this body, it's not me, I'm not Ben, and car horns are honking and tires are skidding and someone is cursing me, and then I'm running, I'm running as fast as I can and it feels good, it feels right, and I'm laughing and I'm crying, and it feels liberating, it feels **normal**—

Jimmy Carter is credited as the first president to routinely jog. He did it mostly for stress release. But since then almost every president has jogged except Reagan, who was probably too old to do it regularly, and George W. Bush, who had to give it up after knee pain. Reagan was a former lifeguard who preferred swimming, as did Kennedy to relieve back pain, and John Quincy Adams regularly started his days by swimming nude in the Potomac, funny story about that . . .

About the Authors

JAMES PATTERSON has created more enduring fictional characters than any other novelist writing today. He is the author of the Alex Cross novels, the most popular detective series of the past twenty-five years, including **Kiss the Girls** and **Along Came a Spider.** Mr. Patterson also writes the bestselling Women's Murder Club novels, set in San Francisco, and the top-selling New York detective series of all time, featuring Detective Michael Bennett. James Patterson has had more **New York Times** bestsellers than any other writer, ever, according to **Guinness World Records.**

Since his first novel won the Edgar Award in 1977, James Patterson's books have sold more than 275 million copies.

James Patterson has also written numerous #1 bestsellers for young readers, including the Maximum Ride, Witch & Wizard, and Middle School series. In total, these books have spent more than 220 weeks on national bestseller lists. In 2010, James Patterson was named Author of the Year at the Children's Choice Book Awards.

His lifelong passion for books and reading led James Patterson to create the innovative website ReadKiddoRead.com, giving adults an invaluable tool to find the books that get kids reading for life. He writes full-time and lives in Florida with his family.

DAVID ELLIS is a Chicago attorney and the author of nine novels, including **Line of Vision,** for which he won an Edgar Award, and **The Hidden Man,** which earned him a 2009 Los Angeles Times Book Prize nomination.

Books by James Patterson

Featuring Alex Cross

Alex Cross, Run • Merry Christmas, Alex Cross • Kill Alex Cross • Cross Fire • I, Alex Cross • Alex Cross's Trial (with Richard DiLallo) • Cross Country • Double Cross • Cross (also published as Alex Cross) • Mary, Mary • London Bridges • The Big Bad Wolf • Four Blind Mice • Violets Are Blue • Roses Are Red • Pop Goes the Weasel • Cat & Mouse • Jack & Jill • Kiss the Girls • Along Came a Spider

The Women's Murder Club

12th of Never (with Maxine Paetro) • 11th Hour (with Maxine Paetro) • 10th Anniversary (with Maxine Paetro) • The 9th Judgment (with Maxine Paetro) • The 8th Confession (with Maxine Paetro) • 7th Heaven (with Maxine Paetro) • The 6th Target (with Maxine Paetro) • The 5th Horseman (with Maxine Paetro) • 4th of July (with Maxine Paetro) • 3rd Degree (with Andrew Gross) • 2nd Chance (with Andrew Gross) • 1st to Die

Featuring Michael Bennett

I, Michael Bennett (with Michael Ledwidge) • Tick Tock (with Michael Ledwidge) • Worst Case (with Michael Ledwidge) • Run for Your Life (with

Michael Ledwidge) • **Step on a Crack** (with Michael Ledwidge)

The Private Novels

Private Berlin (with Mark Sullivan) • **Private London** (with Mark Pearson) • **Private Games** (with Mark Sullivan) • **Private: #1 Suspect** (with Maxine Paetro) • **Private** (with Maxine Paetro)

Summer Novels

Second Honeymoon (with Howard Roughan) • **Now You See Her** (with Michael Ledwidge) • **Swimsuit** (with Maxine Paetro) • **Sail** (with Howard Roughan) • **Beach Road** (with Peter de Jonge) • **Lifeguard** (with Andrew Gross) • **Honeymoon** (with Howard Roughan) • **The Beach House** (with Peter de Jonge)

Stand-alone Books

Mistress (with David Ellis) • **NYPD Red** (with Marshall Karp) • **Zoo** (with Michael Ledwidge) • **Guilty Wives** (with David Ellis) • **The Christmas Wedding** (with Richard DiLallo) • **Kill Me If You Can** (with Marshall Karp) • **Toys** (with Neil McMahon) • **Don't Blink** (with Howard Roughan) • **The Postcard Killers** (with Liza Marklund) • **The Murder of King Tut** (with Martin Dugard) • **Against Medical Advice** (with Hal Friedman) • **Sundays at Tiffany's** (with Gabrielle Charbonnet) • **You've Been Warned** (with Howard Roughan) •

The Quickie (with Michael Ledwidge) • **Judge & Jury** (with Andrew Gross) • **Sam's Letters to Jennifer** • **The Lake House** • **The Jester** (with Andrew Gross) • **Suzanne's Diary for Nicholas** • **Cradle and All** • **When the Wind Blows** • **Miracle on the 17th Green** (with Peter de Jonge) • **Hide & Seek** • **The Midnight Club** • **Black Friday** (originally published as **Black Market**) • **See How They Run** • **Season of the Machete** • **The Thomas Berryman Number**

For Readers of All Ages

Maximum Ride

Nevermore: The Final Maximum Ride Adventure • **Angel: A Maximum Ride Novel** • **Fang: A Maximum Ride Novel** • **Max: A Maximum Ride Novel** • **The Final Warning: A Maximum Ride Novel** • **Saving the World and Other Extreme Sports: A Maximum Ride Novel** • **School's Out—Forever: A Maximum Ride Novel** • **The Angel Experiment: A Maximum Ride Novel**

Daniel X

Daniel X: Armageddon (with Chris Grabenstein) • **Daniel X: Game Over** (with Ned Rust) • **Daniel X: Demons and Druids** (with Adam Sadler) • **Daniel X: Watch the Skies** (with Ned Rust) • **The Dangerous Days of Daniel X** (with Michael Ledwidge)

Witch & Wizard

Witch & Wizard: The Kiss (with Jill Dembowski) •
Witch & Wizard: The Fire (with Jill Dembowski) •
Witch & Wizard:
The Gift (with Ned Rust) • **Witch & Wizard**
(with Gabrielle Charbonnet)

Middle School

Middle School: How I Survived Bullies,
Broccoli, and Snake Hill (with Chris Tebbetts,
illustrated by Laura Park) • **Middle School:**
My Brother Is a Big, Fat Liar (with Lisa
Papademetriou, illustrated by Neil Swaab) •
Middle School: Get Me Out of Here! (with Chris
Tebbetts, illustrated by Laura Park) • **Middle**
School, The Worst Years of My Life (with Chris
Tebbetts, illustrated by Laura Park)

Other Books for Readers of All Ages

I Funny: A Middle School Story (with Chris
Grabenstein, illustrated by Laura Park) •
Confessions of a Murder Suspect
(with Maxine Paetro) • **Med Head**
(with Hal Friedman) • **santaKid**
(illustrated by Michael Garland)

For previews and information about the author,
visit JamesPatterson.com or find him on Facebook
or at your app store.